THE WHISPERS OF THE FALLEN
REBELLION

J.D. NETTO

OFTOMES PUBLISHING
UNITED KINGDOM

DEDICATED TO THOSE WHO ARE NOT
AFRAID
TO FIGHT FOR THEIR DREAMS

SEA OF CINDER

MAC
MEL

SILVER MOUNTAINS

VILLAGE OF
VALLEY HILLS

BILLYTH

GATES OF
THE FOURTH
DIMENSION

VILLAGE
OF AHNOR

WOODS
OF MARSH

ROAD
OF IRON

SWORDSMOUTH

LAKE
OF FIRE

SCARLET
MOUNTAINS

GREAT RIVER

BORDER
OF JUST

VILLAGE
OF BRAVOR

HILLS
MEHN

AGALMATH

SEA OF FIRE

W · E

S

*"WE ARE EACH OUR OWN EVIL,
AND WE MAKE THIS WORLD OUR HELL."*

OSCAR WILDE

Xylia

Petra

Adara

Ballard

Dahmian

ISAAC

I

DARKNESS—THAT WAS all I could see. I looked down, trying to catch a glimpse of my feet as they trampled upon the unseen ground.

An invisible force pulled me while I listened to the sound of many voices. It was bitter cold; my fingertips grew numb with every step I took. It was quiet here—too quiet. My heartbeat sounded like drums softly played by weak hands.

Something lay in the darkness ahead of me. My eyes squinted in an attempt to better visualize the unrecognizable. My breathing failed once I realized it was her—it was Nephele.

Emotions stirred within me; rage shadowed my mind as I approached her body.

She attempted to stand to her feet, feebly moving her arms. It was apparent that an invisible power pinned her down. My wings made their way out of my back as rage continued to take over. I grasped my sword, marching in her direction.

I knelt next to her. Our eyes met.

Without hesitating, I pierced her left hand; blood flowed like a waterfall. Her body trembled as she opened her mouth to scream, but no sound came forth.

You deserve to die, I thought, standing back on my feet. The memories of all the pain she had caused me played over in my head. I placed my right foot on her skull, pressing it against the ground.

I sank my sword into her chest. I was clueless of my whereabouts, but happy to know that my mortal enemy lay here, defenseless.

The sound of her slowing heartbeat invaded my ears. I lifted my foot from her head, kneeling next to her once again.

"You see," I whispered in her ear. "Even with all of your dark powers, Nephele, in the end, you will never win."

O

"HOW ARE YOU feeling?" I heard a faint male voice say. The image of Nephele faded rapidly.

With unclear vision, I tried to make out who it was.

"I will survive." There was a rasp to my voice.

I felt the mattress rise as whoever was next to me stood back up on his feet. It wasn't long until I recognized him.

"Nathan." A feeling of relief took over me.

"I am glad to see you are well. I was worried about you." His lips curved into a narrow smile. Dark circles rested under his hazel-green eyes. His fair hair was tied back; cuts and bruises adorned his pale face and sharp nose.

I rested my back against the bed's wooden headboard. My muscles ached. My eyes surveyed the room, absorbing

every detail. The dark wooden bed was ornamented with floral carvings; the carpet was a shade of purple, stretching throughout the entire room; matching curtains draped around the mullion windows. The fireplace burned and a fresh scent of cinnamon lingered.

"When did we get here?" I asked with a broken voice, confused.

"As soon as I rescued you from Erebos's attack, I flew to Bellator." Nathan paced around the room, his hands crossed behind his back.

"How are the men that aided us in battle?" Vivid images of the battle of Justicia invaded my mind. For a moment, it was as if the screams of those men were as audible as my own voice.

"Many perished against the Nephilins. The men of Aloisio knew they marched to their demise once I mentioned where we were heading." Sorrow flowed with every word he uttered. "They cared not if they walked to their doom…they just wanted to avenge those that the Nephilins and the Fallen Stars had taken from them. They also sought vengeance because of King Marco's decision to side with Lucifer."

I wanted to remember the face of every man that had fought alongside us, but that was not something that I could do.

"They were not warriors?" My eyes narrowed as some of their faces appeared in my mind.

Nathan bowed his head, pressing his fingers against his chin.

"War brings out the warrior in all of us, does it not?"

I knew what those men would become. The thought that their souls would be controlled by the Fallen Stars once they turned into Shadows ignited rage inside of me. For a moment, I was tempted to think that all was in vain. My journey through the Wastelands of Tristar had been dark and perilous. I had seen more than I could ever fully fathom.

Amidst the chaos that crowded my mind, I remembered the words Raziel had spoken to me once he found me: *"Death is conquered. One greater has come."* Those seven words resounded in my heart like a loud horn played in the battlefield. Regardless of how triumphant my return may be, my heart ached at the thought that the Aloisians were fooled by King Marco and were murdered by the Fallen Stars and Nephilins.

A sharp pain invaded my head. Nephele's face flashed in my mind once again; her piercing blue eyes gazed at mine. I grunted, pressing my hands against my skull.

"Are you alright?" Nathan's brows furrowed. He darted me a concerned stare.

"We have not been anywhere else besides this room since our arrival?" I quavered as I composed myself.

Nathan approached me. "No," he affirmed. "Is everything alright?"

"I am not sure," I said after a brief silence. "I saw...her."

Creases appeared on Nathan's forehead.

"Her?" His voice was deep and filled with worry.

I shared with him what I had seen. To me, it had been more than just a vision or a dream. As my words painted a vivid image of Nephele, Nathan's expression grew bitter.

"That cannot be true, Isaac." He scowled, nodding his head. "It must have been a dream. We have not been anywhere else besides this room since our arrival."

I was startled by a sudden knock on the door.

"Is he well?" I heard a low, hoarse voice coming from the other side the moment Nathan opened it.

"Yes," Nathan whispered.

A man walked into the room. He appeared to be in his mid-forties. A thin silver crown sat on his head. It had seven spikes that protruded from its base. His beard was dark and short; his black hair touched the nape of his neck. He gave me a warm smile.

"Isaac," Nathan said as the man strolled toward me. "This is Demyon, king of Bellator. It was his army that found us once the castle of Justicia fell away from Tristar onto Elysium."

Behind the king, I caught sight of my friend—the one who, more than anyone else, understood and knew of the darkness I had witnessed in the Wastelands. It was Demetre.

"You are finally awake." There was a broad smile across his face. "You have kept us all waiting for too long." The last time I recalled seeing him was in Justicia when the men of Aloisio joined us in the garden in front of the castle.

"Demetre!" I shouted with joy. "I am relieved to see you are well."

"There are many who would not believe that you have returned from the Wastelands of Tristar, young ones," King Demyon said in a soothing voice. His dark eyes seemed to smile as he spoke. "We are all relieved to see you two

alive—and that the Diary and the other Books remain in the possession of their bearers."

"Where are the others?" I inquired with a heavy heart, apprehensive and afraid of their response. "Are they alive? Are they well?"

Nathan sat on the settee located by my bed. "Yes, Isaac. All the others are here. Devin, Petra, Xylia, Adara, and Ballard are all safe."

I sighed with relief as I reclined my head against the bedpost.

Demetre shot King Demyon a sudden stare.

"How did you find us, king? How did you know we were going to be at one of the borderlines of Justicia and Elysium? Your riders flocked to the burning castle as the Shadows sprung from the woods."

"I hope you will find joy in knowing that even after all these years, some of us still keep watch over Elysium, Demetre, son of Paul and Lune Aliward." King Demyon approached Demetre with calm footsteps, his eyes set on Demetre's.

Demetre raised both of his eyebrows. "You knew my parents?" he asked, surprised at King Demyon's words.

"Not only knew them. I was with your parents, and Isaac's, when they escaped Justicia and fled to the village of Agalmath eighteen years ago. Unfortunately, I was not aware of the vow your parents had made with the Darkness." King Demyon sat at the foot of my bed.

Nothing Demetre could say or do was able to hide the curiosity that was stamped on his face.

"I was there on the day the attack occurred. Queen Lylith and I had crossed over to meet Athalas when we

18

found Justicia enveloped in smoke, shadow, and flame." I observed King Demyon's face filling with sorrow. "We rode to the burning castle, where we fought against the Nephilins and Shadows."

I burned with curiosity as his words filled my ears. I missed my parents. I wanted—I *needed*—evidence that they were dead or alive.

"We crossed paths with Diane, Dustin, Paul, and Lune as they fled Justicia. They demanded we follow them." King Demyon lowered his head.

The crackling of the burning torches seemed to grow louder as King Demyon spoke. Every word that drifted from his mouth made me anxious. I felt a sharp pang of fear. Surely the worst was true—death had found my parents.

"Paul claimed that Athalas had informed them of a box that contained the Dark Book, which we now know was a fake. Even with watchful eyes, I failed to see the master plan behind Athalas's decision. *'This is ours to keep safe,'* Paul declared once he revealed to us the rugged, locked—"

"You said Paul, king?" I asked, confused at his latest remark. "Paul showed you the box containing the Diary?"

King Demyon cleared his throat.

"The Diary was not handed to your parents initially, Isaac. It was Paul and Lune Aliward who were chosen to keep the Diary safe at first." I took a deep breath. "Athalas was no fool. The day he sold his soul to Lucifer, he erased from the Council's memory the choice they were once given."

I was afraid of setting eyes on Demetre after receiving this new information. My heart raced in my chest. Nathan moved toward Demetre, who rested his head on his hands.

"Lylith and I saw the box—a perfect replica of the original. As I touched the obscure object, the sound of whispering voices penetrated my ears. That was the moment when Paul, Lune, Diane, and Dustin informed the queen and I of their plan to hide away in the village of Agalmath, located next to the Forest of Hathar, where one of the borderlines of Justicia is located."

"The borderline we crossed with Devin…" My voice trailed off as I recalled the day when we had first set foot in the Fourth Dimension.

The howling of the wind resonated outside. Through the glass window, I caught sight of the blinding snowstorm that had descended upon Bellator.

"Of course, Diane and Dustin were aware that Athalas had surrendered his life to Lucifer. They knew of the conditions on which Paul and Lune were allowed to escape the battle of Justicia." King Demyon's gaze pierced mine. "Your mother trusted me with her secret. She developed the gift of foresight a thousand years after the Creator entrusted the Council with the Diary. Apart from me, only your dad knew of her powers. It was because of her ability that she saw what Paul and Lune had done before they left Justicia—and why they had all been spared." King Demyon let out a soft, disappointed sigh. "They knew you would both be hunted by the Darkness when you reached maturity."

I was frozen in shock. "Foresight?" I shook my head in disbelief. To me, she had always been just an ordinary woman. "My mother could see the future?"

"And your dad possessed the gift of meddling with memories," Nathan added in a soft voice.

My heart ached at the sound of Demetre's weeping. I didn't know what to do or say. After all I had lived through, I was still unaware of the truth behind my own family.

"Dustin erased the memories of Paul and Lune ever getting the Diary from Athalas. They stole the Diary, hiding the book away, never speaking of its powers, but unaware of the curse that rested upon the fake copy they carried." King Demyon's voice was filled with angst.

Demetre could not hide the sorrow that overtook him as he heard the king's account. He gnawed on his bottom lip; his eyes welled up with tears while he gazed at the corner of the room, turning from the king's stare.

King Demyon turned his face to the window. He watched the snow descend. "It was only after you were both attacked by Cyro that a special device came to me through Diane and Dustin."

"My parents came your way? What did they bring you?" I attempted to hold back my tears, but the feelings that whirled within me were too strong.

"When the Council was created, the Creator not only entrusted the Diary of Lucifer to its members, but he also gave them a device that helped keep watch over Elysium. This device is named Lion's Stare. Unfortunately, it does not function as well as before. After the fall of the Council, the Lion's Stare was limited to showing only what its owner feels most important."

Demetre wiped the tears from his red cheeks; his eyes were red and swollen. "When did you learn about the Fallen Star that dwelled inside of me?"

"When Diane and Dustin Khan walked through these doors informing me that Cyro was after the both of you, I looked into the Lion's Stare and saw the truth behind Athalas's plan. That was also the day she revealed to me what she had seen when they left Justicia."

Demetre's upper body shuddered as he listened to King Demyon answer his question. He lowered his head, resting it on his hands.

"Athalas erased from the Council's memory the truth about their immortality." King Demyon stared at Demetre in grief. He laid one of his hands against his back. "You see, the Creator also gave them a choice. If any Council member chose to have a child, immortality would be taken from them. Due to Diane's gift, she knew of Athalas's actions, but remained silent. One month after they fled Justicia, Diane was pregnant with you, Isaac."

My lips quivered as King Demyon's words drifted into my ears. My parents had renounced immortality because of me.

"While Lune was still pregnant, she and Paul rode to Bellator, seeking my council. Unaware of the memory they had been deprived of, they informed me of their commitment to Lucifer, but they never told me that their child had been destined to be a host to a Fallen Star," King Demyon added.

Demetre raised his head. The salt from his tears had dried against his skin, leaving a trail down his cheeks. I was concerned for my friend.

Silence lingered over us. Nathan reclined against the wall, his hands crossed on his chest. With a despondent stare, he watched the snow fall from the sky.

King Demyon turned to Demetre. "On the morning Cyro attacked Diane and Dustin, they managed to go to your house, Demetre, only to find your parents' lifeless bodies. Diane and Dustin brought their bodies here, to the castle—"

"Athalas said they died in the fields, along with Isaac's parents." Demetre shook his head, gnawing on the left side of his bottom lip.

"It is no surprise that Athalas lied." King Demyon raised his eyebrows.

I leaped up from my bed, wrapping my arms around my friend.

"They didn't know the outcome of their choice, Demetre. You mustn't blame them for wanting a child…for wanting you." King Demyon stood to his feet, making his way to the door.

Nathan knelt next to Demetre. "Do not weep over unwise choices. Smile for the choices you can make— choices that will shape the future of many."

Demetre lifted his head and his bloodshot eyes met King Demyon's.

"How…how did my parents die?" Demetre's voice was caught in his throat.

"Bravely." King Demyon's lips curved into a smile.

Demetre took a shallow breath. "I need to be alone," He trailed his fingers across his dark hair. "I need to…"

"Of course." King Demyon darted his gaze toward Nathan. "Show Demetre to the garden, please."

"Of course." Nathan rose to his feet. "Follow me, Demetre. I believe you will be able to gather your thoughts in the garden of the castle."

Demetre fumbled his way to his feet as I helped him stand. His complexion made it seem as if he had slept out in the bitter cold for hours. All were silent as he trudged out of the room.

I felt the king slip something into the palm of my left hand.

"What is this?" I stared at an old piece of parchment paper, stamped with a red lion-shaped seal.

"Your parents brought me this. It is a letter that they found in Demetre's home." As I twirled the paper in my hands, I saw Demetre's name written in Lune's handwriting.

I felt my chest constrict as my tears returned again.

"You want me to give this to him?" I feared his answer.

"You are the only one that can give him this letter right now, Isaac," King Demyon affirmed.

I touched the scarlet seal of the lion that had been pressed into wax on the parchment, then analyzed the tears and rips on the edges. I held the last words my best friend's parents had written to him—words that might contain answers to so many questions.

King Demyon laid his left hand on my shoulder. "We will have a special banquet prepared for you and the others tonight. Let Demetre have his time in the garden. I will have someone come and escort you both to the throne room."

I heard the door lock after King Demyon stepped out of the room. All the darkness and loneliness I had experienced

in the Wastelands felt insignificant compared to what this letter meant to the both of us.

I approached the window. The dark clouds and falling snow covered Bellator. Towering gray mountains surrounded this kingdom, reaching beyond the cloudbank; their peaks were covered in a permanent white blanket.

So much darkness, I thought.

I closed my eyes in an attempt to disconnect myself from this present situation. I had just awakened but I felt burdened; a weight rested on my shoulders. I searched for memories that could spark joy within me, ones that had the power to reawaken hope.

I struggled to ignore the fact that the dark memories easily overshadowed the joyful ones. I saw my parents' faces, tried to remember the sound of their laughter, but in an instant, the ash-covered terrain of the Wastelands erased their faces from my mind; the memory of the corpses of those that lingered between the Abyss and Tristar haunted me. Apparently, hopelessness was clouding my mind, keeping me from regaining strength.

I tried to visualize the mornings I would go up the Hill of Mehnor with my father, Paul, and Demetre to go fishing at the river. Life was not burdensome back then. My mind tried to remember the color of the grass, the smell of the field of flowers, the clear water of the river. These memories were also shattered by the invading image of the Wasteland Desert. The only sound I could remember was the howling of the frigid wind that created sandstorms of massive proportions under the red and purple skies. The scarcity of life in the Wastelands had deprived me of the ability to find joy inside of myself. Defeated by my own

memories and thoughts, I opened my eyes and wept bitterly, wondering how I'd had so much strength, courage, and will to fight for the Creator, yet so little hope and joy within my own heart.

II

I FOUND SOME clothes folded on top of the fireplace: a simple white, collarless, laced neck shirt with a dark beige pair of pants. My boots rested next to the settee. A heavy brown coat hung next to the fireplace.

I picked up the shirt and was startled by the sound of an object dropping from atop the fireplace. Sorrow took me as I stared at the book on the ground—the Diary of Lucifer. I laid the shirt on the bed, bending over and picking up the object. The moment the palm of my hand touched it, voices and whispers echoed in my ears and my hands began to tremble. After a while, the voices ceased.

How can such a small thing hold so many secrets? I thought. I placed the book on top of the fireplace along with the letter, fighting away the tears that tried to return.

Through the foggy windows, I was able to see a glimpse of my reflection. My eyes could share stories of their own if they had the ability to speak. I touched the bruises and wounds on my body, knowing they were reminders of the battles and struggles we were all going through.

As I analyzed my fallen countenance, I heard soft knocks on the door.

"Come in," I ordered in a broken voice, rubbing my eyes with the back of my hands.

I looked over my shoulder and caught sight of Nathan walking toward me. "Isaac, Demetre needs you right now."

Silence hovered over us for a moment. His statement burdened my heart.

"Show me the way to him." I gazed at the letter for a couple of seconds; thoughts, questions, and answers coursed through my mind as I reached for the piece of paper.

In a friendly gesture, Nathan rested his left arm on my shoulder.

"Remember the things that give you hope, Isaac."

I lifted my eyes. He had a soft grin stamped on his face. Little did he know that the memories that gave me hope were being overtaken by those that brought me fear.

I absorbed the beauty of the castle as we began to make our way down the grand hall. Silver chandeliers hung from the dark wooden ceiling, holding white candles that burned with a bright blue flame.

"Why do these flames burn blue?" I asked Nathan, my eyes set on the strange-burning fire.

"These candles were made with white dragon's blood, which gives the flames their odd color," he replied.

"The dragons that aided us in battle," I said.

I absorbed the details of the mosaic that covered the top ceiling. Its bright colors depicted mountains surrounded by clouds with waterfalls that cascaded like a bride's veil, creating a flowing river at the base. As Nathan and I continued to amble down the hall, the colorful mountain

depiction changed to a dark night sky with a full moon in the middle.

Purple flags drooped from the high-top ceiling, touching the gray floor. They had the emblem of a white dragon. Canvases with beautiful painted landscapes hung throughout the hall, meticulously placed on every empty spot.

We proceeded in silence, coming to a round staircase. The newels were shaped like white dragons; the balusters created curvilinear patterns that trailed all the way to the bottom, merging onto the statue of a white dragon, its open mouth revealing a set of razor sharp teeth. Its scales were similar to a snake's; its wings were expanded to full length.

My grasp on the letter tightened with every step as I descended. The aroma of cinnamon invaded my nostrils. Torches burning with bright blue flames were placed around us. Servants dusted off the expensive vases, statues, and furniture. Above us was a glass dome with a chandelier crowded with melting candles.

We stopped in front a double wooden door. Patterns were etched throughout its surface; the knob was of a silver color.

"He is on the other side." Nathan's voice was low.

"You aren't coming?" I asked, hopeful. Maybe it would be easier to give Demetre this letter with someone accompanying me.

Nathan shook his head. "No, Isaac. I know what it is you carry, and you alone must hand Demetre this letter," he answered. "I have matters to discuss with King Demyon."

"Alright." I grasped the knob with one hand. I opened the sturdy door, expecting to feel the frigid air, but was surprised once I saw the scenery in front of me.

The grass was green, and the trees bloomed with flowers—their fragrance intoxicating the air. Little rivers flowed in peaceful streams. Wild vines were laced around the trunks of the trees, which had their branches colored with red apples.

Throughout the garden were statues of white dragons. The same incandescent blue flame I had seen inside the castle burned inside their mouths. The garden had been built inside an enormous glass room.

What a place, I thought, contemplating the massive monument.

My thoughts were interrupted by the sound of low sniffles and sobs. The sounds led me to Demetre, who sat next to one of the streams. I removed my coat, laying it on the vine-covered bench under the apple tree.

He shot me a mournful glance over his shoulder; his glistening eyes met mine.

"This place reminds me of home in the summer," he whimpered. "The streams, little rivers, the trees…"

I sat next to him.

"I miss home." The sound of a small stream filled my ears like a soothing melody.

A moment of silence reigned over us. I didn't know if my presence was improving things or causing Demetre more pain.

"We have been friends all of our lives." I cleared my throat. "And I always felt like I could save you…tried to, at least."

"You have done more than that, Isaac," he whispered, letting out a half smile.

A whirlwind of emotions stirred inside of me.

"I am afraid I cannot save you from this, though." My hands trembled as I handed him the wrinkled letter. Some of the red wax from the lion seal had stained the palm of my sweaty hand.

Demetre frowned.

"What's this?" He looked down at the paper.

I let out a soft breath.

"The last words from your parents. My mom and dad found the letter when they entered your house before Cyro attacked us that morning."

My heart accelerated. Demetre caressed the letter, analyzing every detail. He touched the seal, the torn edges, and then he saw his name.

"My mother's writing" He narrowed his eyes, biting the left side of his bottom lip.

With great care, he scratched off the seal.

"Read it!" he suddenly exclaimed, handing me the letter. My eyes widened. "Please, read it," he repeated with a whimpering voice.

"Are you sure?" I asked with a gaping jaw.

He nodded in silence, deviating his eyes from me.

Demetre, we know not where you will be when you read this letter. Our bodies grow weak as we pen these words. We know they will come for you at dawn, for in

31

dreams we saw this day coming. Our minds were unveiled to memories that had long been stolen from us. Please forgive us for not revealing to you the danger we have put you in. It was not because of immortality that we surrendered our bodies to the Darkness; it was because truth was stolen from us.

Your dad and I desired you, but we failed to wait. Uncle Dustin and Aunt Diane will share the truth with you once you show them this letter. Know that we have loved you always. We long for the day we will see each other again.
Farewell.
With Love, Mom and Dad

Every word felt like a dagger going straight through my heart. With trembling hands, I folded the wrinkled paper and handed it back to him. Demetre was silent, gazing at the clear waters of the little river. The tears had stopped

rolling down his face. He had his fingers pressed against his forehead.

"I am sorry," I said, wrapping my left arm around him.

He exhaled a sign of relief.

"I needed to hear those words" His chin quivered. "I needed to hear from them what had happened." He gave me a half-hearted smile as he wiped his nose.

I am sure he understood my puzzled expression.

"It is one thing to have strangers tell you what happened, what my parents' intensions were," he continued. "And another to have your mother and father inform you themselves. My heart feels comforted. I thought they had fled, without any warning, without caring." His face turned to me. "I thought they were cowards…"

We remained seated in silence, gazing at the flowing waters of the small river. I was relieved that his parents' words did not bring him such a heavy burden.

"Their bodies are here," Demetre muttered. "In this garden." He trailed his hand across his hair.

My eyes widened in surprise.

"How do you know this?"

"Nathan," Demetre affirmed. "See those statues?" He pointed at two white statues that sat far to our left. "King Demyon built those as a memorial. Their bodies lie under the ground beneath them."

Even from afar, it was obvious that the statues were built in the likeness of a man and a woman.

"Are they…were they made to look like your parents?" I feared that my thoughts were right. Demetre responded with silence.

"But I don't want to see them." He bowed his head, resting it on his hands. "I am not ready—especially my dad."

My hope was that my presence alone was enough comfort for him at this moment. I had no words that could ease his pain.

"We overcame the darkness of the Wastelands. I will be fine, Isaac." By the sound of his breaking voice, I knew he once again was holding back his tears. "I wish they could see us now," Demetre continued. "I bet never in their wildest dreams did they think we would get as far as we did." He raised his head to me, letting out a thin smile. "I wish my dad could see me now…"

"I cannot disagree with you on that one," I affirmed. "I still wonder about my parents' whereabouts. King Demyon mentioned that they came to Bellator and left. I wonder where they went."

Demetre grabbed a small pebble and tossed it in the stream.

"Be glad that there is at least hope that they are alive," he said. My left hand covered my mouth, making its way to my forehead as I nodded. Demetre was right.

"To my father, I was always so weak and fragile. I presume he saw in me the outcome of a his wrong choice." There was a distant stare in Demetre's eyes.

"Regardless of what he saw in you, my friend, in the end, only you can decide what your fate and journey will be," I said.

Demetre nodded his head. His cheeks were red and his face swollen.

"I wonder how they built this place," I said, trying to diverge from the subject.

"It is quite a sight to behold, isn't it?" Demetre replied in a low voice. "The blue flames keep this garden warm."

"How do you know that?" I asked, standing to my feet.

"Nathan shared a lot on our way here," he responded. "I suppose he was trying to comfort me."

"King Demyon said they are preparing a banquet for us this evening. He said all the book-bearers are to be there."

"Where is it?" Demetre suddenly inquired as I helped him stand, disregarding my previous comment.

"The Diary?" I asked.

"Yes," he said with an edge to his voice. "Is it safe?"

"The Diary is in my room. I found it when I was getting dressed. I believe Nathan put the book there, along with my other things." I started making my way back. "We should head back. We don't want to keep them all waiting."

"I hate dinners. Ever since we left Agalmath, they never seem to go so well," he said, catching up to my pace. I let out a soft laugh.

"Let us hope this one goes better."

As we proceeded toward the door, I glanced over my shoulder, looking at the statues behind me. With my gifts I knew I might have been able to see the last memory they had before dying. Not going to them felt like a betrayal to me. Though I knew Demetre's heart was too weak for such a sight, my heart felt heavy leaving them behind.

"We will see them when you are ready," I said. Demetre shot a quick glance at the statues. His lips turned into a hard line.

"We will…" his voice trailed off.

III

AS I REACHED for the silver handle, the door swung open.

"Isaac, Demetre, you must come with me." Nathan's breath was heavy, and his eyes were tight and worried. "There is an urgent meeting."

"What is it, Nathan?" I was alarmed by the urgency in his voice.

"King Demyon is calling us all to the throne room. We must meet the others now."

The secrecy killed me. As we walked through the halls of the castle, I could not keep myself from thinking of what might have happened. Could it be that Shadows had attacked again? Were Nephilins destroying more people? Had they reached us?

I analyzed the guards and the servants of the castle. It seemed as if they were all unaware of any emergency. The servants calmly dusted off the furniture; the guards, as still as statues, stood at the doorposts and in front of the massive white columns. I tried to read the hearts of those present in the room. I was caught by surprise when I realized no image came to my mind. I tried once again but nothing was shown to me.

"I can't see anything." My lips quivered. "I cannot read their souls." Demetre darted me a surprised look.

I felt my wings slither under my skin. "I can feel my wings but I cannot see hearts anymore."

Anger and doubt arose within me. Was Lucifer doing this? Memories of Aloisio flashed in my mind—moments of weakness where my powers vanished like the mist.

"Are there Nephilins?" Demetre asked Nathan, grabbing ahold of his arm.

Nathan pulled his arm away. "Not now, Demetre. All questions will be answered before the king."

Seven bald men dressed in blinding white robes walked by us. They chattered amongst themselves. Their ears and noses were pierced with silver jewelry. Two of them had markings shaped like white dragons painted onto their bodies. Of course I did not miss their eyes glaring at me as they walked past us.

"It seems the Wise already know you both," Nathan said.

We followed the seven men. Demetre was quiet, his footsteps apprehensive. Nathan kept rubbing his fingers against each other at every step he took. Confusion stirred inside of me as I realized the Wise walked toward a massive wall. No picture frames hung on the wall, and no torches adorned it.

"Is this the right way?" I asked Nathan, to which he made no reply. My eyes looked at the wall again, seeing what many would believe to be a myth. One of the seven men cupped the palms of his hands and blew on them. A

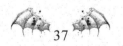

dancing blue flame appeared, burning with great strength. His hands diverged from one another, touching the wall. Like wax, the wall melted to their feet, unveiling the throne room.

Joy filled my heart when I saw Devin and Petra chatting Their faces broke into wide smiles once they saw us. The Wise approached the king, silently standing next to him.

"Am I glad to see you both," Devin said, spreading out his arms as he walked toward us.

"I am relieved to see you are both well," Petra said, walking next to Devin.

When we were within reaching distance, Devin embraced us both. He let out a soft laugh.

Petra's brown eyes overflowed with joy. "Even though our time together was short, rest assured that I am happy to see you far from harm's way."

The sweet smell of cinnamon was once again strong. The throne room walls were built with cobblestones, precisely aligned. An enormous round iron chandelier hung above the room.

The king was seated on his white throne. With a pensive expression, he rested his chin on his hand. Never once did he look my way. Bones that had been melted together gave structure to the throne and its dragon-skull shape. The macabre sight caused me to tremble inside.

"He wants to wait until all are gathered," Devin said, walking closer to the burning fireplace on our right.

"Darker days lie ahead of us." Petra scratched his chin. "The uncertainty of the coming days is troublesome to all those that are aware of this Darkness."

"I am sure word has reached many kingdoms of the destruction of Mag Mell, Aloisio, the overtaking of Billyth, and all the other attacks," I said.

Petra scoffed as he crossed his arms; the wounds on his wrist became visible. "But that is the most frightening thought, isn't it?" He shot me a worried glance. "Many know the truth and yet they still choose to ignore it. One must wonder what kind of thoughts permeate the minds of such men."

Echoing footsteps resounded in the room.

"Am I late?" a boy with long brown hair and light hazel eyes said as he walked toward Devin.

"No, Ballard, you are just in time," Devin responded, a smile curving his face. "Isaac," he turned his gaze to me. "Allow me to introduce you to Ballard Radley, keeper of the third book—the Book of the Destroyer."

Ballard gazed at me for a while. I tried to read his mind but my powers failed me yet again.

"Finally we formally meet, Isaac. Devin spoke of you after he rescued me and the others from Nephele in Aloisio." An odd feeling stirred within me as I gazed at his face—he looked familiar.

I tried to gather any memory I had after King Marco and Nephele bled me like a wild pig, but all I could remember was the darkness that overtook me as I closed my eyes to this world. The memories that came after— those I would always try my hardest to forget.

"What happened, Devin?" I insisted as I collected myself. "After I...passed on to the other world?"

"After the Soul Exchange was performed on you, I was taken prisoner along with Petra, and we were placed in the

Prison of Despair." Devin narrowed his eyes, taking a deep breath. "We were locked in the lowest level, the floor between the Abyss and Tristar. Ely came to us as we lay against the cold prison floor bruised, wounded, and weak."

"The darkness of the lower grounds was frightening. The only sound heard was that of tormented screams and the roars of beasts," Petra added with an edge to his voice. His empty eyes watched the flames dance in the fireplace. "At times, I had the feeling that the walls were caving in on us, suffocating the life that was still left."

"That was until we saw the circle with three lines shining with great strength on the mildewed walls. The symbol multiplied, covering every part of the cell with a bright light, until the prison vanished and we found ourselves standing in front of the cathedral, surprised at the war scenery we gazed upon," Devin said as he grabbed more wood and cast it into the fireplace. "The monuments were turned into ashes, and the Desert dragons burned and mutilated the innocent."

"Until I found you." Ballard set his eyes on Devin, a soft grin stamped on his face. "The moment I set foot on Aloisio, the symbol on the cover of my book was taken by a bright light. I wrapped it in old rags, trying not to draw too much attention. It wasn't long after my arrival that the Shadows invaded and the attack commenced. Doubt overshadowed my mind. Like a poisoned rat, I shambled my way around the battle until I stood in front of the cathedral. Seconds later, Devin appeared with Petra and Ely."

"Appeared?" My head recoiled back.

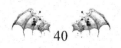

He nodded in return. "Yes," he said. "One moment they weren't there, and the next they were."

"We found the others hiding in the flames of the Council of Many Meetings. Of course, Nephele had found one of us first," Petra said. "I do not think Xylia will forget that encounter any time soon." He gnawed at his bottom lip as his right hand rubbed his chin. "Neither will I…" His weary voice trailed off.

"It is a miracle that you are alive, Ballard," Devin added. If you hadn't been able to escape the Prison of Despair in Justicia after Nephele and Adawnas found you, you would not have been standing here today."

For a short while, I kept my eyes focused on Ballard. There was something familiar about him. Then it became clear to me.

"You were in Justicia on the day I returned to my body, weren't you?" The memories played fervently in my mind.

Ballard smirked. "I see that your memory does not fail you, Isaac. It was a miracle that guided me to Justicia on that day."

Demetre's face was pensive. "What led you there, Ballard?"

"In a dream, I saw you and Demetre running through a great wasteland; the scarlet sky painted with stars sat above you as you desperately traveled down the torturous path. Both of you looked frail and weak, your lips dry and bruised, your bodies feeble and restless. Out of the nothingness a creature appeared. Its scaly body dragged on the dirt like a snake, its long arms crawled, giving it more strength. The creature looked sad…lost." He narrowed his eyes.

My eyes glistened while I wiped my nose with the back of my hand, trying to contain my sobs as he shared his dream.

"Both of you approached the creature. You talked to it, for quite some time. A sudden glare of light cut through the red sky and touched the dry ground. A cloud of dust arose, blinding my vision, but I could still see that the light had taken the shape of a six-winged lion, its eyes as scarlet as blood. The lion let out a fierce roar, causing the ground to tremble. You and Demetre held on to each other as the earth beneath you caved. The creature vanished like a cloud. Then a voice spoke to me. *One greater than death has come.*"

Words did not come to me. I felt the warmth of the flames coming from the fireplace.

"How do you know this? Demetre asked, his face shrouded in confusion. "We never shared this tale with anyone."

"Sometimes, I see things in my dreams." Ballard's voice turned into a whisper as he looked at me. "When Nephele and Adawnas had me prisoner, I knew you'd come back, both of you."

"Why did you go to Justicia alone?" I inquired.

"Because of the dream. I knew I would find you there, and we needed you. I didn't know the Underwarriors had planned an attack on Justicia upon your return."

All was becoming clearer. Raziel had probably ordered Alexander and the Underwarriors to come aid us once we had left the Wastelands.

Ballard let out a deep breath. "I must indeed be grateful for the Underwarriors. They rescued me from that prison…I was too weak to carry on."

"It was also because of the Underwarriors that we were able to escape Aloisio. We must indeed be grateful for their service," Devin said.

"They fought alongside Demetre and me in the battle of Justicia, along with the men of Aloisio. I am forever in their debt," I said. Vivid images of the battle flashed in my mind. As they all shared their tales of peril, I tried not to be consumed by my own memories. "Even in the Wastelands, Raziel found me."

"Where is Ely, Devin?" Demetre said as his eyes circled the room.

"Ely rode to the Kingdom of Watermiles upon the king's request. I believe Demyon is calling up a meeting," Devin replied.

A moment of silence loomed over us.

"My heart grew frail and weak when I saw you bleed over that book," Devin continued. "Unbearable pain stung me when Adawnas walked into the room and looked me down as if I was some chained beast."

One of the servants made his way toward the king, holding a tray with a silver chalice and a metallic jar. The king stared at the young boy with a smile.

"Perfect timing, Pathmus. Pour me some wine."

Gently, the ashen-blond boy poured the purple drink into the chalice. King Demyon watched us with an apprehensive stare.

"Are the others coming, Pathmus?" He picked at the throne's armrests while he looked around the room.

"I apologize for our delay, king," a voice affirmed before Pathmus could reply. I looked over my shoulder and was astounded at the girl's beauty. Her flaming red hair hung below her shoulders, and her eyes reminded me of the green grass of the Hills of Mehnor. Beside her stood another girl with dark hair that cascaded down in waves. Her chestnut eyes were filled with sorrow, her pale skin reminiscent of the purest silk. Our eyes met, but she quickly deviated her gaze from mine.

"Xylia, Adara, welcome," King Demyon said, sipping his wine. "We have much to discuss today."

Both girls bowed their heads and proceeded to stand next to me.

"You must be Isaac," the redhead said. "I am Xylia. Such a pleasure to meet you." She wore a gray hooded coat that trained down to her knees. Around her waist, she had an under-bust black leather corset. Her charcoal boots sat below her knees.

"And I'm Adara," the brunette said with a smile. Dressed in green tones, she wore a corset in shades of lavender atop her gambeson. Her brown boots were ornamented with swirls and patterns.

"You will all have time to chat after we are done. Shadows were seen in the Weeping Mountains around Bellator. Mountain spies sent a message through our Watch Birds, informing us that they caught sight of some creatures emerging from the Ruins of Madbouseux. As we all know, there has been no sign of life in those ruins for thousands of years."

"What kind of creatures?" Ballard took one step in the direction of the king.

"That they were not able to say," one of the Wise men responded, crossing his hands.

I shot him a cold stare.

"What do you mean?" I asked, bearing my eyes into his. "I am assuming the soldiers of Bellator know Nephilins, Shadows, and Desert dragons, given they aided us in battle not long ago."

"I assumed your trip to the Wastelands would have enlightened you about the armies of Lucifer, but it seems you have remained a fool after all." The Wise man's eyes sparkled with anger.

"My good sir, it is not the foolishness of the question that frightens me, but the thought that the creatures Demetre and I saw in that world are coming to Elysium." Silence loomed over us. The corners of his lips trembled. I noticed his hands had turned to fists. "Trust me when I say—better to fight Nephilins and Shadows than the devilries we saw in that abyss."

Devin's lips went as rigid as a rock.

"Isaac," Demetre whispered, avoiding the Wise man's gaze.

"Be quiet, Draevor," ordered one of the Wise men. His companions watched him as he stepped forward. He stood next to Draevor, bearing his ashen eyes into his. The markings of the white dragon covered his bald head.

"What do these creatures look like, Sathees?" King Demyon asked with a fearful voice. "I tried looking into the Lion's Stare but it does not show me anything beyond our borders right now. Thus the reason for fear within me. I am afraid that these creatures are heading toward Bellator."

"One of our scouts said that these creatures resemble humans, despite the greenish hue of their naked skin."

King Demyon's jaw dropped. "Were those the only creatures seen?" Keeping his eyes set on Sathees, King Demyon placed his chalice on top of the throne.

"No, my lord," Sathees replied. "One with red eyes and olive skin was seen leading them."

"Red eyes…" King Demyon's voice faded, his eyes grew distant.

"His garments aged and torn, they said," Sathees added.

Silence reigned over the room for a while. With empty expressions, we tried to make sense of these creatures that had emerged from the ruins.

"Could it be that the tales of my forefathers are true?" King Demyon mumbled, scuffing his fingers against his chin.

"What do these tales say, king?" Devin asked.

King Demyon walked down a short set stairs. "The tale speaks of blood-drinkers. Men that discovered a dark power hidden inside a book called the Book of Letters. Their king fed them his own blood—blood tainted with the darkness of Lucifer. The tale says that the men that drank his blood found eternal life, but in order to remain immortal, they had to drink blood forever. The Creator sent Stars from Tristar and punished the king and his kingdom, sending them all to a place called The Heart of Elysium."

"Can these blood-drinkers change others into what they are?" Seconds felt like minutes as I waited for King Demyon's response.

"The curse can only performed if they have possession of the Book of Letters," King Demyon answered.

"Has there been any word on any other attacks by the Nephilins and the Shadows?" Adara asked with a soft, soothing voice.

"No news," Nathan replied, crossing his arms against his chest. "We have not heard of Nephele, Erebos, or the Nephilins since the fall of Justicia."

"The good news is that we have Ohmen, king of Swordsmouth; Folletti, king of Watermiles, and Valleree, queen of Tarsh coming here to discuss defensive strategies against such powers. They will be here in about two days," Demyon said.

Xylia ran her hands across her red hair, rolling her eyes to the back of her head.

"What are we to do until then?" She spread out her arms. "Are we to sit here and wait for a decision while these creatures roam Elysium?" Her green eyes were filled with rage as she walked closer to King Demyon.

A smirk appeared on his face. "What do you know of war, little girl?" King Demyon raised his voice. "How many battles have you fought in?"

"More than you could ever know." She pressed her eyebrows together.

King Demyon shook his head.

"I do not see how that could be possible," he said.

"King, my whole life has been a battle. My parents died the day I was born into this world. My uncle Ihvar found me two days after they were murdered. I have battled and fought against the rage that burns inside of me. Do not think that just because a crown sits on your head you

47

understand everything there is to know about battles. You might lead soldiers, but you cannot lead hearts, unless they believe in you."

All had their eyes set on her. King Demyon gave her a half-hearted smile while rubbing the corner of his bottom lip.

"King, send out soldiers to patrol the area near the kingdom," Sathees said. King Demyon turned his eyes to him. "May I also suggest that you send Xylia with them? But give her a white dragon. Her bravery is admirable."

"That is not a bad idea, Sathees," the king responded to his servant's request.

"It will be an honor. Better to be prepared than to be caught by surprise." She raised her right eyebrow and crossed her arms. "dragons do not frighten me."

"Xylia, it is too dangerous out there." Adara walked to her side. "We are being hunted. Do not do this just to prove your courage to others."

"I am not trying to prove anything, Adara." She darted her a cold stare. "We cannot just sit here while our enemy destroys everything we hold dear."

"I will go with you also," I said. "I will accompany the soldiers and the dragons."

"Maybe I should ride with you as well, Isaac." Demetre placed his hand on my shoulder.

"Stay here, in case something happens," I said. Considering the fact that my ability had failed me, I had to assume our enemies were close.

"I will also stay with them, Isaac," Devin said.

Nathan came at me. "I will ride with you. Let the other book-bearers remain in the castle while we patrol the area."

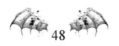

"Pathmus." King Demyon turned to the boy. "Be sure to give them swords prior to their departure."

"Right away, my lord." With great reverence, Pathmus bowed his head and headed out of the room.

"You have two hours. Return before nightfall." King Demyon climbed his way up the stairs, grasping the chalice of wine before sitting back on his throne. "Do not fly beyond Bellatorian borders." He turned his eyes to Sathees. "Lead them to the dragon tamers. Prepare a dragon for Xylia and the soldiers."

Xylia's eyebrows shot up on her forehead. She looked confused. "What about them, king? Do they not get dragons?" She cocked her head in my direction.

"They can fly, girl," King Demyon replied in a snide tone.

Xylia shrugged her shoulders, walking to Nathan.

Pathmus walked back into the throne room holding three swords inside their scabbards.

"Here." He handed a sword to each of us. I gazed at mine as I removed it from its case. Its black grip was adorned with purple stones. At its pommel was engraved the symbol of the white dragon. I caught sight of the other swords that had been handed to my companions. All of them were of similar design and shape.

"Follow me." Sathees turned and walked toward the exit of the throne room. Xylia, Nathan, and I were at his heels.

The moment we crossed the limits of the throne room, there was a loud rumbling sound. Behind me I saw the wall mounting itself up again, hiding everything behind its massive structure.

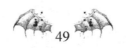

IV

WE MADE OUR way through the somber halls of the castle. The crackling sound of the blue flames on silver torches sounded like a well-rehearsed symphony. Oil paintings of landscapes hung on the monumental pearly white walls. Sathees led the way without making any effort to have a conversation.

Hopeful, I tried to read Sathees's soul, but my attempt was unsuccessful. My fingers clenched into fists. I let out a sigh of frustration.

"Nathan," I whispered. "I can no longer read souls. I don't know what is going on." The troubling thought that our enemies were close shrouded my mind. Creases appeared between Xylia's eyebrows as she wrinkled her nose.

"When did this start?" Nathan looked at me, confused.

"After I—"

"You had the ability to read minds, Isaac?" Sathees interrupted, glancing over his shoulder.

"Yes." I was astonished at his attempt to carry a conversation.

"And I am assuming you lost that ability ever since you returned from the Wastelands, correct?" There was coldness to his voice.

"What business is it of yours?" Xylia spread out her arms. "What do you know about his abilities?"

Sathees came to an abrupt halt.

"My dear." He turned to face us. "I am part of the Seven Wise. I may know more than you give me credit for." Sathees's eyes narrowed. "You saw an enemy."

My heart accelerated inside of my chest.

"Yes…" My voice trailed off as the memories returned to me.

"Now, was there a reason why you would see this enemy? Do you have any unresolved situations with the one you saw?" He sank his eyes into mine.

I bowed my head, cracking my fingers. "If you are as wise as you say, you know the answer to that question."

A soft smile brushed his lips. "Dear one, only a man may know his own heart." He turned his back to me. "You have not lost your ability. It has," he clicked his tongue as he raised his finger, "changed."

"To what?" There was urgency in my voice. "Changed to what?"

He looked over his shoulder. "If I am correct, Isaac, you entered your enemy's mind. How you were able to do so, that I cannot answer." He shied his eyes away from mine. "We must carry on."

My hands tightened into fists.

"Damn it," I whispered, frustrated.

Ahead of us was a set of silver stairs; their rails were made of pure iron, shaped like trees. As we descended, I

noticed Sathees's face growing grim; his lips curved, his fingers clenched. For some reason, he avoided looking at one of the canvases that hung in front of us.

Amidst the paintings that depicted beautiful landscapes hung one showing a woman.

"Who is she?" Xylia stopped, raising her eyes to the painting.

The woman depicted on the painting had a sorrowful look in her chestnut eyes. Her long dark hair cascaded down her shoulders; her smile was thin and shy. She wore a simple scarlet dress.

Sathees turned to face the canvas. In silence, he gazed at the depiction of the woman with a smile on his face. He extended his right hand, trailing the tips of his fingers across the painting.

"That is Queen Lylith—King Demyon's deceased wife." He cleared his throat.

"What happened to her?" Nathan inquired. "How come we have not seen her yet?"

Sathees lowered his head as sorrow overtook his face.

"If we were to see her, endless joy would fill my heart. She died when giving birth to their son, Isakaar." He tightened his eyelids; a soft smile brushed his lips as he shook his head. "I can see her in my memories, walking down the castle halls as the servants readied for the birth of the child."

"Where is the child?" Nathan watched Sathees. "What happened to him?"

Sathees unveiled his eyes, looking at the painting once again.

"He died." He trailed his hands across the canvas with a sorrowful expression. He turned his back and continued to make his way down the stairs.

If only I had my abilities now, I thought while we all exchanged a confused look. I did not need my powers to know that Sathees was hiding something.

The stairway ended in front of a wooden door with corroded black handles.

"Get ready for the soft breeze." There was a snide tone in Sathees' voice. He reached for the door handles, twisting them. At the creaking sound of the opening of the door, the chilling wind touched my face. I shivered, setting my eyes on the snow that descended from the ashen sky.

Sathees made his way out of the door, his long white robe dragging on the ground, merging with the snow. He walked through the storm as if he was immune to the sub-zero temperature.

My companions and I followed him. With every step we took, there was the sound of the snow being crushed beneath our feet. Sathees looked like an apparition as he walked ahead of us. His robes moved with the blowing wind.

Nathan and Xylia walked to my right. Xylia rubbed her hands against her arms in an attempt to protect herself from the cold.

"I figured you'd be used to this weather by now." A soft smile brushed my lips as I watched her.

"How can you endure this weather?" Her teeth chattered at every word.

"It has been so long since we have seen sunlight that I am used to it by now." I took in a deep breath as memories

53

of the bright summer mornings in Agalmath flashed through my mind. I missed the sound of the chirping of birds, the smell of freshly baked bread, the sound of my parents' voices while they talked in the early hours of the morning.

She scoffed, rolling her eyes. "It does not matter how long I walk under this weather, my body could never get used to it. I grew up in the village of Dragonhall, close to the kingdom of Watermiles. Our summers last ten months."

"Sathees!" Nathan shouted, raising his head in an attempt to better see him. "Are we close?"

I gazed ahead, trying to see Sathees through the falling snow.

"Indeed we are!" he yelled in response. Amidst the snow, the shadow of a hill appeared. The closer we got to it, the more trees I saw. They bowed in the wind; the sound of breaking branches merged with the relentless howling of the storm.

I narrowed my eyes, trying to see the landscape ahead.

Without any warning, Sathees started making his way up the hill.

He raised his right hand, turning his face in our direction.

"Stay down there," he ordered. He turned his face away from us. His hands grasped the branches of the trees as he struggled to climb.

"What is he doing?" Xylia had her eyes fixed on him.

Once he reached the top, he knelt down. He lowered his head, sinking his forehead into the snow. He buried his hands under the coat of white that sat on the ground. Not

54

long after, the markings of the white dragon that were on his body glistened with a silver-blue light. The light irradiated from the markings, making them visible even amidst the storm.

Nathan, Xylia, and I watched in fervent curiosity. None of us uttered a single word or turned our eyes from him.

Cracks and holes emerged on the surface of the hill. The ground trembled as the strength of the light increased. A cloud of dust arose, merging with the falling snow, making it impossible to see Sathees. A loud rumbling echoed around us.

A few seconds later, all that was left of the hill was a pile of dirt and dust. In haste, I approached the location where the hill had once stood.

Xylia walked beside me.

"Where is he?" she asked with an edge to her voice.

"What is this place?" Nathan surveyed our surroundings. "I should fly and survey the area."

"No, Nathan." I set my eyes on him. "I am sorry, but with this wind, it is too much of a risk."

"We must help him." Xylia hastened her way toward the remains of the hill.

"Sathees!" I shouted at the top of my lungs.

I narrowed my eyes once I caught sight of the shadow of a man emerging from the cloud of dust. Xylia's stumbled back as she took in the unusual sight.

The shadow strolled its way in our direction.

"I apologize for the mess. This is the only way to get to the dragons." It was Sathees. He dusted off his white garments while looking at us.

"You could have given us some type of warning. We thought you were dead." Xylia rested her hands on her hips.

"There is a price to be paid if one chooses to carry the magic of dragons," said Sathees with a serious tone. "I do not owe you an explanation, young one. You must trust me."

There was anger in Xylia's eyes.

A low rumble came from behind Sathees. He bowed his head, shutting his eyes.

I watched in disbelief as a short gray-stone well emerged from the ground behind him. Its rocks were covered in mold, foliage, and branches.

"How did that just appear?" I shot Sathees a confused stare. "What is that well?"

Sathees opened his eyes. "Our way to the dragons, of course." He turned his back to us. Without any trace of fear, he climbed atop the well, standing on its edge. "This is how we will get to the tamers." He took one step toward the nothingness that stood between him and the mouth of the well. I tried to grab ahold of him as his body fell inside but I missed his hand.

"Is he mad?" Xylia ran to the well. "Does he expect us to follow him? We could die."

The darkness of the well was intimating.

"What other choice do we have?" Nathan lowered his eyes, gazing at the blackness of the well. "We cannot just linger here in this storm."

As the words drifted from his mouth, the rumbling noise resounded once again. I looked behind me to see the hill rising from the dirt.

Xylia took a deep breath, climbing on top of the well.

"Since we have no other option." She looked over her shoulder, setting her gaze on me. "I will see you on the other side, boys." She lowered her head and jumped.

"Well, if she can do it." I gave Nathan one last look before I jumped inside.

My eyes could not see anything around me. I felt suffocated while I plunged down. Not long after I had fallen, I heard Nathan follow me.

After a couple of seconds, I felt my ankles touch the water. When I'd least expected it, I was submerged under frigid water. My wings slithered under my skin in a sign of defense.

Though my eyes were open, the darkness of the water hindered me from seeing anything. I swam through the dark, struggling to bring my body to the surface.

I gasped for air once I reached the surface. There was a dim light shining from what seemed to be the shores of an immense lagoon. I flapped my feet and arms, making my way toward the light. The water was so cold it felt as if my skin was being pierced by one hundred blades at once. It was not long until I caught sight of Sathees and Xylia standing next to a torch that burned against the walls of a cave.

"Over here!" I heard Sathees's strong voice as he beckoned me closer with a slight flick of his wrist.

While I swam my way to them, I realized that no splash had followed mine. Alarmed, I surveyed the water, trying to find Nathan, but there was no sign of him.

"Where is Nathan?" I asked, walking out of the frigid water.

57

"Come stand close to the fire, it will warm you up," Sathees gestured the way with his hand.

"Where is Nathan?" I repeated in a stronger voice, approaching the blue flames of the torch.

There was tension in the silence that had now settled.

"We heard no other splashes after you—"

Xylia was at a loss for words, when suddenly the sound of beating drums reverberated inside the cave. Guttural sounds and terrifying roars joined the repeated beatings.

A cold shiver shot down my spine, and my heart accelerated inside of my chest.

"I know what that is," I wailed as I recalled the last time I had heard those roars.

"What is it, Isaac?" Xylia asked. "What is making this sound?" There was a soft tremor coming from the ground beneath my feet.

"Capios," I answered, turning my gaze to Sathees. "Where are the dragons?"

"They are not far." Sathees stood as still as a statue.

The roars were closing in, growing louder as the beating of the drums increased.

"Lead us to them. We have to leave this place," I said.

Through the darkness we ran. I had the ability to run faster than all of them, but I was clueless as to where the dragons were. I also knew I could not leave them behind— not now.

After my eyes had adjusted to the darkness, I saw that the roof of the underground cave was high; its dark walls dripped with water. The smell of mold lingered in the air.

Ahead of us, a sudden flash of light broke through the darkness.

"There they are!" Sathees cried in tone of relief.

Suddenly, my body was tossed against the cold walls of the cave. A sharp pain spread through my back as I felt the tips of sharp rocks penetrate my skin as I thudded on the ground. A loud, terrifying roar echoed. Disoriented, I reached for my sword.

"Isaac!" I heard Xylia's fearful voice. To my left, I saw her body being dragged by an unseen creature. She tried to claw her way out of the creature's grasp, but the Capios' strength overcame her own.

My wings sprung forth, ripping through my skin and clothes. At full speed, I followed Xylia and the Capios.

"Help me!" she kept on screaming while the Capios let out a high-pitched screech. After a short while, the Capios pulled Xylia deep into the darkness, disappearing from my sight. Her screams faded into silence.

"Xylia!" My breathing had grown shallow. I tightened my hands, squinting my eyes in an attempt to peer through the dark.

I heard the echo of the Capios' distant growls, followed by Nathan's agonizing screams.

"Nathan!" I attempted to run through the obscurity of the cave.

The screams were followed by the sound of massive rocks falling to the ground. In a matter of seconds, a dust cloud that lingered in the air invaded my nostrils.

Once again my ears were stung by Xylia's cries for help. I rested my body against the moist walls of the cave as weakness crawled into my heart.

The sudden sound of wings flapping through the darkness stirred me with hope. I pushed my body away

from the walls of the cave, narrowing my eyes in an attempt to see whatever approached me.

"Fly toward the light, Isaac!" Nathan's voice boomed from the blackness. A strong wind blew as I heard him fly above me. With my wings spread to their full length, I followed him.

Is he holding Xylia? I kept thinking while I headed to the light.

The light shone from a gap in the walls of the cave. Once I flew through it, I found myself staring at an open space that sat high above the ocean. The sound of crashing waves merged with the howling of the wind.

I landed next to Nathan, losing my breath once I caught sight of Xylia lying on the ground, unconscious. Most of her nails had broken off of her fingers. Her face was covered in scratches and wounds.

"How are you feeling?" I asked, relieved to see them.

"I will be fine," Nathan responded with a whimpering voice, looking at the gashing wound on his arm. The cut was deep, and the skin on his shoulder and forearm dangled, revealing his muscle tissue.

"We must go back." I narrowed my eyes, disturbed at the sight of his wound. "We cannot carry on like this."

The smell of burnt charcoal entered my nose. From the corner of my left eye, I saw a shimmering cloud of silver smoke flowing through the cracks in the wall of the cave. Piercing shrieks and growls echoed from the other side.

Nathan rose to his feet, staring at the rising smoke.

A sudden thud created a long gap in the wall's surface.

In an attempt to better hear what was taking place on the other side, I pressed my face against the cold wall.

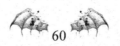

Amidst the growls and roars was the sound of the distant agonizing screams of men.

My eyebrows came together. "There are men on the other side. I believe the Capios are attacking them."

"We must help them," Nathan said.

The muffled screams pained me as, in my mind, memories of the Wastelands once again tried to take over.

I tightened my grasp on my sword as I stood in front of the wall. How would we break it? How would we help the men on the other side?

"Isaac," Xylia mumbled in a broken voice, raising her head from the ground.

"Xylia!" I rushed my way to her. "How are you feeling?"

"I have seen better days."

I extended my hand, helping her stand on her feet. She sank her eyes into mine. "Where is Sathees? Do you think he is…"

Her voice trailed off as the ground beneath us started to tremble.

"What is going on?" Nathan asked.

I turned my eyes to the wall. Cracks continued to appear throughout its surface as a cloud of dust arose, merging with the silver smoke that lingered. The trembling of the ground intensified at a great speed. It was not long until the wall was turned into scattered rocks.

The growls were now louder; the smell of decayed flesh burned my nostrils. The afflicted cries of the men were almost as loud as the roars.

Once the cloud of dust had settled, I walked through the crater that was now in front of me. A shiver shot down my spine as my eyes absorbed the sight of a dead soldier lying

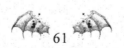

on the ground. His face was deformed, his jaw dislocated. His torso was exposed—wounded with burn marks. I approached the body only to find that his right arm was missing.

The ground in front of me disappeared, falling into a massive crater. Inside, white dragons were chained to the walls, fighting the unseen creatures that tortured them. Their snouts smoked as bright blue flames gashed from their mouths. The beasts fluttered their wings, trying to break free from the silver chains that bound them to the walls. Men feebly waved their swords, struggling in their battle against the Capios. A round metal staircase led to the bottom of the crater, though the darkness below did not allow me to see far.

Unexpectedly, a white dragon soared out of the bottom of the crater at great speed, letting out a mighty roar. Mounted on the beast was one of the tamers.

I was alarmed when I heard Nathan's harrowing groans. I looked over my shoulder and saw him lying on the ground with his hand pressed against his wound. Xylia stood beside him.

I stomped in their direction.

Sweat rolled down his forehead; his eyes glistened with tears. His breathing was rapid and shallow. Blood oozed from the wound in his arm, dripping between his fingers.

"Xylia." I bore my eyes into hers. "Watch Nathan."

Xylia furrowed her brows, looking in the direction of the crater.

"You will try to free them by yourself?" Her eyebrows slanted upward as her eyes widened.

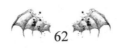

"What other choice do I have?" I looked down at Nathan's trembling body. "Those men need my help."

She grasped my hand. "Be careful." Her face looked pinched as her eyes glistened.

My feet left the ground above me as I plunged downward. I dodged flame and rock, trying to approach the white dragons. My body shivered at the sound of drums bellowing around me. I knew they were coming. My eyes absorbed the macabre sight of bodies hanging from rocks like ornaments. The round staircase was covered in blood.

I landed next to one of the white dragons. The beast agitated its wings, trying to pull its neck free from the heavy chains. With great strength, the animal wagged its tail. I was discouraged when I realized the thickness of the chains.

I cannot break this, I thought while watching the animal.

I was alarmed when I heard ominous shrieks and growls around me. A strong force gripped my arm, pulling me to my knees. I waved my sword in the hopes that I would wound its unseen body. The dragon grew even more flustered; its breathing deepened while smoke billowed from its nostrils.

The growls ceased as I felt the invisible creature release me. Relieved, I pulled my arm away.

"Are you Isaac?" a reedy male voice asked. I turned my eyes to the man standing behind me.

"Who are you?" I asked. "Where is the Capios that had ahold of me?" The middle-aged man had scruffs of hair on his chin and a scar across his nose. Whatever was left of his silver armor was covered in blood, which also flowed from a wound on the right side of his neck.

"Othar, head of the Dragon Tamers," he replied in a broken voice.

"I am Isaac. I have come to help you." I attempted to ignore the helpless screams that echoed throughout the cave. "Tell me what you need."

His eyes trailed across the blood-covered staircase.

"Can you save all my men?" he asked, his voice filled with despair.

"I am not sure if I can save them all." I laid my hand on his shoulder. "But I give you my word that I will try."

"Help me free all the white dragons." He circled the cave with his eyes. "I cannot leave my men to fight alone."

"What do I have to do?"

"At the bottom of the cave is the Chamber of Bellator. Inside, you will find a lever amidst the spikes at the foot of a statue. Pull it and the chains will disintegrate. We built it as a defense mechanism in case an attack ever occurred."

"I am assuming that the bottom of the cave is overrun with Capios."

Sorrow overtook his face. "The men that were there never got out," he said with glistening eyes.

"My friends are here—one of them is badly wounded." My chest tightened at the thought of my suffering companions.

"The only way to save us is to release the dragons. Their flames can destroy Nephilins and Capios."

I looked at Othar, knowing that the chances I would meet him again were scarce.

"It is a shame that we had to meet in a situation like this, Othar." I let out a soft breath.

64

"Do not feel sorry for the circumstances in which we have met, Isaac. It is better to know a warrior for a moment on a battlefield than to walk beside a coward for a lifetime." He turned around, rushing his way up the staircase, returning to the massacre that was happening in the crater.

I jumped into the darkness, finding courage in the simple thought that I could help all of these men defeat the Capios. At the same time, I wondered if Demetre and the others were safe. Had the Capios reached the castle? Were the books secured? The darkness seemed to inspire my mind into thinking ill thoughts.

V

THE BELLOWING ROARS of the white dragons faded along with the shouts of the men as I descended. A light shone from the darkness beneath me. As I drew closer, I noticed that it came from the flames that burned on a torch pinned to the wall of the cave. I felt a warmth rise through my body when my feet touched the ground. My eyes surveyed my surroundings, in case enemies sat hidden in the shadows.

I reached for the torch, shuddering once my fingers wrapped around its cold base. My wings rested on my back as I trod through the unknown. Visibility was limited and a foul odor lingered in the air.

It was quiet—too quiet. The hairs on my neck rose as I listened to the sound of my own heart beating in my chest.

After a few steps, I caught sight of the chamber Othar had mentioned.

The entrance had been sculpted into the wall of the crater. Seamless designs ornamented the doorway; writings from an unfamiliar language had been carved on the walls.

I continued walking until my toes kicked something hard. My eyes darted to the ground, catching sight of the remains of a destroyed wooden door. My wings fluttered in a sign of warning.

The unfamiliar words glistened with an incandescent blue light as I walked through the entrance of the Chamber of Bellator. Water dripped from the walls, creating puddles on the ground. The echoes of the raging battle echoed faintly around me.

My heart skipped a beat when I heard the terrifying drumming sounds start again, this time even closer to me. I quickened my pace, looking for the lever Othar had mentioned. In my desperate search, I came across a crater located at the end of the tunnel.

I hastened my pace, making my way inside as the sounds continued. Ahead of me, I saw the statue of a white dragon sculpted atop a blue stone. As Othar had mentioned, spikes protruded from its base.

A sudden light illuminated the small chamber. I realized the flame on my torch burned brighter, causing the blue stone to reflect a kaleidoscope of colors; the ancient writings on the walls exuded light.

I sat the torch next to the statue, searching for the lever as the guttural sounds continued to echo. With all my strength, I pulled one of the spikes toward me. The palm of my hand stung with a sharp pain. I screamed, bringing my hand closer to my eyes. Despite the precarious lighting, I saw blotches on my skin.

My hand closed into a trembling fist. All the spikes looked identical, making it difficult to find the lever.

There was no time to waste. Without much thought, I continued to pull every spike, hoping to find the lever that sat hidden among them.

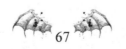

The pain was excruciating. My hands burned with a throbbing pain. I was relieved when one of the spikes shifted. I released it from my grasp, listening to the thundering roars that now echoed in the air. The bright colors emanating from the stone began to fade; the light from the ancient writings dissipated. It was not long until the only light source I had was my torch.

There was a loud thud to my right. I grabbed my torch and looked down, finding the body of a soldier lying on the ground. The thudding continued. Like a rehearsed symphony, the noise echoed. What my eyes saw brought me great terror. Dead bodies of Bellatorian soldiers started to appear around me. It was a macabre sight to behold: Their mouths had been sliced with such ferocity that they merged with their noses—or whatever remained of their facial features. Their eye sockets were empty.

As fast as my legs could carry me, I ran through the narrow small tunnel, heading to the main entrance of the Chamber of Bellator. The mutilated corpses kept piling behind and ahead of me. A stomach-curling odor permeated the air.

Once I stepped out of the chamber, I beheld the corpses falling from atop the cave. They mounted on top of one another, spilling their innards as they hit the ground.

The mighty roars of the white dragons intensified as I made my way out of the depths of the crater. The creatures had set the staircase aflame. Riders mounted on their beasts fled while others hovered inside, burning everything in their path.

I was mesmerized by how the Capios burned. Once the fire touched their unseen bodies, one could see the fire

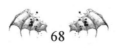

outline their grotesque shapes. Silhouettes of hollow eyes, abnormally long hands with elongated fingers, and legs similar to an amphibian's with human feet were enveloped and consumed by the flames.

"Isaac," I heard a voice shout from atop the crater. "Hurry!" To my surprise and relief, the voice sounded much like Sathees'. I kept on rising in the direction of where I had first left Nathan and Xylia. Silver smoke lingered, creating a thick curtain around me.

As I soared, to my left I saw Othar mounted on his white dragon. His eyes bore deep into mine as he gently nodded his head.

"Tell Demyon what you saw here. Warn them that they are coming!" he shouted in a loud, strong voice. I gave Othar one last look before my eyes refocused on my trajectory. Many dragons clung to the walls of the crater—most of them had their riders on their backs.

Once I had reached my destination, a mighty explosion roared. Frightened, I looked over my shoulder and saw that the crater—and all that was inside of it—had been set on fire. Inside the flames, I saw white dragons turning to ashes, their riders burning alive as they fell away from the beasts. The pungent smell of burning flesh arose.

I distanced myself from the explosion, searching for my companions. My mind also found time to worry about the others in the castle. I needed to go to them.

I was apprehensive the moment I realized my companions were nowhere to be found.

"Xylia! Nathan!" I yelled in the hope that they would hear me, but there was no response.

The heat of the flames brushed against my skin. There was no time to waste. Once again, I looked around me and, at the top of my lungs, shouted their names repeatedly, but silence still lingered.

I left, flying through the tunnel that had led us all there. Weariness took over my body as I traveled through the darkness, struggling to maintain my altitude and speed. My mind could not help but think of what could have happened to Nathan, Xylia, and Sathees.

As I recalled the Capios dragging Xylia through the tunnel, fear filled my heart and mind. How come my powers seemed to have diminished after my return from the Wastelands? It grieved me to think that I had come from that place only to see my companions perish.

An unexpected object shimmered in the obscurity of the tunnel. Curious to see what it was, I landed beside it. It was a sword—similar to the one King Demyon had handed us prior to our departure. Blood was smeared on the blade, and there were cracks on its grip.

She is not dead, I kept thinking to myself. My breathing grew shallow as the air thickened with smoke. I tightened my grasp on the sword, determined to find them.

There was a sudden tremor in the walls of the tunnel. I was startled by the sound of rocks falling beside me. Standing back on my feet, I attempted to run, but a sharp pain took over my head. Disoriented, I fell on my chest, feeling the pebbles pierce through my skin. A cloud of dust arose from the ground.

I laid my hands on my head, feeling an open wound that gushed with blood. For a while, I lay motionless, trying to

figure out what had just happened. I grunted in pain, struggling to stand to my feet.

I managed to rise. Disoriented, I rambled my way through the tunnel using my left hand to support my body against the wall.

In a matter of seconds, the cloud of smoke seemed to have thinned out. I reached out through the darkness around me, trying to find something to hold on to, but my hands found nothing.

The lagoon is ahead, I thought. *The well should be above me.*

My eyes narrowed in an attempt to better see my surroundings. My heartbeat quickened as I still failed to see.

With caution, I continued to walk through the dark. My head pained me greatly; dizziness tried to take over me. After a couple of steps, I felt the cold waters of the lagoon touch my feet.

I got on my knees. My teeth chattered as I submerged my hands beneath the freezing water. After taking a couple of drinks, I washed the painful throbbing wound on my head.

A soft bubbling sound came from the lagoon. Alarmed, I tightened my grasp on the sword's grip. I heard the waters move, feeling the ripples touch my calves as the soft sound continued. My wings spread to their full width; I kept looking around, hoping to see any movement. From the lagoon, a red light came forth. The scarlet glare increased as it rose from the bottom.

I did not know what to expect. My mind raced at full speed. What sort of devilry lingered in places like these?

The light moved to my left side at a slow pace. I dared to take two steps into the lagoon to better see where the

light came from. When I looked down at the water, my breathing failed as I saw the reflection of a pair of enormous moss-green eyes gazing behind me. I turned to find a macabre creature. It let out a high-pitched growl as it lifted its long snout. From the corner of my eye, and despite the limited lighting, I saw its slender body covered in thick scales. They rattled as the creature slithered out of the lagoon.

The grotesque beast moved around me in a circular motion. There was a red light shining from the tip of its tail. Like a snake, it positioned its body for an attack.

Without any sudden moves I gazed at the creature with my sword in hand. Three uneven horns protruded out of its nostrils; its gills were colored with a green pigment that glistened in the dark. The smoke cloud grew thicker, making it difficult to breathe. I had to leave this place if I wanted to find the others.

The moment my feet left the ground, the creature snapped, hissing as it tried to sink its teeth into my flesh. I managed to wound its body, slashing its neck with my sword as I turned from its violent attack. It let out a deafening screech, recoiling to the ground. Darkness once again hovered as the light on its tail went out.

My body trembled as I continued to soar into the nothingness, unaware of how far I was from the roof of the cave. The creature's roars bellowed once more. I looked beneath me and saw nothing but darkness, which was soon broken by a pair of green eyes that approached me at a rapid speed.

I quickly swayed to my left, trying to avoid the creature's attack. Light once again shone from its tail. The beast

reared upon the anterior portion of its scale-covered body as it extended its long neck. Its bright teeth glistened as it opened its mouth, trying once again to wound me. I dodged its attacks; its eerie screeches pierced my ears.

Every time the creature tried to wound me, it would strike its head against the walls of the tunnel, causing rocks and boulders to fall.

To my relief, I caught sight of the roof of the cave above me. Despite the falling rocks, I was able to reach it. Of course, the question now was how to escape this place.

The creature let out a loud groan as it returned to the bottom of the cave, the light on its tail dimming out and sinking into the darkness.

My breathing was now the only sound I could hear. I struggled to keep myself from giving in to despair. I felt the razor-sharp rocks touch the palms of my hands as they trailed the cold roof of the cave, trying to find an escape.

A loud roar resounded as a bright scarlet light flashed throughout the place. I was quick to see that the creature had ascended from the lagoon, its body positioned for a final strike. I plunged down, causing the creature to strike its odd-looking skull against the roof of the cave. In an instant, rocks rained down, creating a massive crater above me and revealing the white landscape. Flurries of snow made their way inside the cave.

With painful groans, the creature recoiled back to the bottom of the cave, slithering its way into the cold waters of the lagoon.

With all the strength I could muster, I made my way out. The frigid wind brushed on my face as I ascended toward the gray skies. In haste, I surveyed the landscape, trying to

find the well that had led us to the cave, but it was nowhere in sight. I struggled to fly through the snowstorm, but my eyes failed to see through the thick curtain of white. I used the back of my hand to wipe the blood that oozed from the wound on my forehead.

The sounds of drums echoed in the air once more. I wondered where they were coming from. They seemed to be all around me, but I could not be sure of their exact location.

It was at this moment that my mind recalled the Wastelands of Tristar, the red sand of the deserted landscape, the scarlet sky painted with silver stars—the emptiness of not knowing whether I would ever leave that place. I recalled the foul shadowed creatures that tortured me as I strolled around the lonely hills.

I have not returned to die here, I thought, filling my mind with memories that brought me strength. I remembered the Creator; Raziel informing me that Death had been conquered; Demetre being brought back to life along with me; the men of Aloisio that had aided us in the Battle of Justicia.

No matter how intensely Lucifer's army plotted against me, I knew it was my duty to overcome all their evil schemes.

With a great struggle, I landed in front of the old door of the castle. As my legs sank deep into the soft snow, I stood still for a couple of seconds in an attempt to regain some of my strength. Flying still took its toll on my human body. I felt the stinging pain coming from my hands and my head; my wounds dripped with blood.

The high towers of the castle were hidden by the storm. My wings retracted under my skin as I opened the door.

Once inside, I discovered that the torches that had been scattered with great precision throughout the hall no longer burned; an eerie silence lingered in the air. My eyes absorbed the sight of the countless bodies of Bellatorian soldiers scattered on the floor like mere objects. Blood flowed from their wounds; their golden suits of armor were reduced to shards. Human limbs hung from the chandeliers.

Anger stirred within me. I made my way among the bodies, trying my best not to touch them. The canvases lay broken, their pieces spread across the somber hall. I felt as though the sub-zero breeze that blew through the cracks in the windows could touch my bones.

There was fear in me that the worst had happened to my companions. I struggled to make my way up the staircase once I saw all the decapitated corpses piled on top of each other. I tried to capture the last image these men had seen before they died, but none appeared in my mind. I sighed in frustration as a feeling of impotence tried to find its way inside of me. With every step I took, the soles of my boots touched the blood that covered the ground like a long scarlet rug.

The hall that led to the throne room sat in darkness. Flags with the emblem of the white dragon lay on the floor, torn and smeared with blood.

Ahead of me, amidst the destruction, was a man resting on a chair. He had his head bowed. In his hands, he held the head of a soldier; the skin around the soldier's neck had

been ripped from his body. The remnants of his victim lay against the man's left leg.

"Who are you?" Rage flowed with my words as I marched to him.

The man shot me a surprised, cold stare, but he seemed unbothered by my presence as he let out a soft chuckle.

"What do we have here?" There was a snide tone to his words. The pale man dropped his victim's head on the floor. My eyes analyzed his flaming red hair, and green irises that seemed to have been painted on his face. His thin lips pursed into a cunning smile, revealing a set of fangs.

"Pardon my appearance, young one. I had to feed," he said, using his tongue to wipe the blood that was smeared across his chin. His ragged brown coat was punctured with holes, and his white shirt was also covered in bloodstains.

I scowled at him, confused.

"Who might you be?" I watched him with attentive eyes.

The man cackled. "My name is Dahmian, servant of Bartholomew, King of Madbouseux."

"Then you serve a dead king, Dahmian." With caution, I stepped my way to him. "We all know that the inhabitants of that kingdom vanished thousands of years ago."

Dahmian bit the right side of his bottom lip, taking two short steps in my direction.

"There are always three sides to a story, boy: my version, your version, and the truth. If only our disappearance could be so simply explained." His right eyebrow rose up to hide under his flaming hair. "We did not just simply vanish into thin air. We became…special." His tongue caressed his fangs.

76

I recalled King Demyon's account of the blood-drinkers. Could it be that Dahmian alone had killed all these men?

"I assume you are responsible for this doing?" My gaze was fixed on the body that lay next to him.

"We all need to eat, young boy." He knelt next to the headless man; his fingers trailed the blood that poured from the body's wounds. "I must confess that I cannot wait to taste royal blood." A cunning smile appeared on his face.

With sword in hand, I moved in his direction. My wings once again appeared despite of my body's exhaustion. I swung my blade, certain that it would wound his pale skin, but I was caught by surprise when I felt my sword burn the palm of my hand.

I released it from my grasp, staring at him in disbelief.

"What is your name?" He clasped my face with his right hand. "You are surely not ordinary."

I pierced his eyes with mine.

"No matter." He tightened his grasp and then released me. "You will answer me soon enough." He let out a menacing laugh, turning his back to me and facing the wall behind him.

"Now, where is that old man?" Dahmian strolled around the empty hall, humming a disturbing melody.

"What are you doing?" My eyes followed him. Dahmian approached an iron chest that sat near the fireplace.

"Are you in there, my friend?" He kicked the chest three times. "It is time to get out."

His olive eyes looked over his shoulder. "I must speak to the king. We have urgent matters to discuss." His lips pursed into a thin smile.

77

He bent down, opening the two locks on the iron chest. There was a muffled male voice behind the creaking sound.

It was one of the Wise. His clothes were smothered in blood; his eyes and mouth were covered with black rags and his garments had been ripped around his shoulders and waist.

With bare feet, the man crawled out of the chest. I looked for the markings on his skin, but there were none. His hands trembled as he got on his knees.

"You know how to get us to the throne room, don't you, old man?" Dahmian grabbed the nape of his neck, tightening his grasp as he led him near the wall. "Work your magic and get us to the other side…please."

For a second, Dahmian had his back to me; his full attention was focused on the wall. Without much thought, I risked another attack. I swung my sword, aiming for his right thigh. At full speed, the blade penetrated his skin. A loud scream came forth.

I waited for Dahmian to strike back. To my surprise, he led his right hand to his thigh and covered the wound.

"You still do not understand." His eyebrows pressed together. "We cannot be defeated, boy."

He grabbed the man's head and cocked it to his right.

"You brought this upon him."

I heard the painful groans as Dahmian sank his teeth into the left side of the man's neck. With trembling hands, he tried to push himself away from Dahmian's grasp.

A tingle of fear rushed down my spine as I contemplated the wound on Dahmian's right leg, which was now closing up. The bleeding had ceased.

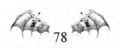

"I won't kill you…yet." Dahmian's lips and chin were smeared with blood. "Now, show us the way."

"You need to uncover his mouth." I recalled the way the other Wise men had opened the wall earlier. With a fallen countenance, the man nodded his head in agreement with my statement.

Dahmian narrowed his eyes, scowling at me.

"Do you lie, boy?" His eyebrows rose. "If you are lying," he pointed his finger at the man, "this old rag will die a very painful death."

"I am not lying." I tightened my hands, bearing my eyes into his.

He removed the rag that covered the man's mouth. I expected him to shout, but no sound came from him.

"What is your name?" Dahmian knelt beside him.

The man lifted his tired eyes, clearing his throat.

"Othaleeon."

Dahmian slapped the right side of the man's head. "Do not keep me waiting, Othaleeon."

"I was entrusted…to keep the secrets of Bellator safe. Do…not expect me to simply open the—"

Dahmian's right fist collided with the man's face, opening a wound on his cheek.

"Do you take me for a fool? Show me the way."

Othaleeon bowed his head.

"Let him kill me." I was startled by a strong voice that echoed inside my head. *"Let him take my life away. Do not fight back."*

My eyes turned to Othaleeon. His tongue trailed across his bleeding lips as he looked at the wall.

"I may be of old age, but knowledge is one of my weapons, and I am afraid I cannot show you the way into the throne room." He pressed his eyelids together, expecting Dahmian to strike him again.

"You—"

"This is no time for games, Dahmian." A loud voice boomed behind me. I looked over my shoulder, finding a man of high stature standing next to a blond woman. "If we do not enter the throne room soon, our attack will be delayed. Why have you not fulfilled the task I entrusted you with?" The man marched in our direction. His tattered brown coat covered his body down to his knees.

"Who might you be?" He scratched his chin, looking at me as if I was an insect.

"That is none of your concern," I replied, reaching for my sword, which was lying on the ground.

The man scoffed and continued making his way to Dahmian. His dark hair was tied back; his crimson eyes shimmered in the dark. The woman made no effort to move from her place; as still as a statue, she watched us with her hazel eyes.

Dahmian pointed at the despondent man. "The old man is the only one that can show us the way in, Bartholomew."

Bartholomew? The King of Madbouseux? Had he returned from his grave as a red-eyed killer?

"Dahmian, how loyal are you?" Bartholomew placed his finger under Dahmian's chin, lifting his head.

His green eyes widened. "I followed you in your rebellion against the Creator and Elysium when you sold your soul to Lucifer. We rode together to war and to our grave, and never was I disloyal to you."

80

Bartholomew's lips went rigid. "Make sure that does not change during this battle." His head cocked in my direction. "The winged boy is still breathing."

"The winged boy might be important, my lord." The woman spoke. Her golden locks bounced as she strolled toward Bartholomew, her hazel eyes looking at me. Her waist was strapped in a black corset. "Do you not recall Nephele mentioning that there was one who was the keeper of the Diary of Lucifer? It is clear that this boy is not ordinary."

"Do you take me for a fool, Nylora?" He looked at me. "Of course I remember."

A cunning smile appeared on Bartholomew's face. "Old man," he said, shifting his gaze to Othaleeon. "If you do not show us the way, we will feed on you in front of this boy."

Do not help me. Othaleeon's voice boomed inside my mind once again. I let out a frustrated breath; my hands trembled.

Why should I not help you? I thought, hoping he would answer me, but there was only silence.

Bartholomew walked around the suffering man. Othaleeon's eyes swam with tears.

"I will ask you one last time." The sound of breaking bones merged with Bartholomew's voice. He crushed the man's right leg with his left foot. Othaleeon let out a deafening scream, which turned into copious sobs. "Lead us to the throne room."

I tightened my grasp on my sword while I watched the horror in front of me. For a moment I thought my heart

was going to jump out of my chest. What was this man's plan?

Othaleeon did not utter a single word. Nylora trailed her hands across his head, kneeling beside him.

"Since you have denied our request, we will have to find someone else. You are becoming a burden to all of us." A smile appeared on her face. She looked over her shoulder, bearing her eyes into mine. "I believe his lack of cooperation makes him guilty, don't you think so, boy?"

Tears of frustration rolled down my left cheek.

"That makes him loyal...you beast." My chin quivered as the words drifted from my mouth.

Bartholomew slapped Othaleeon's face with the back of his hand. "So keep in mind that it was loyalty that led this man to his grave."

The bloodbath began. They mounted Othaleeon's body. Nylora dismembered him, pulling off his arms and drinking from the open wounds. Dahmian sank his fangs into his face, ripping apart his nose and eyes.

"Let them kill me." His voice once again spoke to me, only this time it sounded more like a fading whisper.

Bartholomew tore Othaleeon's garments from his body. With his hands, he ripped the man's stomach open, spilling his guts on the floor. As they feasted on Othaleeon's flesh, the wall started to melt like ice. My heart pounded as fear arose inside of me. Were my companions on the other side of this wall? Had they been captured? Were they alive?

"I guess the old man was not so loyal after all," Dahmian laughed, pointing his blood-covered finger at the wall. All three stood to their feet, their clothes, hands, and faces smeared in blood.

VI

THE THRONE ROOM sat in darkness. My eyes surveyed the room, searching for my companions, but they were nowhere to be seen. I did not know if I was to feel joy or sorrow at this moment. Had they escaped? Had they been kidnapped?

"Where are you?" Bartholomew shouted, kicking one of the chairs to the ground. "We know you are here, Demyon."

All the furniture lay untouched. A low fire still burned in the fireplace.

"How did you find us?" I asked Bartholomew as he paced around the room.

"That is none of your concern," Nylora snapped as she, along with Dahmian, approached the empty throne.

"Well, Nylora. I can answer my own questions." A smirk appeared on Bartholomew's face. "We followed the Capios here. Once Xavier came to encounter Nephele and Erebos in the Heart of Elysium, we knew we had a chance of finding the book-bearers."

A cold shiver ran down my spine when I heard the name of the one that had brought me so much rage.

"You saw Nephele?" My mind was polluted with memories of the last time I had seen her.

Bartholomew pursed his lips. "Is she any of your concern?" He narrowed his eyes.

She was of my concern. I wanted her dead.

Bartholomew pressed his fingers against his chin, turning his face to Dahmian.

"This boy annoys me. How come he is not dead yet?" he asked.

"I do not think you want to kill him." I was relieved to see Devin walk out from one of the doors behind the throne.

"Devin," I shouted, relieved to see him. "You are well."

Nylora marched in his direction; the sound of her heels clicking against the floor reverberated.

"Well, what do we have here? If only you had been the one to have awakened us from our sleep." Her voice was like an entrancing melody. She extended her hand in an attempt to touch Devin's face, but he recoiled.

"Awoken you from your sleep?" Devin asked. With sword in hand, he paced around the room, his eyes focused on the blood-drinkers.

"Where is Demyon?" Bartholomew grew impatient. He rubbed his fingers against his forehead. "We must speak to him."

"What business do you have with him?" Devin pointed the tip of his sword toward Bartholomew.

"Our business is our own, Nephilin," Dahmian said. "Must we kill all the inhabitants of this kingdom in order to see its king?"

84

"You and the other Nephilin…Nephele…you are both very stubborn." Bartholomew said, giving Devin a half-hearted smile. "There are ten of us here in Bellator. I wish I could tell you where the others are."

"What business do you want with me, Bartholomew?"

Bartholomew's jaw opened and he intertwined both of his hands.

"Oh my," he said with a smile. "The king walks out of his chamber." He spread out his arms, bowing his head in mockery.

"All my life, I thought the tales of the blood-drinkers were legend. It is repugnant to see what you and your people have become," King Demyon said.

"My people?" Bartholomew raised his right eyebrow. "Always so quick to judge, Demyon. Always so willing to pass judgment without knowing the truth." Bartholomew rushed his way toward him.

"How far have you fallen?" King Demyon looked at him in disgust.

"Hopefully, I have fallen so deep into the darkness that no one will dare try to bring me back to the light." He bent his neck to the left, cracking his bones.

"May I go fetch the others?" Dahmian asked.

"Yes. I want them all here." He furrowed his brow, narrowing his eyes at King Demyon.

Dahmian paced his way out of the throne room, humming the same haunting melody from before. Bartholomew clicked his tongue repeatedly; his eyes focused on King Demyon.

"I know they are here, Demyon." Bartholomew crossed his arms. "You know of whom I speak."

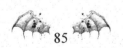

King Demyon observed Nylora as she walked to his right.

"Will you tell us where they are?" she asked as she grabbed the nape of his neck, licking away the blood that had dried on her lips. "I do not think it is necessary to say what will happen if you do not."

"Do not think we will allow you to wound him." Devin stooped his body forward as he used both of his hands to grasp the handle of his sword.

Bartholomew let out a snide laugh. "Let's see what the great Nephilin is capable of." He grasped King Demyon's arm. "Try to stop me." His teeth sank beneath Demyon's skin.

From the corner of my eye, I saw Devin's garments ripping like a veil, his dark feathered wings springing from his body. My wings slithered underneath my skin, ripping their way out of me in an instant. Like a torrential river, anger rushed through my veins. I did not hesitate. I tightened my hand into a fist and struck Nylora's jaw.

Her right hand tightened around the nape of my neck. My nerves twitched beneath her grasp. As the blade of my sword penetrated Nylora's side, a throbbing pain took my head.

My surroundings were as black as the night. I saw no one else but a grotesque monster ahead of me. Instead of its skin, a clear substance covered its frail-looking body. Its once vivacious blond curls were now lifeless. Despite the gruesome appearance, I could tell by the facial traits that this monster was Nylora. Why did she look so decomposed?

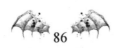

Her body shivered at every step I took. Low snarls came out of her as she wrapped her exposed chest with her skeletal arms. For a while, I gazed at the creature. A part of me was aware that this was the moment to wound her, but for some reason, I pitied her. What had led this woman to be this way? She had once been human and now she was a monster. My thoughts were drowned by the vivid images of how she and the others had killed Othaleeon and the Bellatorian soldiers. My hands pulled on her hair, lifting her chin to me. Empty cavities had taken the place of her eyes. For a few seconds, I stared at her, despising everything she had become. I rested my blade beneath her chin.

"Death," I whispered, feeling my sword cut through her skin. A thick, dark liquid poured from the gushing wound.

The darkness faded like smoke. I took in a deep breath as I surveyed my surroundings. All in the room gazed at me with fervent eyes.

"Isaac…" Devin's voice trailed off. "How?"

Something wet touched my boots. I gasped when I caught sight of Nylora's bleeding body lying on the floor. Her beautiful pale skin disintegrated, revealing the clear substance that covered her skeletal body.

"Bastard," Bartholomew declared, surprised at the sight. He tightened his trembling fists; his eyes bore into mine.

Confusion stirred inside of me when I saw my sword smeared with Nylora's blood.

Wings similar to those of dragons sprung from Bartholomew's back.

"No one can kill us!" Bartholomew shouted. "Who are you, boy?"

"My name is Isaac Khan and I am the bearer of the Diary of Lucifer."

"Nylora was right when she said you were no ordinary boy." Bartholomew pursed his lips and spit on Nylora's decomposed body. "She was…always weak anyway."

By now, Nylora's body was nothing more than a pile of bones buried in a puddle of blood. The stench that rose from the decomposed corpse was reminiscent of a dead animal's carcass.

From behind me, loud footsteps resounded. When I turned, all the courage inside of me vanished. Dahmian marched in front of them. Their wings were extended to their full width, some being longer than others. I counted, and with Dahmian they were a total of eight blood-drinkers. They stopped in a perfect line.

"Can you defeat us all, Isaac?" Bartholomew let out a malefic laugh as he walked to them. "See that boy?" He pointed to me. "He killed Nylora."

"What are we going to do about that, Bartholomew?" Dahmian asked, crossing his hands.

The blood-drinkers had their eyes fixed on me.

"You will all pay for this," one of them shouted in a high-pitched voice. "No man can kill us." They broke out in animalistic growls and roars. The noise resembled a pack of lions roaring in the wilderness.

It was in that moment that a sudden blue fire appeared inside the fireplace. Confused, I gazed at the bright flames, wondering where they had come from. The cold air inside the room gave way to a rising temperature.

"You are all fools." My heart skipped a beat when I recognized the voice that reverberated around us. It was

Sathees'. A ghostly image of him appeared next to the empty throne. He was clothed in his white robes, and the markings on his body burned with an incandescent blue light. His eye sockets were consumed by flames.

A loud explosion occurred where Sathees stood, filling the air with a blinding silver.

"What are you trying to do, old man?" Dahmian shouted. "Scare us all with your cheap tricks?"

Loud roars echoed in my ears. My knees trembled when I saw wings appear. The smoke receded, revealing a beast that now stood in the room with all of us. A white dragon, armored from head to tail.

Bartholomew and the others stared at the beast with fearful eyes.

I looked at him with a smirk on my face.

"Cheap tricks?" I mouthed the words to him.

The blood-drinkers were agitated. They exchanged confused looks as they stepped away from the throne room.

"I will kill you," Bartholomew screeched, pointing his finger toward me. "I will kill you."

In a matter of seconds, their bodies turned to smoke. They flew through the windows, reducing them to shards as they broke through the glass.

"Cowards!" Devin shouted, watching our enemy flee.

For a while, I stared at the magnificent creature. How did Sathees know that we were here? Devin and King Demyon approached me.

Like the early morning mist, the white dragon's body started to dwindle. The temperature in the room dropped.

The flames inside the fireplace ceased to burn. Darkness settled once again.

Sathees lay on the ground, unconscious. To my relief, next to him were Xylia and Nathan. All three of us tended to them.

"Are the others safe?" I asked Devin as he knelt next to Nathan.

Devin shot me a cold stare.

"They are." His voice was cold. By the look on his face, I knew what question lingered in his mind. Little did he know that I was also unaware of how I had been able to take Nylora's life.

"Where are they?" I asked him. I grasped Xylia's cold hand; my eyes trailed across the wounds on her fingertips. Her face was covered in cuts and bruises.

"In the dungeons," King Demyon replied from my right. "I ordered them to wait for us there."

Once again I looked at Devin. He shied away from my gaze.

All three of them lay like the dead.

"What is wrong with them?" I feared for their lives.

"Sathees protected them by using the dragon Shield. The shield will protect the body but it will put it into a dormant state. They will wake soon," said King Demyon. "Devin," he continued. "Take Xylia and Nathan to where the others are. I will care for Sathees."

"Alright," Devin mumbled in response to the king's request. With steady hands, he set Nathan on his shoulders.

My entire body trembled as I grabbed ahold of Xylia. I was weak.

VII

KING DEMYON CARRIED Sathees, exiting the room through the center door located behind the throne. Devin made his way out using the doorway located on our right. I followed. We were led down a long and narrow passageway.

At every footstep, I felt a weight growing in my mind. I tried to understand how I had been able to defeat Nylora. I had lost my abilities after my return from the Wastelands, but this newfound power was undecipherable to me. Devin seemed apprehensive, his eyes never looking at me once.

The precarious lighting made it difficult to see. Torches had been sporadically placed on the mildewed walls of the passageway.

"When did the blood-drinkers' attack commence?" I asked Devin, attempting to start a conversation.

"Moments after you left with Xylia, Nathan, and Sathees, one of the Bellatorian guards barged into the throne room, holding the head of a man. His ears had been lacerated, and on his forehead the word 'war' had been carved." He made no effort to look at me. "Shortly after, the Bellatorian soldiers flocked inside the castle as the sound of drums resounded. They wanted to protect the king." He shook his head from one side to another. "King Demyon ordered the book-bearers to stay hidden in the dungeons until he felt it was safe for them to come out."

I slowed my pace, allowing Devin to go ahead of me. Even if just for a short while, I wanted solitude. Despite the alarming situation we were all in, I still wanted to find the answers I was looking for.

I noticed the passageway led us in the direction of a stone wall.

"Any plans on how we will get to the other side?" I asked.

With his right hand, Devin reached inside the satchel around his shoulder, taking out a turquoise jewel shaped like a circle.

"What is that?" My eyes were fixed on the object.

"The Lion's Stare." His hand tightened its grasp around the object. "King Demyon said it would reveal to us the way out of the passageway."

I felt a tremor beneath my feet. Startled, I gazed as the wall in front of us opened wide like a door. I was surprised to see that it had led us to the hallway where my room was located.

This side of the castle was untouched. The flames still burned bright and a sweet aroma still lingered in the air. Through the window I saw that the snowstorm had ceased.

"Lay her in that room." Devin cocked his head to the right. "I will be waiting for you here." There was tension in his voice.

"Alright," I said.

He walked in the opposite direction, entering one of the other rooms.

I twisted the doorknob, stepping inside the room. The crystal chandelier was the first thing that caught my eye. The satin curtains were as white as a dove's feather.

I laid Xylia on the snow-white mattress. I grabbed one of the pillows and placed it under her head. I sat beside her, holding her cold hand. There was something entrancing about this girl. She seemed so bold, yet so fragile. Though I knew so little about her, through her actions I could tell that her past was filled with ghosts.

That was the moment when I felt the weight of my responsibility. I had returned from the Wastelands of Tristar not only to protect a book, but to guard the people of Elysium. The Creator had sent these bearers my way for a reason that I was yet to discover. Regardless of how long it took for this reason to be revealed, I wanted to protect them.

I rose to my feet as I heard footsteps and whispers outside of the room. I gave Xylia one last look before I headed out. I wanted to know how Sathees had managed to escape. Where had he gone during the attack in the mountain?

I stepped outside of the room and was relieved to see my companions standing next to Devin. Demetre gave me a half-hearted smile.

"We were worried about you." He greeted me with a hug. "I wanted to come out and fight."

"We had strict orders from the king to stay hidden until it was safe," Ballard remarked with an unsettling voice.

Demetre had a rugged brown satchel hanging on his shoulder.

"I knew they were going to come looking for it." He extended the satchel to me. "It was the first thing I went after before we went into hiding."

"Thank you." My hands reached for the object I despised. "Where are the other books? Are they safe?"

"We all have our books, Isaac," said Adara with her soft voice. "We were not fools to leave them behind."

"Why did you take so long to return?" Sweat descended down Petra's brow. "Were you all attacked while you were out there?"

"Before Isaac answers that question, I would like him to tell me something first," Devin said, biting his bottom lip. "How did you kill the blood-drinker?" He scowled at me.

"I wish it was that easy to explain, Devin." I trailed my hand across my hair while shaking my head. "Ever since my return from the Wastelands, my powers have…changed."

An uncomfortable silence hovered. They expected me to elaborate on my answer.

"You stood in front of her as still as a statue, and in a matter of seconds, she fell down dead." Devin stabbed his finger toward the ground. "You must know what you did."

"You can enter the mind, Isaac?" Petra's mouth gaped open, his chestnut eyes widening in amazement.

"I could sense their souls and see the last images they saw before they died, but I was never able to enter the mind," I affirmed, confused.

"Isaac, entering the mind is a dark and dangerous power." Devin walked toward me. "Look at Nephele. She can enter the mind of her enemies through their dreams. She can inflict pain with a simple thought." He shrugged his shoulders. "Why would you possess such power?"

"Nephele," I mumbled to myself, recalling the images I had seen when I awoke in my room. *Had I killed her? Had I destroyed her?* I thought.

"Demetre," Adara said. "Is there anything different about you ever since your return?" Her brown eyes glistened.

He was silent for a while, thinking.

"I had no abilities before, and I have none now," he answered.

"Sathees," I said. "I believe he knows. As we made our way to the Dragon Tamers, he mentioned something about me entering the minds of my enemies."

"We will wait for him to—" Devin was interrupted by loud shouts and screams of men coming from outside of the castle.

"What is that?" Creases appeared between Petra's eyebrows as he approached the window.

I felt my heart skip a beat once my eyes caught sight of the violent scene. Outside the castle walls, a riot was taking place. The people of Bellator had gathered at the foot of the wall around the castle with torches and spears, clamoring and shouting.

"What is going on?" Demetre's voice was caught in the back of his throat.

I heard rapid footsteps approaching. I glanced over my shoulder and saw King Demyon walking in our direction, accompanied by five of the Seven Wise. Next to them walked a young boy. His vacant eyes trailed across the room. His clothes were covered in dirt and blood.

"What is happening out there, king?" Devin asked, looking at the boy. "Who is this? What happened to him?"

King Demyon approached the window.

"They want answers, Devin. The people want answers," he said, resting his head against the glass. "This boy ran to the castle before the riot began. One of our soldiers helped him."

The young boy's body shivered as his jaw chattered. There was an empty stare in his brown eyes.

"Young one." With his mouth open, the boy lifted his eyes to King Demyon. "Tell us what happened."

"They came earlier today," the boy started with a brittle voice. "One had red eyes…and teeth like a mountain lion's." He released a long breath, shivering as tears ran down his face.

"He speaks of the blood-drinkers," I whispered as my eyes caught sight of the bruises that covered the boy's arms.

"Were they the ones that barged their way inside the castle?" Adara asked, watching the boy with glistening eyes.

"Yes," I replied.

"They started killing everybody. There was no mercy in their eyes. They murdered families, hundreds of them. They said they were looking for a dark book." The boy's words turned into weeping.

"Are they fighting for Lucifer?" Petra asked.

"We are not yet sure where their allegiance lies," one of the Wise Men replied. He resembled Sathees; he had no hair, and his eyes were of an olive color. There were markings on his skin.

"They said they wanted the Book of Letters," the boy continued. "One of the creatures said that the book was inside the castle. He claimed that they would only stop slaughtering the families if the book was handed to them."

"We do not have the Book of Letters in our possession. Why would they think the book is with us?" Adara asked in an alarmed voice.

"You do have the book," King Demyon stated in a somber tone. "Only, you were not aware that you had it."

The clamoring of the people grew louder as we all fell silent.

"Who is the bearer of the book?" Adara's eyes trailed across the room, looking at each one of us.

King Demyon strode his way toward Ballard.

"Ballard is the bearer of the Book of Letters," he affirmed.

Ballard's eyes widened. He reached inside his battered satchel, taking out the mysterious object. The book resembled the Diary, except for the symbol etched into the cover: three straight lines inside a circle.

"My boy, your book is also called the Book of the Destroyer. Like all of the other books you bear, it was written by Lucifer. The difference is that this one has been opened before." King Demyon placed his hand atop the dark object. "Your book led the Kingdom of Madbouseux to its doom. Bartholomew found it hundreds of years ago, soon after the attack against the Council in Justicia. Upon selling his soul to Lucifer, he opened the book and learned its forbidden secrets. It contained a curse that allowed mankind to live forever if they consumed human blood. The curse can only be performed in the presence of this book."

I felt tension rise the moment King Demyon uttered the last words. Not only did we have to deal with Fallen Stars,

97

Shadows, and Nephilins, but we also had a new enemy rising.

"They were the ones that attacked us today," King Demyon continued.

"How many blood-drinkers were there?" Ballard asked.

"There were ten of them." King Demyon turned his face to me. "Until Isaac killed Nylora."

The roar of the crowd emerged as a battle cry. My eyes looked outside; fear rushed inside of me. The people that we were bound to protect had turned against us.

"To think that those that died here today will turn into Shadows," Adara said in a sorrowful voice, resting her hand against the window.

"Even if the blood-drinkers are not fighting for Lucifer, the Fallen Stars will still benefit from their attack." Devin lowered his head, reclining against the wall. "Will this evil ever cease?"

"I fear that is not the worst that could happen," King Demyon said. "If the Book of Letters is taken by them, they will once again be able to transform humans into blood-drinkers, creating an army that no weapon can destroy."

Ballard looked at the ground, pressing his fingers against his chin.

"What must we do?" Demetre whispered, turning his eyes to me.

King Demyon was silent for a short while.

"Give me the Lion's Stare, Devin," he requested, extending his hand.

Devin handed him the round jewel.

I noticed a circling mist hovering inside the Lion's Stare as King Demyon held the object close to his eyes. The blood seemed to have left his face as his jaw opened.

"No, no, no," he kept repeating in a frantic voice. "The blood-drinkers are waiting for us outside. The riot is only a diversion. Once we leave the castle, they will come for the book." King Demyon turned to the Wise. "Is there any way to warn Ohmen, Folletti, and Valleree? They will be here soon."

"Unfortunately, there is no effective way to communicate with them. We are not sure of their location. Even if we send our Watch Birds, they would still not find them," replied one of the Wise Men. He had eyes the color of honey.

"King, we cannot linger. Is there a passageway that can lead us out of the castle unseen?" Devin asked, his hair dripping with sweat.

King Demyon scowled. "How do we leave the castle when Xylia, Nathan, and Sathees still recover? Do we leave the other servants behind to face their doom while we escape?" He pressed his eyelids together, reaching for the crown above his head. He opened his eyes, setting them on the crown he now held in his hands. "My people have turned against me." His hands released from their grasp the symbol of his authority, letting it fall to the ground.

Bellatorian soldiers mounted on their horses gathered atop the wall while the remaining warriors grouped at the foot of the gate. The sound of their blaring horns reverberated.

"Then I leave with the book-bearers," Devin affirmed. "We could take the Road of Ahnor. It will lead us deep into

the Weeping Mountains. From there, we might be able to intercept Ohmen, Folletti, and Valleree."

"That road will also lead us to the Ruins of Madbouseux," Ballard stated in a worried voice. "We will be walking to our graves if we take that road."

"We have no other choice," Devin said, the veins on his neck protruding beneath his skin. "We need to take this chance. If the people make their way inside the castle, you will be the first one to die, Ballard."

Ballard opened his mouth to contend with Devin but no words came out of him. He knew Devin was right.

"What about Xylia?" I asked, trembling at the thought of leaving her behind. "What are we to do with her?"

"What about me?" I heard her voice coming from behind me. She stood by the doorway; dark circles surrounded her green eyes. There was no color to her lips.

My arms wrapped her in a sudden embrace.

"I am relieved to see you are well," I said through heavy breaths. My heart hammered beneath my chest as I felt her tender embrace.

"Thank you," she whispered in my ear. "For everything."

We explained our current situation to Xylia. Judging by her fallen countenance, she was still tired.

"We leave without Nathan and Sathees?" Her eyebrows shot up her forehead.

"We have no other choice. If we stay here, we will all be killed. Those people are terrified of the blood-drinkers and they will do all that they can to give them the Book of Letters," I said.

"Sathees protected Nathan and me during the attack." She trailed her right hand through her flaming hair as she closed her eyes. "I cannot just leave them."

"They will be safe, Xylia," King Demyon assured her. "The Wise and I will protect them."

Xylia lowered her head, walking toward the window.

"Those we were sworn to protect have now turned against us," she mumbled as her right hand rested against the hazy glass of the window.

"They are afraid." Adara crossed her arms. "Fear can steal a person's sanity in a matter of seconds."

"It would be wise to allow them to leave, king," one of the Wise Men affirmed. "Let them take the secret passageway. The blood-drinkers will never suspect they took the Road of Ahnor. They do not know you possess the Lion's Stare."

King Demyon's silence made me anxious. He scowled at the rioting crowd while rubbing both of his hands together.

"Follow me," he said, walking in the direction of the throne room.

We were at his heels. There was fear stamped on all of our faces as we traveled down the halls of the castle.

"What is on your mind, Demetre?" I noticed he had a vacant expression on his face as we walked.

His lips turned into an impassive smile. "I am debating whether it would have been better for us to have stayed in the Wastelands rather than to have returned to Elysium." He shook his head, letting out a short breath. "At times like these, I wonder if we can indeed win this war."

"I see the Wastelands as a test of our perseverance. We cannot surrender because the road is getting narrower." My

right arm wrapped around his shoulder. "My friend, we must not lose hope."

Of course, it was easier to say that to him than to believe it. In my heart, I struggled to maintain the hope living inside of me. Could we really keep the darkness at bay?

I avoided looking at Nylora's decomposed body once we stepped inside the throne room. I knew the lifeless corpse would be a reminder of the confusion that stirred within me.

"Help me move the throne, Devin," said King Demyon, grasping the left side of the throne with both of his hands. With a confused look, Devin walked up to him. They both dragged the throne from its place, revealing a hidden stairway that led down an obscure path.

"Go down the stairs and follow the passageway. At the end, you will see the ocean. Follow the trail through the cliffs. It will lead you to the Road of Ahnor." King Demyon frowned, using the back of his hand to wipe the sweat from his brow.

"I will watch over them." Devin's lips pursed into a thin smile. "Thank you for everything."

King Demyon's glistening eyes trailed across the room, looking at each one of us. He struggled to catch his breath.

"Come on, all of you." He beckoned for us to go down the stairway. "You must all leave."

I bowed my head, paying respect to the man who had shown us all great devotion and courage.

"Be brave, young ones." His voice was brittle. "The task that rests upon you is dangerous. Do not lose heart."

Tears strolled down King Demyon's cheeks as he saw us disappear into the darkness. I knew in his heart he did not know whether he would see us again. In his mind, he probably wondered if he was going to survive this attack.

"Farewell, book-bearers," I heard him whisper as we walked away.

VIII

I SHIVERED AS I felt a cold air blowing inside. I rubbed my arms against my body, trying to make myself warm. Small torches lighted the passageway; their flames burned low.

Despite the poor lighting, my eyes did not miss the writing on the walls. Etched into the stones, the mysterious words were similar to the ones I had seen in the Chamber of Bellator. Throughout the passageway was also the symbol of the white dragon I had seen on the flags hanging inside the castle.

I heard low sobs coming from behind me. I saw Petra weeping as his body sagged against the wall.

Devin looked over his shoulder. "Petra, we cannot linger." He made his way to him.

Petra slid his body against the wall until it reached the ground. He embraced his legs with his arms and continued to cry, ignoring Devin's remark.

"Give him time," Demetre said, looking at the others.

Adara strode her way to Petra, kneeling at his side. She rested her hand on his head. "We are all afraid," Adara said in a whimpering voice. "But we cannot allow this fear to stop us."

"That is easier said than done." Petra lifted his face to her. "Don't you think?"

She narrowed her eyes. "Yes, but we must still fight against our willingness to give in to fear."

"Isaac," Petra said in a broken voice, wiping his tears with his wrists. "Can you answer me one thing?"

"Yes," I responded, fearing his question.

"Do you fear the outcome of our journey?" He pressed his back against the wall, standing back on his feet. "You have returned from the Wastelands of Tristar with Demetre. One would assume fear would be a foreign feeling to you by now."

I looked at all my companions. They watched me with fervent expressions, waiting for an encouraging answer.

"Fear became more imminent after our return," I declared. "In the Wastelands, minutes are like days, and days like years."

"How did you both manage to return to your human bodies?" Adara meddled with her fingers.

The horrific memories flashed through my mind. I glanced at Demetre, waiting for him to answer the question.

"The last image we saw before we returned to our human bodies was of a white-winged lion with eyes as red as blood." All gasped the moment Demetre mentioned the animal we had seen. "It let out a mighty roar, creating a crater in the ground. We fell and, as fast as rays of light hit the earth in the early hours of the morning, returned to our bodies."

"You mean to say you saw the Creator, Demetre?" Petra asked in a surprised tone, taking a step in his direction.

"Yes," Demetre answered. He looked at every single one of their faces. "Have you not all seen him before?"

"No," Devin replied. "Only Isaac and Petra have seen the Creator in the form of a white lion."

"I saw the animal you speak of in a dream," Ballard contested. "But never have my eyes gazed upon him."

I was surprised at this newfound information. Could there be a particular reason why only Petra and me—and now Demetre—had seen the Creator with our own eyes?

My body grew numb with fear as I felt the ground beneath my feet tremble. Moments after, shouts, growls, and screams echoed from above us.

Petra widened his glistening eyes. "They have entered the castle grounds. We are doomed." He pressed his hands against his head.

"They do not know where we are," Devin asserted in a strong voice, looking at the roof of the passageway.

"We need to continue." I put my left hand on Petra's shoulder. "Now, more than ever, you need to be brave. We must leave this place."

"Find them!" I heard a strong voice echo from above. *"They have the book the red-eyed killer wants!"* Raging shouts followed; the strong stomping of their feet caused the roof to shake.

Our pace quickened as the blatant shouts of the angry crowd loudened. Amidst so much peril, I still needed to remain focused on our goal.

There was a drastic change in temperature; the walls of the passageway were now covered in a thick layer of ice. As we continued on, a dim light appeared ahead.

"That must be the way out!" Demetre shouted between heavy breaths.

The bitter cold cut through my skin. The wind's chill felt like knives entering through my flesh. I realized Demetre's assumption was correct as we approached the light.

We slowed down our pace as we tried to catch our breaths. With careful eyes, I surveyed our surroundings, ensuring that we were not followed.

From the corner of my eye, I noticed Devin approaching the gap that led to the ocean. The look on his face shot a cold chill down my spine.

"What is it, Devin?" I asked, bending my body forward, my hands resting on my knees.

"The tide is rising." His voice was a low whisper.

My throat closed once I heard his statement. I walked to him and glanced down the gap, shivering at the sight of the furious waves that crashed against the rocks. The others approached me, standing by my side. I looked to my left and noticed that the only sight to be seen was that of a cliff that towered above us.

"Where is the path that will lead us to the Road of Ahnor?" Xylia asked, probably expecting the worst answer imaginable.

Despair settled in once we realized the path was nowhere to be seen.

"We should fly, Isaac," Devin suggested, looking out into the ocean.

"They might see us, Devin," I said, struggling to hide the fear in my words. I narrowed my eyes, looking out into the raging ocean.

The crashing sounds of the waves were drawing nearer. Despair found its way into every single one of us.

"We climb." Ballard pointed to the cliff. "It is not that far."

An unsettling silence lingered for a while. There was fear in all of our faces.

"We will be going to our death." Adara shook her head, pressing her hand against her forehead.

My shoulders shrugged up. "Are we not already fighting for our lives?" I turned my gaze to hers. "We must be brave."

I marched to the edge of the cliff. Without much thought, I grasped one of the rocks to my left; my body hung in mid-air as my right hand struggled to find a safe grip.

For a couple of seconds, I stood still—my eyes danced as they studied the cliff. The clashing sound of the furious waves caused my heart to beat faster as I inhaled the frigid air.

"Come on!" I beckoned them to follow me. I glanced down, realizing the water was still rising.

My hands latched onto the rocks around me as I attempted to make my way to the other side. Some of the rocks were as sharp as shards of glass, cutting the palms of my hands. I had to ignore the sharp pain, knowing that if I let go, I could fall to my doom.

From the corner of my eye, I saw Demetre, Petra, and Ballard already climbing their way across the cliff.

I was startled by sudden abrasive shouts resounding from above.

"Where are they?" I heard the faint voice of a man.

"We must find them or the blood-drinkers will murder us all!" a female voice cried in response.

I panicked. It was not going to be long until they found us hanging on the side of a cliff.

"Isaac!" I heard Demetre scream. "We are not going to make it."

I looked over my left shoulder, realizing that Xylia, Adara, and Devin had not yet begun to climb. The sea was an arm's length from reaching the passageway.

My wings slithered beneath my skin for a couple of seconds. The moment my hands released the rocks, they sprung from my back. I was aware of the risk of having the blood-drinkers see us if we were flying, but that was a chance I was willing to take at this moment.

In a matter of seconds, I clasped Demetre's and Petra's hands, carrying them toward the sky.

"Isaac, what are you doing?" Petra shrieked as I continued to fly.

"Improvising!" I yelled with a smirk on my face. "Hold on to me."

I flew beside the rocks of the cliff, struggling to hold on to my companions.

"What about Ballard?" Demetre shouted. "We cannot leave him."

"I will return for him as soon as we land." My eyes searched for a landing spot. It was not long until I caught sight of a valley located a safe distance from the riot.

I felt my eyes throbbing as I neared the valley. There was a sharp pain spreading throughout my body. Flying still took its toll on me.

My legs were immersed in the snow when I landed. My body was relieved when I released Petra and Demetre from my grasp. They trudged through the snow, sitting on the scattered rocks. The valley was quiet; the pine trees stood tall, surrounding us like monumental walls.

"Is that Devin?" Demetre narrowed his eyes, looking to the sky.

My chest tightened as I realized he only carried Adara and Xylia. I marched to him once he landed; his dark wings retracted, resting behind his back. Adara and Xylia rubbed their hands against their arms, trying to remain warm.

"Where is Ballard?" My heart hammered inside my chest.

Deep creases appeared on his forehead.

"I did not see him when we were flying," he said. "I thought you had brought him with you."

"We must go back," I declared, my mind already crowded with thoughts of what might have happened to him. Had he fallen to his death? Had he been found?

My feet left the ground, and Devin followed.

The crowd's ravenous cries intensified. As we ascended, I could faintly see Bellator as it sat hidden behind a cloud of smoke. Monuments and houses burned like torches. We decreased our altitude, flying beside the cliff, looking for Ballard.

"There!" Devin pointed to the ocean; his dark wings maneuvered his body down.

Despair took me once I saw Ballard—his body floated atop the violent waters, his arms and legs spread wide.

Devin grasped his right arm, pulling Ballard's body out of the frigid waters. His lips were a shade of purple; his skin had lost its vivid pigment and his arms and legs dangled lifelessly.

We rushed our way to the valley. Despite the speed with which I had gotten to the valley previously, the present situation made it feel as if this was the longest journey yet. *Was Ballard dead? Had the waters taken him?* I thought as sorrow and rage crept their way inside of my heart.

"Hold on, Ballard." I watched him as we flew.

The incessant shouts of the crowd continued to ring through the air. I wondered if they had entered the castle. Had they killed King Demyon? Were the blood-drinkers still amongst them?

We plunged down toward the valley at full speed. My companions wore death-stare expressions when they saw Ballard.

"Give me your coat, Demetre" Devin demanded the moment his feet sank under the snow. "We need to warm his body."

"What happened to him?" Adara rushed to my side. "Is he alive?"

"I don't know." I bore my eyes into hers.

"Let's lay him over there." Adara pointed to one of the rocks.

"Use the coat to cover the rock, Demetre," Devin ordered while carrying Ballard's body.

Demetre removed his coat, laying it on top of the dark rock. Ballard's brown hair looked like thorns covered in ice.

Devin laid him on the rocks and wrapped him with the coat. He bent his head down, laying the right side of his face on Ballard's chest.

"I feel his heart," Devin remarked. "It is weak."

"His breathing is frail," I murmured as I saw the almost non-existent movement of his chest.

"Why did you leave him, Isaac?" Xylia exclaimed in rage. "Could you not have—"

"Could I not have what?" I felt my heart thundering in my chest. "If I had helped him, Demetre and Petra would have fallen. I had not the strength to carry all three." I stomped my way closer to her as anger burned inside of me. "You and Adara were the ones that could not even climb your way out of that cave. Don't you dare presume to tell me what I should or should not have done."

"Quiet, both of you!" Petra shouted in a breaking voice.

An uncontrollable anger slithered its way through me. Like a snake that wraps itself around its prey, I felt my patience being crushed by Xylia's remarks.

Once again, everything around me disappeared. I was surrounded by darkness. My eyes could only see one thing—Xylia. *Is it happening again?* I thought.

As I looked at her, I saw that her eyes were as black as the night, and blood ran down her cheeks like tears. Her skeletal body was covered in rags. Wisps of hair sat on her head.

An uncontrollable hatred fueled me. I wanted to kill her. How dare she presume to tell me what I had to do? Maybe she thought she was better than all of us.

I can't do this, I thought, surprised at my current desires. *How can I be willing to kill her?* What was this will that was

now finding its place in my heart? She was my companion. How dare I desire to take her life?

Moments later, the scene before me vanished. I was back in the valley.

What is happening to me? The question lingered in my mind as I watched Ballard.

"He is gone." A shiver went down my spine when I heard Devin utter these words.

"What do you mean, 'gone?'" Adara pushed Devin to the side, her hands grasping Ballard's shoulders. "Ballard?" she asked as her voice turned to sobs.

"No, no, no..." Petra's voice faded as he lowered his head.

My eyes swam in tears. I stared in disbelief at Ballard's frozen body. Like a sword that sinks inside an enemy's body, the cries of my companions penetrated my ears.

I shot Devin a morbid look. He sat still in the snow with arms crossed over his knees. With a vague expression, he gazed at Ballard.

Demetre leaned over Ballard's body and grabbed his hand. He shivered at the touch. He was silent as the tears rolled down his red cheeks.

Xylia rested her head on Ballard's chest as her right hand caressed his frozen hair. "I need to hear your heart beat again, Ballard," she begged with a breaking voice. "Please, do not leave us."

Sadness drowned all other sounds around me.

"We must move on," Devin affirmed as he stood to his feet, wiping away his tears.

Xylia turned her gaze to his.

"Move on?" She furrowed her brows. "One of our companions just died."

"And we will die with him if we do not continue to move toward the Road of Ahnor," he contested. "Those men, and the blood-drinkers, are still after us."

"Give us a moment to mourn," Demetre requested.

"Our mourning may cost us our lives. We are being hunted—all of us. We must leave this valley." Devin raised his voice.

I turned my back on all of them, venturing into the woods. There was a desire in me for solitude and silence. I shuddered as I recalled the image of Ballard clinging to the side of that cliff when I'd left him to meet his demise. My knuckles struck a dry tree trunk. I let out a shout, kneeling down; my bleeding hand rested on my thighs.

"Where are you?" I mumbled through shallow breaths, struggling to contain my urge to cry. "Where is the winged lion that breathed life back into me?" My hands tightened. "Amidst the chaos, the task you have appointed to us seems too burdensome to carry. I know humanity chose to fall away from righteousness, but can those who have chosen to fight for you not find mercy?"

I reached inside my satchel, touching one of the objects responsible for all this chaos. I wanted to toss the Diary in the raging ocean and let it sink to the bottom. In my heart, I desired to be the young boy who knew nothing of Lucifer or Fallen Stars right now.

"Despite all the pain and the loss, this task is greater than any of our needs and desires." I looked over my shoulder and saw Demetre approaching me. "There can be no victory without peril, no life without death, no strength without pain."

"Do you think we will live to see our victory?" I managed to stand back on my feet.

He lifted his eyes to the sky. "Do you remember the Song of Brave Heroes?"

"Of course." My eyes narrowed. "Your dad sang it to us whenever we went fishing." My chin quivered while the memories of those days flooded my mind.

> *"Brave heroes of the west.*
> *Glorious in conquest and victory.*
> *Brave ones who knew fear, yet overcame the enemy.*
> *Brave heroes of the west.*
> *Darkness was not your worst enemy.*
> *Fear found room amongst ye*
> *Yet through the darkness, thy light appeared."*

"The songs of glory and triumph forget to mention the trials and struggles those heroes had to endure in order to achieve their victory," said Demetre in a low voice.

I bowed my head. Would there be songs about us? Would we live to see the days when the gray clouds that hovered in the sky would no longer cover Elysium? Would we once again be able to return to Agalmath and see the fields ready for harvest?

"Hopefully, when they write songs about our journey, they will not forget to add verses that mention our trials," I murmured.

I felt his hand reach for my shoulder.

"You see, Isaac." He managed to smile. "Our songs will speak of our struggles and battles because we will be the ones to write them." His tearful eyes met mine. "Never doubt for a second that we will live to see our victory, my friend."

Demetre wrapped his arms around me.

"You are not alone, my friend," he said. Though hope was a foreign feeling at the moment, I had to believe that better days were yet to come.

IX

IN SILENCE, WE made our way back to our companions. The frigid wind brushed against my cheeks, sending shivers throughout my body.

I was startled by the sound of crackling branches and twigs coming from my left.

"Did you hear that?" Demetre's eyes turned, surveying our surroundings as he quickened his pace.

It was not long until we found our companions. Petra had his eyes fixed in the direction the sounds were coming from. Devin had his sword in hand, ready for an immediate attack.

"Whatever that is, it is heading this way," I heard Adara's high-pitched voice say.

I unsheathed my sword. The faint cries of the rabid citizens of Bellator could still be heard from where we stood.

My heart skipped a beat as the sound of an agonizing shout rose from the woods.

"Help!" a broken male voice yelled. "Please, help me!"

"We are coming!" Adara cried, running to the woods. She halted once she realized none of us followed her.

"Will you do nothing?" Her eyes looked at each one of our faces.

"What if it's a trap?" Petra asked.

Adara let out a quick breath, marching in the direction of the voice.

"Stop," Devin ordered, grabbing ahold of Adara's right arm.

"We must help him," she insisted, struggling to get free from Devin's grasp.

"Please," the stranger continued. "Help me!"

"Let me go, Devin," she requested, her left hand battling against Devin's hold.

"Listen—"

My jaw dropped when I saw Adara's fragile hand encounter Devin's face. A brief silence lingered.

"I do not care how dangerous our journey may be. I will not lose my humanity and compassion," she said, her eyes brimming with tears. She turned her back to all of us and ran to the stranger.

"Wait!" Demetre shouted, running after Adara.

We were all desperate. Ballard's death was a vivid sign of how fragile we all were. Powers and abilities amounted to nothing when compared to the growing darkness.

"What if he is one of them?" Xylia asked, walking in my direction. "What if he is a blood-drinker in disguise?"

"That is a chance we will all have to take now," Petra said with a worried look.

After a couple of minutes, I heard their footsteps approaching.

Devin sheathed his sword, crossing his arms.

"If he is one of the blood-drinkers, Adara and Demetre will deal with him." He shrugged his shoulders. "I care not."

They emerged from the woods. The man rested his arms on Adara and Demetre's shoulders. He seemed to be in his mid-forties. His dark skin enhanced the color of his tired hazel eyes. His bald scalp was covered in bleeding wounds.

The man struggled to move his legs. He let out painful moans every time the soles of his feet touched the ground. I watched as he tripped on a rock that was covered by snow. His body thudded to the ground.

I rushed to the man's aid. I looked back and was surprised to see Devin walking into the woods. His face was shrouded with rage.

"Devin," I mumbled, watching him disappear.

"I have seen better days." The man spoke in a hoarse voice.

"Save your strength," said Petra.

Demetre and Adara knelt next to the weak man.

"Thank you for coming to my rescue, my dear." With great struggle, he reached for Adara's cheeks, touching them with his fingertips. "Your bravery will surely change the fate of many."

The wounded man cringed, gritting his teeth. I noticed that there was a flow of blood coming from beneath his right hand, which was pressed against the left side of his waist.

"They attacked my family." He squinted his eyes. "My son and daughter...murdered in front of me."

"You will make it through this," I affirmed, trying not to show the whirlwind of emotions that stirred inside of me.

"They murdered the king." His breathing grew ragged. "King Demyon did not stand a chance against them."

"Mu-murdered?" Xylia inquired. She lowered her head and her shoulders drooped. I did not need my abilities to know what was in her mind. She wanted to know if Nathan and Sathees were safe. I was not sure if I could withstand the loss of so many in such a short time.

"Dead," I mumbled to myself.

With chattering teeth, the man closed his eyes.

"What is your name?" Demetre asked.

"That does not matter," he answered with a discontent smile. "If I tell you who I am today, you will not know me for who I will be tomorrow."

We all shared a confused look.

I heard footsteps coming from behind me. I glanced over my shoulder and saw Devin making his way in our direction.

"Doubt not that your choices will lead you down perilous roads," the man said with his gaze set on Ballard's body. "The boy sleeps."

I jumped back, surprised at his remark. Xylia scowled at the man.

"Sleeps?" Adara darted her finger toward Ballard. "He is dead. Do you not see it?"

"Your friend…sleeps," he repeated.

"Stop saying that," Xylia shrieked through clenched teeth. "He is dead." Her lips trembled.

A smile pursed the man's rigid lips. I laid my hands on him and felt the temperature of his body dropping at a rapid pace. His chest stopped moving. His eyes rolled back in his head, hiding underneath their lids.

Demetre laid his head against the man's chest, trying to listen to his heartbeat. Low sobs and sniffles echoed around me as we all realized that the man had indeed passed away.

"I believe we should get used to losing everyone around us," Xylia said in a bitter tone.

"We should just give them the books," Adara said, standing to her feet. "That way, maybe our loved ones will be spared."

"Spared?" I frowned in disbelief at what she had said.

"Do not say such things, Adara." Demetre darted her a furious stare.

"Why not?" Adara snapped. "Look at this man." She pointed to the lifeless body. "What do you think will happen to him now? Do you believe he will find eternal rest?"

In our hearts, we all knew he could not cross over to Tristar or the Abyss. I turned my face away from the scene, trying to avoid setting eyes on the man's dead body.

"I do not believe any man or woman has yet crossed over to Tristar," she affirmed in a strong tone.

My mind recalled the moment when Death took me down that door in the Prison of Despair and I saw the multitude of people that rested beneath the scarlet sky in the Wastelands. While the Fallen Stars in the form of Shadows controlled their souls, their spirits remained asleep, unable to cross over.

"Thus the reason we cannot surrender to them," Petra retorted, marching in her direction. "Ever since the Council began guarding the Diary, the souls of men have never found rest. We must be the ones to bring the truth to light so the dead can never come back again."

"We should not be the ones to go to war for the mistakes of the past." Adara closed her hands.

"Why do you say this, Adara?" We were all startled by the strong, unfamiliar voice that spoke. "Will trials have the power to change your decisions?"

A soft breeze caused the snow to lift from the ground. It danced in a circular motion, creating a tall curtain of white. I saw that the snow took the form of a well-built man. Bright golden eyes appeared below ashen hair that cascaded down his shoulders. For a while, I could not believe my eyes. Wings appeared. This time, the being had not only one but two pairs of wings emerge from his back.

"Who are you?" Devin asked, raising his eyebrows.

The being gave him a smile.

"I am Leethan, one of the Higher Stars from Tristar," he replied, his body still hidden by the curtain of snow.

"You were the one that retrieved the Diary from the Abyss," I said, recalling the day Devin shared the tale with me.

"And you are now its bearer," he affirmed as the curtain of snow receded, revealing silver armor covering his body. Three spikes protruded from both gauntlets. Etched on his breastplate was the emblem of the six-winged lion.

"Yes, I am." I was mesmerized at the sight of him.

"And here are the other book-bearers." His golden eyes analyzed every single one of us. "It is a pleasure to meet you all…in person." He bowed his head.

It was hard to miss the long, thin sword that was attached to his waist. Devin held his head steady, not showing any emotion to the Higher Star.

"What brings you here, Star?" Devin asked.

122

"I see one of your companions is dead." He tilted his head in the direction of Ballard's body. "I have come to bring him back to life."

"Bring him back?" My jaw dropped.

"He has been dead for quite some time. I do not believe his body can live again," Adara stated, wringing her hands together.

Leethan lifted his head toward the sky, watching the snow that fell.

"Can you answer one question for me, Adara?" Leethan turned his gaze to Adara. "Do you believe it is impossible for you to stay alive until this war is over?"

With calm steps, he made his way to Ballard.

Adara's throat closed. She bit her bottom lip, turning her eyes from Leethan's firm gaze.

"No," she replied after a brief silence. "I do not believe it is impossible."

Leethan knelt beside Ballard, grasping his hand.

"Then why do you think it is impossible for this boy to live again?"

Ballard gasped for air as he opened his eyes. His skin returned to its fair complexion, his green eyes shone bright.

"Ballard!" Adara shouted. We all rushed our way to him. There was a labored heaving of his chest; his eyes had a vacant stare.

Wrinkles appeared on Devin's forehead while he watched us.

"How do you feel?" Demetre asked, his right hand gently shaking Ballard's shoulder.

"I am well," he replied with a dry voice. "Where is my satchel?" He narrowed his eyes.

123

"Here," Devin answered, lifting up the ragged object.

Ballard released a breath of relief, running his fingers through his chestnut hair. He gazed at his satchel for a while.

Leethan had a soft smile stamped on his face.

"Why did you doubt, Adara?" he asked in a soft voice. "Would the Creator send me to you in vain?"

Her iridescent eyes were set on him.

"Doubt is not as burdensome as belief." She bit her top lip, setting her eyes on Ballard.

"The easiest road will not always be the safest way, Adara." Leethan rested his hand on her shoulder.

She shook her head, trailing her fingers across her lips. "Those are just empty words." Wrinkles appeared on her forehead. "Would you like to know why believing is so hard for me?"

We all fell silent.

"My parents served King Marco in Aloisio. My father was the king's right hand, aiding him in important decisions concerning the kingdom. When my father discovered that King Marco had fallen, he informed my mother. That evening, the king's soldiers barged inside my home, raped my mother, and hung my father in our living room." Adara leaned her body forward, resting her elbows on her knees. "One of the soldiers held my head up, ensuring that I watched every single moment. You ask why I doubted?" She lifted her eyes to Leethan. "I do not care if you are a Higher Star or if you serve the Creator. All I know is that I watched my parents die and no intervention came from the Creator when I needed him the most."

"Do you know why they died, Adara?" Leethan's voice deepened.

She rubbed the back of her hand against her nose. "Because they knew the truth," she said in a broken voice.

"No." A soft smile curved his lips. "They died protecting the truth. War brings loss and pain to many." He placed his hand beneath her chin, sinking his golden eyes into hers. "A real warrior will know the moment that he has to lay down his life for those that he loves."

"They never laid down their lives, Leethan. They were murdered. I presume you don't know what it means to have those you love taken from you," Adara said in a cold voice.

A storm of emotions raged inside of me. A part of me rejoiced with Ballard's life, while another focused on Leethan and Adara, wondering where this argument was going to lead.

"Have you forgotten that many of us fell with Lucifer long ago? Do you not think that, deep in my heart, I miss them? Can you image the pain of being separated forever?" Leethan asked Adara as her eyes fidgeted. "You have been alive for eighteen human years, whereas I have been roaming Tristar and Elysium for ages. Your parents perished for a greater cause while my companions destroyed themselves because of pride and an unquenchable thirst for power."

Adara gulped, bowing her head.

Ballard's shoulders drooped forward as his feet touched the snow-covered ground.

"The important thing at the moment is that Ballard is alive," Devin mentioned, trying to turn the conversation from the current subject.

"Look," Petra whispered, observing the location where the man's dead body lay. "He is fading."

A white mist enveloped the body of the stranger that Adara and Demetre had helped.

"If I can comfort you, Adara," Leethan started as he approached the man's body, "your parents have gone to Tristar. They did not die ignorant of the truth."

Her jaw dropped as her eyes widened. "They crossed over?" she asked.

The moment Leethan was done speaking, the mist began to circle around him. Moments later, both Leethan and the body of the lifeless man vanished from sight.

Without uttering a word, I looked at the faces of my companions.

"We are alive," I said with a shy smile. For a moment, I allowed myself to enjoy the fact that Ballard lived and that we were all standing here—together. We broke out in laughter, sharing tears of joy as we embraced one another.

"We are alive," I kept repeating. Even if it was just for a short moment, I wanted to enjoy the feeling that all was going to be well. I knew our enemies were still close. I knew we were being hunted. Despite all these facts, I wanted to revel in this moment as much as possible.

Xylia touched the right side of my face. "I am sorry I tried to blame you for his death."

"There is nothing to be sorry about." My fingers touched her hand. "We were desperate."

She gave me a shy smile.

"Are you able to carry on, Ballard?" she asked him, adjusting her satchel around her shoulder.

"Yes," he replied, arching his back as he stretched out his arms.

Ballard's eyes were taken by sorrow. If they had the ability to speak, they would probably have much to share.

"Do you know the way to the Road of Ahnor from here, Devin?" I asked.

"I do," he said. "We go northwest. The Road of Ahnor will lead us to the Weeping Mountains, bringing us close to the Ruins of Madbouseux. That is the most probable path that King Ohmen, King Folletti, and Queen Vallerre have taken."

"Let us also not forget that Madbouseux is also the place where Bartholomew and the other blood-drinkers were first seen." I trembled at my own remark. I noticed the faces of my companions growing worried at my words.

"This way," said Devin, walking ahead of us. I hastened my steps until I walked alongside him.

"My heart is greatly troubled," Devin remarked, his eyes set on the forest ahead of us.

"Why do you say that?" I asked.

"In my heart, I do not believe Bartholomew and the others will stop their hunt just because they don't find us." He shook his head. "They will come for us. I've heard stories of how King Bartholomew and his army slaughtered thousands, conquering the neighboring villages and peoples." He glanced over his shoulder, setting his eyes on Ballard. "They will not stop until they have that book within their grasp."

"I fear that Nephele and the others are also plotting against us," I added.

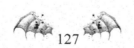

127

"That is a fact." Both of his eyebrows rose up. "Lucifer and the Fallen Stars silence themselves when they plan an attack. It took them ages to come for you and the others. They are patient."

A loud cry sprang forth from behind me. Ballard crouched his body as he bent his knees; both of his hands covered his ears.

"Ballard!" Demetre yelled, grasping Ballard's right arm. "What is wrong?"

He continued to scream, falling to the ground.

"We have to help him," Adara said, kneeling next to him.

"Make it stop," he said under clenched teeth. "Please." Sweat trickled down his forehead, the veins on his neck lifting beneath his skin. He crawled on the snow, his nose bleeding, his breathing ragged.

"It must stop," he screeched. "I cannot..." He never finished his sentence.

Petra reached for Ballard's satchel.

"Look." He pointed at the object. There was a faint light shining from within the satchel. "It is coming from the book," he affirmed with a confused look. Ballard's cries were deafening.

Petra grabbed the book from inside the satchel.

His eyes closed tight. His breathing grew heavy and I noticed his chin trembling.

"No," he mumbled. Petra opened his eyes wide as blood poured down his cheeks like tears. He knelt down, pressing his hands against his eyes.

"What is happening?" Xylia inquired, watching in horror.

"Inside Petra's satchel." Adara pointed to the object, which also had a faint glowing light shining from within.

"Will we also suffer like that?" Xylia asked with a tight voice.

I watched both of my companions writhing on the forest floor. I was not accustomed to this feeling anymore—it crawled inside my heart like a dangerous insect, ready to infuse me with its poison. I felt vulnerable and weak. I did not know how to help my companions now. I stared at them, thinking about a way to release them from their suffering, but I couldn't. I recalled the words Adawnas had spoken over me: *"Even though your inner man is strong, you won't be able to completely rid yourself of your human desires."* Once again I felt like the naïve boy I had once been. My right arm trembled as I clenched my fists.

"Demetre." I set my gaze on him. "Grab the Book of Letters."

He gave me a confused look.

"You…you…want me to grab—"

"Just do it," I insisted. "You are the only one who is not a direct bearer. The moment Petra touched that book, its power struck him down." I was hoping my thoughts were correct. "Grab it."

Demetre looked at Ballard and Petra as they crawled on the ground; their screams were like howls. Blood drops stained the snow. He bent down as fast as he could, grasping the Book of Letters and Petra's book. The light that shone from the symbols etched into the their covers disappeared.

Demetre and I exchanged a surprised look. Ballard and Petra ceased their screaming. Ballard shrugged his shoulders as he attempted to stand to his feet.

"Are you both alright?" I knelt beside them.

They both nodded. With the back of his hands, Petra wiped the blood from his face. Ballard had his hand over his chest.

"Can you please tell us what happened?" Xylia requested.

"It'd be best if we kept on going," Devin said in an assertive voice, his eyes surveying the woods around us. The faint cries of the crowd were still audible.

"Wait, Devin," Petra said, rubbing his eyes. "I need to rest for a short while." He sat on tree bark located next to Ballard.

Devin gnawed on his bottom lip, shaking his head. "We will be caught if we stay here. Bellator is still not far behind us." He grew impatient.

"Please," Ballard said, quavering. "I need to rest—even if just for a short while." Sweat streamed down his forehead, reaching his cheeks.

"Do as you wish." Devin spread out his arms. "Let me know when you would like to continue. Let us hope we are not too late to encounter the kings and queens." He reclined his body on one of the trees.

"What happened?" I asked, standing back on my feet.

They both looked at the snow-covered ground with despondent stares.

Ballard ran his fingers through his chestnut hair. He narrowed his eyes, probably trying to recall everything that had happened.

"I remember the moment you snatched Demetre and Petra from those rocks," he started, his eyes meeting mine. "I was no fool. I knew you could not carry all of us to safety at the same time. I looked to my left and saw Devin, Adara, and Xylia still standing inside that tunnel. The waters rose at a ferocious speed." His fingers clenched over his knees. "Moments later, I saw Devin soaring, holding the girls. That was when I felt a weight on my shoulder. I recall my book feeling as heavy as a rock. My hands lost their grip and I plummeted into the freezing waters."

"So you were not attacked?" Adara asked in a tone of confusion.

"No, I wasn't." He crossed his hands. "I tried to swim, but my book continued to grow heavier, pulling me to the bottom. When I tried to remove the satchel from around my shoulder, my arms failed to respond." He fell silent for a moment and then continued, "That is the last thing I remember before I stood…before I saw…him."

"Him?" I asked with a gaping jaw. In my heart, I knew whom he spoke about.

"The lion with wings." Joy filled his eyes.

"You saw him?" Petra raised his brows.

"Yes, I did," he answered. "He stood right beside me, quietly. His peaceful scarlet gaze brought me comfort. I looked around and saw the greenest grass I had ever seen, and trees as high as castle towers adorned with flowers." He let out a soft laugh. "I saw birds flying in the blue sky."

From the corner of my eye, I noticed Petra staring out to the horizon with empty eyes.

"The Creator and I stood atop a mountain, looking out into a red sunset," Ballard continued. "A gentle breeze

131

brushed my face as I watched his mane moving with the wind, the feathers on his wings dancing with the breeze."

Ballard was quiet. He seemed to be lost in thought, probably recalling the vivid images of his memories.

"After a while, I saw a being flying in our direction. He hovered in the air like an eagle," he continued. "As it drew closer, I was able to see that it resembled a man. It was Leethan. His feet touched the ground in front of me. He knelt before the lion." He narrowed his eyes, curving the corners of his lips. "The feathers on his wings changed color as the light touched them."

As I heard Ballard share his tale, in my heart I felt a burning desire to lay eyes on the lion again.

"'Take him,' the lion declared. His deep voice was unlike anything I had ever heard. When he spoke, it was as if the trees, the rocks, and the sky had voices of their own, uttering the same words that he did."

Ballard rested his head on his hands.

"He sent you a message, Isaac," he said in a soft voice. "I will use the same words that he used."

With curious eyes, my companions looked at me. My heart palpitated. I was anxious to know what he'd said. Though our encounter had been brief, I missed the company of the white lion.

Ballard sighed as he scratched his head.

"He said you asked him where he has been. He wants you to know that he has been watching."

I gasped. Ballard could not have known what I had just asked the Creator. I contained my tears, recalling the words that had drifted from my lips. Demetre approached me, resting his left hand on my shoulder.

"After the lion had ordered Leethan to take me away, he rose to his feet and touched my right shoulder. 'Your companions are waiting for you,' he said. I gave the lion one last look; his eyes were brimming in tears. Like ice that melts under the sun, the breathtaking landscape around me disappeared. Leethan kept his hand on my shoulder until our return."

Ballard grunted, rising to his feet.

"I stood there," he said, pointing to the place where Demetre and Adara had gone to rescue the stranger. "I was surprised when I saw Leethan's wings shrink underneath his skin. His eyes grew dark and his hair disappeared. A few moments later, the powerful Higher Star had the appearance of a fragile old man. 'Your life rests on the actions of your companions. If they rescue me, you will return to your human body; if not, you will be taken back to Tristar,' Leethan said as he lay on the snow. At the top of his lungs, he started shouting for help."

We were all silent. None of us dared to look at one another.

"I did not want to leave you all during such perilous times." He trailed his eyes across our faces. "I watched as you all stood on the other side, debating whether or not the man should be helped."

"And then you saw me?" Devin said in a louder voice. "You saw me trying to stop Adara."

Adara was quiet, shooting Devin a shy look.

"I am not blaming you, Devin." Wrinkles appeared at the corners of his eyes. "You did what you thought to be right. Adara did what she believed to be righteous. Neither

133

of you were aware of the outcome of your choices," Ballard remarked.

"We need to move on." Devin turned his back to us. "Our enemy is still lurking around." He marched toward the woods.

"He is right," I said. "We'd better move."

No one questioned Devin's orders this time. In silence, we all followed at his heels, treading our way through the valley. The shouts of the angry crowd faded as we continued to head to the Road of Ahnor.

Despite all the questions that needed to be answered, some burned within me with greater intensity. Had I entered Xylia's mind? An urge to murder her had taken over in an instant, due to the simple fact that she had not agreed with me. What was happening to me?

A dark memory invaded my mind. I recalled the day Nephele mentioned that Lucifer and me had a special connection—something that the Fallen Stars and Nephilins were yet to discover. Was that the reason why this new ability had developed? What kind of connection did I share with the Dark One?

I set eyes on every single one of my companions, thinking about the situations and struggles that might have led them here. To my right was my ever-faithful friend whom had been with me through all my trials and perils. Despite our journey through the Wastelands, our friendship had remained untouched. To my left was Xylia, the girl I had wanted to kill a short while ago. Judging by her strong attitude, I knew her past had been brutal. Petra, the one that had brought me some comfort when we met, was now quiet, walking with his left hand resting over his ragged satchel, caressing the object that was hidden inside it.

Adara walked next to Ballard. While she tried to be strong, her vulnerable composure showed how fragmented her heart was. They would eventually exchange looks, but I knew Ballard was still thinking about what had happened to him.

Ahead of us was the Nephilin that had remained faithful all this time. Even though he tried never to show his true feelings, I knew Devin struggled with his decision. Evil had run in his blood since birth. I wondered if he ever felt like surrendering to his nature and becoming like the others. Adawnas had not been as strong, and who was to say that Devin would also not meet the same fate?

My return from the Wastelands had left me with a void inside of my heart, one that I felt growing stronger

"Are you alright, Isaac?" Demetre asked, noticing that I had slowed my pace.

"Yes," I replied. "I...I just um...need to think for a while."

With a worried look, he bore his eyes into mine.

"Isaac, do not let—"

"I said I am fine!" I shouted. The others turned in surprise.

"What is the matter?" Xylia asked, fixing her hair behind her ear.

"Nothing," Demetre responded, keeping his eyes fixed on me. "Everything is alright." He picked up his pace, marching his way to Devin.

I kept watching them walk through the valley. If fear was a scent and I was a predator, I would have smelled my prey from miles away. They were all afraid.

Petra came to a stop. He let the others go ahead of him. Once I was by his side, he continued walking alongside me. He cracked his knuckles, gnawing on his lips.

"I must share what I saw," he said in a low voice.

"What do you mean?"

"When I touched Ballard's book, it showed me…something." His breath caught in his throat. For a while, he whimpered as his left hand caressed his satchel. He widened his brown eyes. "The Creator will be killed," he stated in a somber voice.

My throat closed at his remark.

"Killed? How so?" My eyes narrowed.

"I saw the Creator wrapped by a snake; its macabre eyes were hollow, its body covered with the color of night. The Creator's white fur was stained with blood. His wings had been clipped and his mane was the same color as the snake," he affirmed with a rough voice.

"What you saw, Petra, could mean many dif—"

"No, Isaac. I know what I saw. It is a warning. I did not want to tell the others because I can sense fear within them."

My eyebrows came together. "Do you not think that I am afraid?" His jaw opened. "Fear has never left me. I've just learned how to tame it."

He wiped his nose with the back of his hand.

"Then do not share this with them until they also learn how to tame their fear." His pace quickened.

DEVIN

X

THROUGHOUT MY LIFE, a part of me had always longed to be free from the evil that coursed through my veins, while another craved every single destructive desire I had. I recall the day I left Byllith and sought refuge with the Council of Justicia. Athalas received me with opened arms, welcoming me into the castle. For four hundred years, Athalas taught me how to control myself and my natural desires.

It was not an easy thing to see the man that had taught me all that I knew fall into darkness. The worst part was that I had never noticed any signs that his allegiance had changed. Had it all been in vain? Maybe I belonged with the other Nephilins. Was it foolish of me to think that I could find redemption by helping these young ones on their journey? I didn't know how they all perceived me. Little did they know of the daily struggles my inner man endured.

I can't deny that I was tempted to lead them to the Nephilins or the Fallen Stars and hand them the five books. But I knew that if I followed this desire, I would bring destruction upon many innocent lives throughout Elysium. I was torn in two—my desires battled against each other.

"His aloofness is growing every day," Demetre complained, walking next to me.

"Isaac has a lot on his mind, Demetre." I kept my eyes on the trees ahead of me. "Let him be for a while."

The wind picked up. Demetre rubbed his hands against his arms. His eyes carried an empty stare.

"Sometimes I feel as if I do not belong here with all the others." He raised both of his shoulders. "I am not the bearer of any book. I do not have any special abilities of my own." He lifted his eyes, meeting my gaze. "Am I just a burden?"

"What do you think?" I lowered my head, avoiding the thorn-covered branches that hung ahead of me. "Are you worthy of being on this quest?"

He pressed his fingers against his lips, considering his answer.

"A man is as a man sees." I rested my hand on his shoulder. He lifted his eyes to me as his lips curved into a thin smile.

"I remember the day I first met your parents," I said, seeing their faces in my mind. "They were some of the first Council members to welcome me. At the time, they were not yet in love, but their friendship was strong."

Demetre watched me with curious eyes.

"They never seemed to object to the fact that I was a Nephilin and wished to do harm more than good. At that time, I had already lived in Elysium for a thousand years, and never had I found anyone that accepted me as much as they did. 'Be strong, Devin,' your mother said. 'We all struggle with the desires of our hearts. We just need to find ways to strengthen the desires that are pure and righteous.'"

His right eyebrow rose up, hiding behind his dark hair. "She said that to you?"

I let out a brief laugh.

"Yes, she did."

"Why are you telling me this?" he asked. "Why is this relevant to me?"

"Your parents made wrong choices, but these choices do not erase the righteous deeds they performed in the past. I am not sure how much a Nephilin's life is worth, but they helped me—saved me. I want to show you that no matter how weak or unworthy you might feel, these feelings cannot erase the fact that you belong with this company. And though we might not see the reason now, we will find out soon."

Demetre gave me a half-hearted smile.

"Thank you," he said after a brief moment of silence.

We continued making our way through the valley. The snow fell once again. A thick mist settled as the frigid temperature continued to drop.

"Look out!" Ballard shouted at the top of his lungs, his finger pointed toward the sky.

Something fell from the tree branches above us. It thudded on the soft snow, squirming blood on the thistles that covered the ground. I lost my breath when I saw that it was the lifeless body of an old man. He had a rope tied to his neck. The smell of decayed flesh brought tears to my eyes. Xylia and Adara covered their noses, staring at the corpse in horror.

"Look up," Isaac whimpered, his eyes fixed on the branches above us.

Ten naked bodies hung above us. Two of them were children—a boy and a girl. Four were young women who seemed to be no older than thirty. The other four were men. They were missing their toes and fingers; their jaws had been ripped from their faces.

"What is this place?" Petra stumbled back, trying to catch his balance as he stared at the dead bodies.

The sound of hoofs thundered in my ears. I unsheathed my sword, positioning myself for an attack.

"Get your swords ready." My eyes froze inside their sockets, looking for whatever being approached us.

We waited in silence, expecting an attack. The sounds of beating hoofs grew louder. What devilry had come to encounter us? After a while, no one appeared.

"Where is it?" Isaac asked, standing next to me, his eyes surveying the landscape around us.

"I am not sure," I replied, feeling the frigid wind brush against my face.

I was startled by the sound of a loud neigh. I squinted my eyes in an attempt to better see through the blinding mist. With careful steps, I walked in the direction of what sounded like a horse, and the others followed. Walking through this mist set my teeth on edge. I fidgeted at the sound of every branch I trampled upon. My eyes glanced over my shoulder. Adara held her sword with trembling hands. Petra walked beside Ballard, their eyes set on me. Xylia and Demetre hastened their steps, following alongside Isaac.

From the mist emerged an old stall and, from afar, I caught sight of the distressed animal. I let out a quick breath, wiping my forehead with the back of my hand.

"It is just a horse," I said, lowering my sword. The others followed my action.

There was an old two-story house on our far right. It had a large front window with two horizontal shutters next to the door, which lay on the ground, broken into pieces. Some of the roof shingles were missing.

"I am assuming those people lived here," said Xylia, glancing in the direction of the bodies.

"What happened here?" Adara had her fingers over her mouth, and was staring at the old house.

I paced toward the animal and the sound of its neighing increased the moment it laid eyes on me. My right hand stretched as its dark eyes bore into mine. The horse was a dapple-gray stallion.

"There, there," I whispered as I approached it. I saw its wounded hind leg—the injury stretched all the way up to its thigh. The horse tried to escape from the stall by casting its body against the walls. I rested my hand on its head. At my touch, the horse fell silent, its leg twitching.

"What was that?" Adara asked, approaching the animal. Her hands were curled into a ball, resting on her chest. "How did you get him to stand so still?"

I gave her a closed smile. "I can communicate with some animal species—call them when I need them."

"Can you call us some horses so we do not have to walk in the snow?" she inquired, her eyes demanding that I give her the answer she expected.

"I tried the moment we left the valley. Unfortunately, I did not feel any horses nearby," I said.

143

"Then I am assuming your gift is not that effective," Xylia noted, walking toward the horse. Petra, Ballard, Isaac, and Demetre had their eyes set on the old house.

"Why do you say that?" My eyebrows tightened.

"This horse has probably been sitting here for a while. If you can feel and call them, how come you were not aware that this animal was here?" She petted the gray stallion.

She was right. I had used my gift to search for horses just moments ago. Why had I not been able to feel his presence?

"Over there!" I heard Ballard shouting.

Startled, I looked and saw the boys running.

"Where are you going?" I stepped away from the horse, following them. "Wait!"

My body froze in shock when I saw a child walking out of the house and descending the two shorts steps that led out the door. The girls flocked in his direction. The boy closed his small eyes and fell to the ground, smashing his face against the snow.

Isaac knelt next to him. He removed his coat and wrapped the boy with it. He seemed to be around six years of age. His brown hair was covered in blood, his feet were bare, and his chest was exposed.

"Can you hear me?" asked Isaac as he reached under the boy's head, holding him against his chest. Blood dripped from the small cuts on his chapped lips.

The young boy grunted, gulping his throat.

"Mom…Dad…" he whispered in a low voice. He opened his eyes, looking at every single one of our faces.

"You will be alright," Demetre affirmed with a deadpan smile.

The boy raised his left hand, touching Isaac's cheek. His arms were covered in bruises. Isaac wrapped the boy's hand in his.

"Don't worry. We will take care of you," he said, running his hand through the boy's tangled hair.

"Should we check inside the house?" asked Ballard, looking at the boy. "There might still be other survivors."

"I think that is a good idea," Demetre said, looking at me.

"I agree." I turned my gaze to Isaac. "Stay with the girls and the boy." I pointed to Ballard, Petra, and Demetre. "You three, come with me. Let us search the house."

"Be careful." Adara darted us a worried stare. The boy let out weak moans as we strolled toward the house.

With swords in hand, we walked through the doorway.

Shards of clay were scattered on the ground. The shelves on the walls had been smashed to pieces. A putrid stench invaded my nostrils when we approached the kitchen. I absorbed the sight of the eviscerated body of a woman torn in half; her upper body lay atop the table while her lower part was on the wooden floor.

"Are you sure we should continue searching? I don't see how there could be any survivors inside this house." Demetre covered his mouth with the back of his hands as he walked away from the kitchen.

"We search upstairs," I ordered, covering my nose as I followed Demetre.

There was a stairway on the right side of the house that led to the second floor.

"Come on." Demetre turned his eyes to us. "We should not linger for long. Let us search for other survivors and leave this place."

Demetre started making his way up the stairs, resting his right hand on the rail while holding his sword with the other. Ballard walked behind him, followed by Petra. Once we reached the second floor, the smell of burnt flesh brought tears to my eyes.

"Apparently, something died up here as well," Ballard mentioned, covering his nose.

There were three doors in front of us. An old puppet in the likeness of a girl hung on the doorknob in front of me.

"How are we going to do this?" Petra's chest heaved with heavy, panting breaths.

"We each check a room, and then we leave." I turned my face toward Demetre. "Would you mind checking this room with Petra?"

"No, not all," Demetre replied.

I stepped to my left, standing in front of the other door while Demetre and Petra entered the room.

A shiver shot down my body once I turned the cold knob. To my left was a bed that had been made out of brown oak. Three frames hung from the white wall—all had their paintings destroyed, leaving just the remnants of the canvases. A brown rug sat at the foot of the bed.

"Ballard, did you find anything?" I asked in a loud voice.

"There is nothing here!" he replied from the other room.

"Petra? Demetre? Anything?" I shouted.

"Nothing," Demetre answered.

I was about to head out the door when a chill shot up my leg. There was a cold grasp around my ankle that pulled my body. I thudded to the floor. My eyes darted over my shoulder and saw a black shadow shaped like a man. My heart skipped a beat as I caught sight of its skeletal hands tightened around my left ankle.

I tried to land a kick on the creature, but my feet sank under its shadow. With great strength, it lifted me off the ground and cast my body against the roof. A sharp pain spread through my back. Ballard, Demetre, and Petra flocked into the room.

The grotesque being released a growl once it saw them. I managed to stand to my feet as fast as I could.

"What in the name of Elysium is that?" Ballard unsheathed his sword.

I limped my way to my companions, feeling a sharp pain in my chest. I watched as both of the creature's skeletal hands turned into arms, each equipped with four-fingered hands. At the tip of each finger was a sharp, curved claw. The creature's bones slithered beneath its brown skin while its body took a shape similar to that of a dragon. Its elongated skull had a thin snout. Wings appeared on its back, expanding to almost twice the size of the creature's thin tail.

The creature lowered its head, growling as it crawled to its left. Its golden eyes trailed across the room. The pain in my leg worsened as I watched it raise its body. It let out a loud roar.

I jumped in the direction of the creature, attempting to bury my blade beneath its thick neck, but it dodged my attack. The wooden floor trembled as it rushed its way

toward Demetre. The dragon-like beast catapulted in his direction with its teeth in view. Demetre leaped to his left, swerving from its attempt to sink its teeth into his skin. With his sword held up in the air, he managed to land a cut on the creature's thigh. A loud hiss followed his attack.

Quick footsteps echoed behind me. I looked over my shoulder and saw Petra fleeing.

"Where are you going?" I shouted, watching him run down the stairway. The creature raised its head, drawn to the sound of his footsteps. The beast narrowed its glowing yellow eyes. It leaped out of the room, pursuing Petra.

"Coward!" Rage burned inside of me like a furnace. I turned my attention to Demetre and Ballard. "Follow the creature down the stairway."

"What about you?" Ballard asked between heavy breaths.

"I will warn the others." I pointed my finger toward the stairway. "Go. Now."

I faced the closed window in the room. It was locked. Without much thinking, I flung my body against it, breaking it into pieces. The cold wind touched my face as my wings expanded. Isaac, Xylia, Adara, and the boy were still in the same place.

"Run!" I shouted, flying my way toward them. Seconds after, Petra ran out of the door, screaming at the top of his lungs. *Coward,* I thought. The animal was at his heels, sprinting out of the house.

The moment Isaac caught sight of the creature he drew his sword, standing in front of the girls and the boy. The dragon-like monster flapped its wings, letting out a deafening growl. When its feet left the ground, I rushed in

its direction. As fast as a breath, Isaac's wings appeared. We both tackled the creature in mid-air, piercing its body with our swords. Isaac wounded it on its ribs while my blade entered its skull. It let out a blazing screech as its body plunged to the ground. The animal's body touched the snow, assumed its previous shadowed shape, and dispersed itself like smoke. Moments later, its body vanished.

Ballard pressed the heels of his hands against his eyes, resting his body against the doorpost. Demetre sat on one of the steps of the stairs with a gaping jaw. His elbows rested on his knees, and he supported his chin on his hands.

I flew down, landing next to Ballard.

"You…ran," I said behind gritted teeth, shooting Petra a cold sneer. "You abandoned us in that room." My eyebrows tightened when I saw him with his head bowed, biting the nail off his left thumb.

"What do they mean, Petra?" Isaac set his eyes on him. He remained silent.

"Will you not say something, coward?" I marched in his direction, tightening my fists. A sharp pain shot up my leg, causing me to lose balance. I fell to my knees, containing my urge to scream.

"Devin!" Adara ran in my direction. "Are you alright?"

I recoiled from her attempt to lay her hands on me.

"Leave me," I said, darting her an angry stare. She took three steps back, a surprised look stamped on her face. I wanted to kill that boy. How could he have left us? The thought that he was one of the book-bearers enraged me. This boy was not worthy of such a task.

149

"You left us, Petra!" Demetre shouted. "We could have all been killed by that creature and all you cared about was your own life."

"What did you expect me to do?" Petra yelled in response, spreading out his arms.

Ballard shook his head. "You could have used your sword. You could have tried to kill the creature."

They all stared at Petra in anger. Petra covered his face with his left hand, turning his back to us. Silence lingered for a while. Xylia stood next to the young boy, who seemed to be unconscious.

I failed in my attempt to stand on my feet as the pain continued to spread, reaching my lower back. With my hands, I grasped at the snow on the ground, tightening them with great strength.

"Devin, are you alright?" Isaac rushed his way to me.

"I just need to rest for a while." My teeth clenched while my eyebrows pinched together. "The house is empty. We should be safe here...for now."

Demetre and Isaac grabbed my arms, helping me stand. I attempted to move my left leg but the pain was too strong to bear.

"Damn creature," I said, limping as we headed to the house. I looked back to make sure we were all safe. Adara carried the young boy. Xylia had her sword in her hand; her eyes trailed across the trees. Ballard followed behind me. Petra strolled behind them with his hands inside his pockets.

"I have never seen anything like it." I cleared my throat, taking in a deep breath.

"Was it a dragon?" Isaac asked.

"dragons do not turn into shadows. That beast was not from here."

I recalled the frightening words Raziel had spoken after the attack of Mag Mell: "The gates between Elysium and the Fourth Dimension now lie unguarded." He had warned us that beasts had infiltrated our world. Was he still guarding the Gates with the remaining Underwarriors? We had not seen or heard from him ever since. Nathan had returned, but had not mentioned anything about the others.

"I think that beast—" I grunted due to the pain. "I think that beast came from the Abyss."

Isaac shot me a frightened stare. I struggled to walk up the two short steps in front of the doorway. I could no longer move my left leg. Drops of sweat beaded down my forehead.

"Let's put him by the staircase, Isaac." Demetre cocked his head, showing Isaac the location of the staircase.

I lifted my arms from their shoulders, limping on my right leg as I tried to sit on the first step.

"Adara." Demetre turned his eyes to her. "Let's lay the boy in one of the rooms upstairs so he can sleep."

"Alright." She gave the unconscious boy a tender look.

"Let me see your leg, Devin," Ballard requested, kneeling in front of me.

"I will be fine," I retorted with a weak and tremulous voice. My head reclined against the wall while I grimaced—the pain grew stronger.

"Sure you will," Ballard said in a snide tone.

I screamed when his hands touched my leg.

"Hold him, Isaac," he ordered, keeping his eyes on me. "Petra, please go outside and bring me some of the snow. Look for a bucket in the kitchen." He pointed to his left.

In silence, Petra turned and walked to the kitchen.

"I will keep an eye on the door," Xylia declared.

Never in my life had I felt such unbearable pain. My whole leg throbbed as a burning sensation stung my muscles.

"Can you remove your boot, Devin?" Ballard asked, his hand pressed against the wound.

I felt my back muscles constrict while I attempted to lean forward. The pain was excruciating. I cringed my teeth, taking a deep, long breath.

Ballard leaned his body, grasping the edge of my feet. I screamed as he pulled my boot from my leg.

Ballard frowned his forehead upon looking at the wound.

"Your flesh…is melting." He bore his eyes into mine. "I thought only iron or the flames of a white dragon had the power to kill you."

"Then I am assuming that creature had hands of iron." I cringed, struggling for breath. "It burns." I pressed the edges of my hands on my forehead.

"Do you know what you are doing, Ballard?" Isaac asked.

"My father is experienced with medicinal herbs. He taught me some things. The king of Mag Mell asked him to be the overseer of Valley Hills once he was informed of my father's skills," he responded, analyzing the wound. "We relocated to the village four years ago."

Isaac shot me a veiled look, raising his right eyebrow.

"Have you heard from him since you left?" Isaac asked.

"No. My father is too occupied with his affairs. I understand him not sending me any news." He shrugged his shoulders. "I miss him though."

Isaac and I realized that Ballard was not yet aware of his father's death. I shook my head, telling him not to divulge the news now.

My stomach turned when I saw the wound on my left ankle. My flesh throbbed as the wound festered.

Ballard raised both of his eyebrows. "It is spreading fast." He turned his head to the kitchen. "Petra, did you find anything?" There was an impatient tone in his voice.

Ignoring his friend's question, Petra walked out of the kitchen holding a gray bucket covered in rust. With his face turned to the floor, he walked through the doorway.

Ballard ripped the bottom of his shirt, tying the piece of cloth around my thigh. The mere feeling of the delicate cloth touching my skin burned like fire.

"This will help with the bleeding." He wiped the sweat from his brow with his right wrist.

Petra rushed inside with his bucket overflowing with snow.

"Here," he said, handing Ballard the bucket, then stepping away from us.

Ballard reached inside, grabbing a handful of snow. I let out a deafening scream.

"The wound needs to be cleaned, Devin." The right side of his lips trembled as he rubbed the snow on my ankle. My teeth pressed both of my lips together as I held my screams.

"Should we melt the snow?" Isaac asked in an impatient tone.

Ballard shook his head in answer to his companion's question. "There is no time."

"After you clean…the wound, what will you do?" I asked under my breath.

Ballard ignored my question, his eyes fixed on my ankle. I felt my left arm begin to twitch. Was this the end of me?

"I will go search for wood. It will be dark soon," Petra declared, walking outside once again.

Ballard reached inside his satchel, searching for something.

This pain was far worse than when the Whispering Lights had entered my head.

"I can't move my arm," I whispered the moment I realized I was losing feeling in my limbs. "I don't think I will make it."

"Ballard, what are you looking for?" Isaac asked with an edge to his voice.

"Here it is," Ballard said, taking out a small glass vial filled with a black liquid. "This is essence of Green Lilly. They are flowers found on the shores of the River of Abstergo during the summer. This liquid relieves pain and helps the body fight any infection."

Was this his brilliant plan? I was almost certain that this essence had never been tested on Nephilins. Could this really work?

"Hold him, Isaac," Ballard ordered. "Devin," his eyes met mine, "do not move."

He opened the vial, pouring the dark liquid on my ankle. The liquid was cold when it touched my skin, but in a

154

matter of seconds it burned like fire, increasing the pain. I could no longer contain my screams. I shouted at the top of my lungs. Sweat dripped down my forehead and hair, reaching my lips. Seconds later, the pain subsided as my leg grew numb. My left arm was also unresponsive.

My senses started to escape me. I battled against my eyelids, struggling to stay awake. The voices of my companions turned to muffled groans, and my vision dimmed as all sound faded. I closed my eyes.

XI

I WAS AWAKENED by a cold breeze brushing against my face. My eyes caught sight of the small crack on the glass. I moved my left leg, expecting the pain I had been feeling to strike me again, but the pain I felt was bearable—almost forgettable. I rubbed my eyes with the edge of my hands, realizing I lay on the bed of the room where the creature had attacked me earlier. Beside me, on the ground, was a candle that was almost burning out, its dripping wax creating patterns on the floor.

I heard footsteps approaching. Petra walked into the room, holding a new candle. He was startled when he realized I was awake.

"I…um…I found this candle in the kitchen. I noticed yours was burning out." He scratched the back of his head. He knelt next to the bed, holding the wick of the new candle atop the flame. He avoided looking at me.

"Where is everyone?" I asked, managing to sit. I rested my elbows on my knees.

He placed the new candle on the floor beside the burnt wax. "They are all downstairs, sitting around the fire." He arose to his feet.

Anger still burned within me.

"Why did you leave us, Petra?" I asked in a low voice, trying to control my feelings.

He let out a frustrated sigh, turning his back to me. He lifted his head to the ceiling, cracking the knuckles on his fingers.

"A couple of months ago, me and two of my friends decided to go to the Great River for a weekend," he started after a brief silence. "We mounted our horses, picked up our girls, and rode down the Road of Iron, excited for our little adventure." He put his hands inside his pockets. "On our first day, we had a great time swimming, fishing, building our shelter out of tree branches and vines, and talking around the fire." I noticed his eyes filling with tears as the words drifted from his mouth.

Where is he going with this? I thought as I listened.

"On the second day, I awoke to the sound of thunder and rain. Gray clouds had veiled the sun. Our shelter was undone by the fury of the wind and our horses had fled during the night. We were scared." The tears started to roll down his cheeks. "I will never forget the bright, yellow eyes and the disfigured body that stood in the woods, gazing at us all. With a terrifying growl, the Shadow attacked my girl, Freeda. My two friends, along with their girls, fled toward the trees while I watched the grotesque creature devour the one I loved." He sniffed, wiping his tears with the backs of his hands. "You know what I did once I saw my girl dead?" he asked with trembling lips.

"No." I felt my throat closing as I stared at this boy, surprised at the story he shared.

"I ran away, like a coward," he mumbled. "Two other Shadows appeared, chasing my friends. All I heard were their screams of torment as they were devoured. I left them to die. There was no courage in me to help them." He bowed his head. "It took me hours to get to Swordsmouth. I ran through the woods, afraid that I was being followed. The torrential rain made my journey all the more difficult. The howling of the wind, and even the sound of branches breaking, startled me while my mind continued to remember the death of my friends."

"How did you manage to get home?"

He tightened his eyebrows together. "I caught sight of the gates of Swordsmouth, saw the green flag with the emblem of the silver helmet flapping as the wind continued to blow. *Is my family safe?* That was all I could think about once I saw my kingdom. I walked through the muddy gates, my heart racing inside my chest. The guards saw me. 'Petra, are you alright?' one of them shouted as they opened the iron gates. At that moment, I did not care about my well-being. I was concerned about those that I loved. I ran home, ignoring their questions. When I walked inside my house, all I found was a note sitting on the table next to a box with an iron lock and a symbol of a circle and two lines etched into the top.

"'The Book of the Light Bearer is yours now.

Guard it with your heart and mind.

Love, Mom and Dad'

"I called out for them, hoping that they were still there, but my hope was shattered when I realized they had left." His fingers tightened around his hand. "My parents abandoned me when I needed them most. I held that note

158

in my hand and felt the world cave in around me as I looked at the mysterious box lying on top of the table." His eyes met mine. "Maybe that's why I abandoned you all when you needed me. Because that's what I do. I abandon people. Apparently, it runs in the family."

"A man is as a man thinks, Petra," I declared, standing to my feet. "Let not your past dictate your present actions. Your parents might have left, but we, your companions, are still here."

"It is not easy, Devin." His shoulders drooped down. "It is not easy to have everything taken from you. My whole life changed in a matter of hours."

I crossed my arms. "Do you think I cannot sympathize with the pain you are feeling? My father is a Fallen Star and my human mother was turned to Shadow when I was still an infant. I never had them beside me." I clenched my fists, recalling the days when I'd felt abandoned and lost. "It might not be easy, but it is not impossible to overcome such pain."

"Do you truly believe that?" Petra inquired, his eyes begging for an uplifting answer.

For a brief moment, I reflected on all the times I had allowed my past to influence my actions. A part of me was still unsure if helping the book-bearers would give me a chance at redemption from the evil that ran within me.

"Yes, I do," I replied in a low voice, knowing that it was easier to answer his question than to believe in my own answer.

His lips curved into a shy smile. He looked around the room one more time, turned, and walked down the stairs in silence.

We are all flawed, I thought while Petra's words ruminated in my mind. His fear was a reflection of his arduous past. To think that we had the five weapons that Lucifer's army—and other creatures—were searching for struck me with fear for the first time. Pain constricted my heart as I remembered the day Adawnas had abandoned Isaac and me in the forest. How could she? After all the years we had lived together, she'd surrendered to her weakness, abandoning us all. Was she still alive? I found it hard to believe that she had sided with the Fallen Stars.

I descended the stairs; my stomach growled when I smelled the cooked meat. I was surprised to see all the book-bearers sitting by the fireplace, holding their skewers over the flames. To the left, near the door, were the remains of a young buck. I saw the young boy we had found earlier sitting next to Adara. He was wrapped in a ragged blanket, resting his head against her body. Demetre sat on Adara's left. Xylia watched the flames, sitting next to Isaac. Petra had his arms and legs crossed as he reclined his body against the wall.

"Where did you find skewers?" I asked with a grin on my face.

Ballard's shoulders moved as he let out a soft laugh.

"They were in the kitchen." He twirled his skewer in the fire.

"And who fixed the door?" I walked down the last step of the stairway.

"I think the better question would be, 'Who gutted the deer,'" Demetre said with a smile. "Come sit by the fire, Devin. You must be hungry."

"Are you proud, Demetre?" Isaac asked with a laugh. "The deer did almost beat you."

Ballard clicked his tongue. "The deer almost got away," he said.

"You should all be grateful. It has been a while since we have had a decent meal," Demetre boasted as they all broke out in laughter.

"What happened after I passed out?" I walked to the window, my eyes surveying our surroundings. There was no snow falling from the sky, no sign of an enemy nearby.

"Isaac and Demetre went out hunting while Ballard fixed the door. Xylia and I cared for the boy." Adara turned her head, fixing her eyes on Petra. "And he did not leave your side until now."

My eyes shifted to Petra. Apparently there was more to this boy than I had thought.

"Thank you," I said.

"You are welcome," he replied, clearing his throat as he approached the fire.

My gaze turned to Ballard. "Thank you for caring for my wounds."

"No problem. I am sure you would have done the same for me." He brought his skewer closer to his face, touching the meat in the hopes that it was fully cooked.

I watched them as they talked and ate. It was uncommon to find bravery amongst such young boys and girls. There was no choice for me now but to protect them. I had no other option but to believe that my sacrifice was going to be worth something.

I sat next to Xylia.

"Here." She handed me one of the skewers with meat. Petra made himself comfortable beside me.

I felt the heat of the flames on my hands. From the corner of my right eye, I noticed the boy gazing at me with a fervent expression. For some reason, seeing this boy reminded me of the days when I roamed Elysium alone after my mother was transformed into Shadow. His innocent face reminded me of all the other infants that had been made orphans. Like headless insects, we ventured through the woods, not knowing what to do to survive. That was until Nephele and Azaziel found us as they went searching for our kind, hiding us beneath the grounds of the Kingdom of Byllith.

"Are you alright, boy?" I asked, giving the child a half-hearted smile.

With his thumb in his mouth and his eyes fixed on mine, he shrugged his shoulder and turned his face away from me.

"He is fine," Adara replied, wrapping her right arm around the boy. "He is just traumatized. He did just lose his family."

With a vacant expression, the child gazed at the fire.

"Are you sure he is alright?" I felt the creases appear on my forehead.

"Yes." Her eyes narrowed. "He is fine, Devin."

The child recoiled under her arm, holding his knees with his arms.

We were all quiet for a while. I enjoyed the warmth of the fire, the sound of the crackling flames, the smell and flavor of the meat.

"Do you think Ohmen, Folletti, and Valeree are still alive?" Isaac broke the silence, his elbows resting on his knees.

"I am not sure," I answered, watching the flames dance inside the fireplace.

"What do you think, Isaac?" Xylia placed her skewer on the wall, wiping her fingers on her pants.

Isaac winced. "We have to believe that they are alive."

"And what will we do once we inform them of the attack on Bellator?" Ballard asked.

"We continue to look for allies throughout Elysium. I am sure once we inform them of what happened, they will side with us on this quest," Isaac answered.

"I do not want to be the pessimist here," Ballard raised his eyebrows. "But who is to say that they have not sided with Lucifer already?"

Isaac rubbed his forehead with his fingers.

"We must take the risk," he replied with a worried look while cracking his knuckles. For a moment, he gazed at the window behind him. I could tell he was deep in thought, probably thinking of the various outcomes this journey could have. Though I desired to trust him with all my heart, a part of me still questioned if there was something he was hiding. I still could not understand how he had been able to kill Nylora in Bellator.

"I wonder if there have been other attacks." Ballard cleared his throat. "I worry if Valley Hills is still safe." His voice dwindled away.

Isaac shot me a daunting look. I knew at that moment that we were both thinking the same thing. *Should we tell him about his father?* Anatolio Radley was his father and the

163

Overseer of Valley Hills, a village located near the River of Abstergo. I had not forgotten the moment when Isaac and I saw his father's body being devoured by a Shadow.

"Ballard." I dropped my shoulders. "There is something that Isaac and I must share with you."

Ballard scowled, laying his skewer against the base of the fireplace.

Isaac scratched his chin, standing to his feet.

"Devin and I visited Valley Hills. We were heading to Mag Mell, hoping to find allies, when we stumbled across the village."

Ballard leaped up.

"Did you see my father?" he asked with wide eyes. "You probably met him. Why did you not tell me that you visited my village?"

Isaac approached him, kneeling at his side.

"Your village is gone, Ballard." He laid his hand on his shoulder. "They were all attacked by an army of Shadows."

Ballard shook his head in disbelief. Creases appeared between his brows.

"Gone?" he mumbled through short breaths. "And my father?" His lips quivered, already expecting the worse.

A cold shiver went down my spine as the images of the attack continued to flash in my mind.

"He died," Isaac replied. "When we arrived, your father had already been killed."

Fear and sorrow settled in the room. They were all quiet, listening. In their minds, they probably wondered if those that they loved were still alive.

Ballard grunted, punching the wooden floor with such force that blood splattered on his clothes.

Isaac tried to hold him as he continued to strike the floor with his right hand. With great strength, Ballard arose to his feet and pushed Isaac against the wall. With tears streaming down his face, and with both of his hands pressed against his head, he marched his way up the stairs. I heard the sound of a door banging. I glanced up and saw that Ballard had gone inside one of the rooms.

Isaac turned, facing everyone around the fireplace.

"Are you all afraid of our enemy?" he inquired in a loud voice. "Are you?"

Xylia lifted her eyes to him. "Not only do we fear our enemy, Isaac. We fear that we might lose our lives during this war."

"Then you are not worthy of being on this journey." There was anger inside his iridescent eyes. "While you fear for your lives, the ones we love are losing theirs."

"We never asked to be bearers," Petra remarked. "We never asked for any of this to happen."

"But it did," Isaac said with an edge to his voice. "We are the bearers of the five books of Lucifer and we are being hunted by the Fallen Stars, the Nephilins, and now the blood-drinkers." With slow steps, he paced around the room. "Though they are not here, every time fear finds its way into our hearts, they win. We cannot be afraid of our doom if it brings redemption to Elysium. We might have lost loved ones, but there is still a whole world that needs to be saved. Though the darkness might seem to thicken every day, we must believe that there is strength in us to destroy it."

The crackling sound of the flames loudened as silence settled.

165

"Isaac is right," Demetre said. "Those that we have lost must inspire us to fight for those that are alive."

"Your courage is admirable," Xylia retorted, standing to her feet. "Yet you seem to forget that we are not the ones that returned from the Wastelands. We are not as brave as you."

"I heard it said once that a man is as man thinks, Xylia," said Petra, looking at me from the corner of his eye. "We must believe that there is a greater purpose behind us having these books."

"In the Prison of Despair, Death took me to the Wastelands of Tristar and showed me the spirits of those that died without knowledge of the truth. Their souls are being controlled by the Fallen Stars, and while they have that control, those people will never rest. They will always remain in the Wastelands, unconscious." Isaac raised his right hand, closing it into a fist. "It is not that we must not be afraid. We must not allow fear to control our actions anymore."

"So we fight for the freedom of the living and the dead?" Petra asked in a low voice.

"Yes, my friend." Isaac turned to Petra. "If those that we loved died ignorant of the truth about Lucifer and the Creator, their spirits are also prisoners in the Wastelands of Tristar and their souls are being controlled by the Fallen."

All in the room gazed at Isaac. They knew—we knew—that if fear continued to dictate our actions, we would soon meet our doom.

After all were done eating and chatting, they started making their way one by one up the stairs into the rooms. At least tonight we had a roof over our heads.

166

"Are you coming up, Devin?" Demetre asked.

"I will be fine here." I remained seated in front of the fireplace, watching the flames burn the logs into ashes.

XII

THOUGH MY EYELIDS were heavy, I could not sleep. In my mind, I kept seeing the frightening image of the creature that had attacked me. Never in my fourteen hundred years had I seen such a monstrosity. What other devilries had infiltrated Elysium? My mind was too preoccupied with the many unanswered questions that still lingered. I watched the fire burn low while trying to think of logical answers.

My thoughts were interrupted by the sound of footsteps crunching in the snow outside. I heard the faint neigh of a horse and the groans of a man.

I grabbed my sword, rising to my feet. After a couple of seconds, the footsteps ceased. I could still hear the labored breaths of both the horse and the man.

With great caution, I opened the door. The cold air invaded the living room. I stepped outside and caught sight of the animal and its rider standing immobile in front of the door. The man was wrapped in a thick, dark fur cape; his head curved down.

Was he an enemy? Where had this man come from?

He let out painful groans as he lifted his head.

"Help me," he whispered in a broken voice.

"Who are you?" With caution, I took three steps in his direction, my feet sinking beneath the snow.

"Help…" His voice trailed off as he fell unconscious. I ran to him once I realized that he was about to fall from his horse. The moment my hands touched him, I smelled the pungent odor of rotten flesh. I held my breath, fixing my eyes on his narrow face. A gash flowing with blood took the place of his right eye. He seemed to be in his mid-thirties; a tattered dark beard covered his face. The horse was also wounded with a long cut on its neck.

"Devin!" I looked back and saw Isaac running toward me. "Who is this man?"

"I am not sure. He is badly wounded." The man groaned in pain. "Take the horse to the stall while I bring him inside," I said, rushing my way to the house.

Where had this man come from? What kind of creature had wounded him this way?

"Ballard!" I yelled, marching up the stairs. The man let out low groans.

"Yes," he croaked. He opened the door of his room, rubbing his eyes with his hands. Petra stood behind him with a worried look on his face.

"I need you." I barged inside.

"Who is that? What is that smell?" Petra inquired, making his way to the window. He covered his nose.

"I don't know." I laid him on the bed. Demetre entered the room. His face was shrouded with fear once he laid eyes on the man.

"Help." The man struggled to raise his left hand. Sweat poured down his face like a waterfall.

169

"Get me water, Petra," Ballard ordered while analyzing the severe condition of the man's face. Petra rushed his way out.

"What is all this noise?" Xylia stood under the doorpost. Her eyes widened once she saw the horrific scene. "How may I help?" She rushed her way to us.

"Where is Adara?" I asked, worried.

"Sleeping with the boy," she responded, watching the man's wounded face.

"He has a high fever." Ballard had his hand pressed against the stranger's forehead.

Petra rushed into the room holding a silver metal bucket.

"Here is the water," he said, laying the bucket next to the bed.

"Get me my satchel," Ballard said, his lips quivering. I looked at him, confused as to why his eyes were brimming with tears.

Demetre grabbed ahold of the satchel that was on the floor. "Here, Ballard."

Ballard was about to reach for it when he recoiled his hands.

"Inside, there is a small glass vial with a bright golden liquid. Find it, please." He spoke in an agitated voice, taking long deep breaths, fixing his gaze on the man once again. Tears started pouring from his tired brown eyes.

"Why don't you—"

"Please, Demetre!" he shouted. "Just…find it."

Demetre's lips went rigid. He lowered his head, searching for the object Ballard needed.

"Is this it?" he asked, hopeful. In his hand was a vial filled with a yellow liquid.

Ballard shot him a quick glance and gave him a silent nod. He reached for the object with trembling hands.

"Ballard," I grasped his wrist, "this man needs your help. He is dying. Can you help him?"

"Yes," he whispered.

With quivering breaths, he tightened his eyelids together, pressing his fingers between his eyebrows.

I released his wrist. He reached for the vial, pouring the liquid into the bucket.

"Now we wait," he whispered, looking at the man.

"How long?" I heard the man grind his teeth as he groaned. "He does not have much time."

"Just a few seconds," he replied.

"Help," he whispered once again as he tried to raise his left hand.

"You will be fine, sir," said Ballard, grasping the man's weak hand.

Xylia, Petra, and Demetre watched the scene with fervent eyes.

"Where is Isaac?" Demetre's eyes surveyed the room.

"He should be outside. I asked him to take this man's horse to the stall," I replied, keeping my eyes focused on the man.

"I will go find him," Demetre said, dashing out of the room.

"I'll come with you," added Petra as he followed him.

Ballard cupped his hands and submerged them in the golden liquid in the bucket. A fragrance similar to that of blooming daisies arose.

171

He held his hands over the man's face, letting the liquid drip from his palms and fingers. He bit the corner of his lip as the tears once again appeared. With a vacant expression, he watched the drops of golden fluid touch the man's wounds, run down his tattered beard, and drip on the sheets that covered the bed.

Moments later, the man's moaning ceased; his breathing was smooth and steady.

I sighed, resting my right elbow on my knee.

"Good job," I murmured, tapping Ballard on the shoulder.

"My father taught me well." He wiped his nose with his right wrist. He rose to his feet and marched down the wooden staircase.

"I will go check on Adara and the boy." Xylia exited the room.

With my head resting on my hands, I sat for a while in silence.

"Darkness will soon cover all of Elysium," said the man, turning his head to the side.

"Do you have a name?" I asked, crossing my hands.

With an empty stare, he gazed at the door. His chest arose with difficulty as he tried to breathe.

"Why does it matter?" he groaned. "I will probably be dead in a couple of hours."

"Even those that have died have names." My hand strolled across my hair. "My name is Devin."

With great struggle, the man turned his head to me; his moss green eye looked into mine.

"You are not ordinary," he remarked as he analyzed my face. "I have never seen eyes as blue as yours." I felt his

right hand tightening around my own. "Thank you for helping me."

"You are welcome." The sight of his wound caused my stomach to churn. "What happened to you?" I asked, trying to keep my eyes on his face.

For a while, he looked at the ceiling; his throat let out low grunts and moans.

"A man with wings like a dragon and eyes like blood walked inside my home. He claimed that King Demyon had gone insane and stolen a book that could destroy the entire world." Anxiety crawled inside of me. I knew who he spoke about. "He clasped my wife's head with his hand and broke her neck, sinking his teeth into her wrists." His voice started breaking. "Afterward, he told me that we had to find a way to enter the castle and retrieve the book or all the people of Bellator would be killed."

I tried to keep a straight face as I listened to him. Of course I knew who the man with dragon-like wings was, but I assumed he was not aware that we were the ones the blood-drinkers were after.

"What happened after?" I asked.

He gazed at me in silence.

"The citizens went mad," he started. "With torches and spears in hand, some men flocked to the castle while others searched Bellator." He gave a grimace of pain as he arched his back, trying to find a comfortable position on the bed. "I mounted my horse and fled. Whatever damage this book could do, I wanted no part in it."

There were footsteps coming from the stairs. Seconds later, I saw Petra, Demetre, and Isaac approaching the room.

"The horses are agitated, Devin." Isaac looked at the man and cringed at the sight of his wound. Demetre gnawed on the side of his upper lip. "They do not want to stay inside the stall. We searched the woods for any signs of an enemy and did not see anything."

"I will tend to the horses soon," I said, turning my eyes back to the man. "How did you lose your eye?"

The man made an inarticulate sound as he lifted his left arm, trying to touch his wounded face.

"I saw a boy in the woods. He stood alone in the middle of the road..."

"How old was this boy?" My eyebrows furrowed as I recoiled my head.

"He was young." His eyes became thin lines on his face. "He seemed to be around six years of age. I tried to help him. When I approached the boy, his body changed in seconds. His head stood far from the ground, towering above my own. He grew thick and muscular; horns appeared out of his skull, and his eyes were as black as coal. Instead of a nose, there were two small cavities on his face. His mouth was long and thin, his teeth sharp and short."

My heart hammered under my chest. I darted an alarming stare at my companions. Though I did not have the ability to read minds, I could see in their faces that we all shared the same thought.

"The creature attacked me, holding my head against the snow." The man shuddered as he spoke. "It reached for my right eye with one of its fingers..."

Tears rolled down his eyes and onto the sheets of the bed. With his fingertips, he touched the gash on his face.

"I will let you be." I arose to my feet. "Let us know if you need anything else."

"Right now, solitude would be the best thing I could have," he said, laying his hands beside his body.

I made my way out of the room. Isaac, Demetre, and Petra followed. Could it be that Adara and Xylia were caring for the beast that had attacked this man?

"Where is the boy?" Demetre asked the moment I closed the door behind me.

"In the room with the girls." I set my gaze on the room they had chosen to sleep in. My hands tightened around the handle of my sword.

"Girls," I said, knocking on the door.

There was no response.

"Are you there?" asked Petra in a louder voice, unsheathing his sword. Seconds felt like minutes as we waited for them to respond.

"They have to be inside," Isaac muttered, furrowing his brow.

I twisted the knob, pushing the door with my shoulder, but found that it was locked.

"Girls!" I shouted at the top of my lungs. Alarmed, I drew my sword.

"That's it." Isaac landed a kick on the door, smashing it in half.

"Xylia!" Isaac screamed, rushing his way inside.

The room was empty. We looked at each other, confused at the sight.

"Where are they?" Petra's eyes surveyed the room. "Where did they go?"

There were creases on the sheets of the bed. I marched toward the window, looking out at the dark landscape, trying to spot them.

"They have to be in this room," Demetre said, searching under the bed.

Footsteps creaked on the wooden floor of the room. My lips tightened as I turned my face in the direction of the unexpected sounds.

"Do you hear it?" Isaac asked with eyes wide open. The sudden noise ceased. Our breathing was the only audible sound in the room.

"Where is it?" I feared an attack from whatever lurked around us.

Deafening screams came from the other room.

"It's in here!" the wounded man roared. "Help me!"

"Is everything alright?" Ballard shouted from the living room. I heard the sound of his footsteps as he ran up the stairs. We hastened our way to the other room.

My wings moved beneath my skin when I laid eyes on the man.

"He is in here." His entire body trembled. "Listen."

An unseen creature strutted around the room. The continuous creaking noise of the wooden floor raised the hairs on my neck.

The man lifted his body with great difficulty, struggling to stand on his feet. His chest heaved with desperate breaths. While reclining his back on the bedpost, bite marks appeared on his face. His neck was ripped open before he could scream. Parts of his nose and lips were torn away from him. A puddle of blood formed on the white sheets of the bed.

176

"Show yourself, coward!" Demetre raised up his sword.

Petra turned his head, searching for the unseen being that walked around the room.

The man's body twitched as life poured out of him.

A hovering cloud of smoke appeared in front of me. It assumed the shape of a grotesque monster. The creature was tall; its two horns were only inches away from touching the ceiling. It hissed as its dark eyes darted in our direction.

With a strong grasp, the beast held Adara and Xylia under its arms. This was indeed the creature the man had so fearfully described.

With great strength, it slammed its horns against the wall, creating a gap. Cold air flooded the room as the beast jumped its way out.

We were all at its heels.

"Do not let it escape," said Ballard, running as fast as his human legs allowed him. The beast roared as it clumped its way through the soft snow.

Petra, Ballard, and Demetre stayed behind while Isaac and I chased the monster at full speed.

Isaac's feet abandoned the ground as he soared into the air; his white wings spreading wide. I bent my knees, propelling my body toward the beast. As I approached its massive body, I grabbed one of its horns, my feet landing on its back.

With loud screeches, the creature released the girls, tossing them onto the snow. Isaac plunged down from the sky, his hand tight around his sword. At that moment, his gaze alone would have caused the fiercest of men to tremble in fear.

Before he could strike the creature with his sword, it clasped his left wrist, hurtling his body against one of the pine trees. Seconds later, the creature's strong hands gripped my wounded ankle. I gritted my teeth, feeling a sharp pain shoot up my leg.

As my feet rose away from its body, I attempted to wound it with my blade. I pierced its shoulder as I was catapulted into the woods. The creature shrieked. My back collided with the bark of a bay willow tree.

My sword slipped from my hand the moment my body thudded on the ground. Disoriented, I looked up and realized that we were near the dead bodies that hung from a neighboring tree. Isaac lay on the ground, unconscious.

From behind the beast, I saw Ballard, Petra, and Demetre running in our direction. With a loud bellow, the creature stalked toward them.

"Watch out!" I shook my head from one side to the other, trying to remain focused.

The beast attempted to lash at them with its massive hands, but they dodged its every move at a surprising speed. With a determined expression, Petra swung his sword against the creature, which dodged his blade by lowering its head. Demetre rushed his way to Isaac's unconscious body.

The monster tried to sink its teeth into Ballard's arm. He swung his sword at the creature while dodging its swift attack. The beast shrieked as the blade entered its side. Once again, Petra raised his sword, and this time struck the creature on its right shoulder, driving his weapon deep within its body. It fell on its side, writhing in agony.

This lingering pain was something unfamiliar to me. I managed to stand, reclining my trembling body against the tree's bark. I watched all of them. Demetre stood in front of his friend's body. Judging by his stare, he was prepared to die in order to protect Isaac.

For a few moments, Ballard and Petra had vacant expressions in their eyes. In a trance-like state, they stood immobile. The creature continued to thrash its wounded body against the snow. I was confused when I saw Ballard lowering his arms. He bowed his head, dropping his sword to the ground, standing only inches away from the beast. What was he doing? Was it his plan to die again?

Desperate, the beast tried to crawl in the direction of the trees. Ballard's left arm trembled as he clenched his fists. Petra drew closer to the creature. Fear and confusion filled me when I saw Petra laying his right hand on the creature's skull. As fast as a breath, it ceased its movements. Its breathing grew shallow as its growls transformed into murmurs. The powerful monster appeared to be paralyzed. Ballard opened his eyes, raised his left fist, and struck the ground, causing the earth to shake beneath us. Cracks appeared on the ground, creating uneven patterns that extended all the way to the trees. I watched with a fervent gaze as the ground that the monster stood on caved in, swallowing its grotesque body. Like new skin that covers a wound, cracks in the earth quickly closed.

Silence lingered as I stared at Ballard and Petra. Where had such abilities come from?

Ballard pressed his brows together, looking at his left hand in amazement. With a gaping jaw, Petra trailed his fingertips across the palm of his hand. My attention was

179

turned away from them as I limped my way to Isaac. Ballard rushed his way to the girls while Petra marched toward me.

"Are you alright?" asked Demetre, helping me kneel next to Isaac. From the corner of my eye, I saw Petra approaching me.

"Isaac," I said, shaking his left shoulder. "Can you hear me?"

He opened his eyes wide, leaping to his feet.

"Where is the creature?" he asked.

"The creature is gone," Petra said with a confused expression.

"Gone?" Isaac reached down for his sword, which had its blade buried beneath the snow.

"Ballard and me—"

"The girls!" Isaac screamed before Petra could finish his sentence.

Was there honesty amongst us? I thought while watching Isaac rush his way to Ballard and the girls. Demetre and Petra followed him.

How could these abilities have sprung out of nowhere? In my heart, I hoped that they were not keeping secrets from me. Having to fight against the evil within me was already a battle in itself, but to have to fight against their lack of trust would be something unacceptable to me.

"How are you feeling?" asked Isaac, kneeling beside Xylia and Adara.

Adara cleared her throat. "What...happened?" she asked, pressing the edge of her hand against her forehead. "My head hurts."

Petra lurched his way closer to Ballard.

"I would also like to know what happened," I declared, looking at each one of them.

Petra and Ballard exchanged a confused expression. Xylia rubbed her face as she lifted her back from the snow. She squinted her eyes, wagging her head from side to side.

"Where is the boy?" she asked.

Isaac scowled at her, extending his hand.

"The boy was a creature from the Abyss," he said while helping her stand to her feet. "It turned into a beast and attacked all of us. Do you not remember?"

"What do you mean?" Adara's eyebrows knitted together. "The boy wasn't real?"

Xylia's nose scrunched up in disbelief as she set her eyes on Adara.

"The last thing I recall was lying in bed with him," Adara said with a frown. "His innocent eyes looking straight into mine as we both fell asleep."

"You did not hear anything else after you fell asleep?" Demetre rested his left hand on his hip.

Adara narrowed her eyes.

"No," she replied in a low voice.

"I remember checking on her after we tended to that man's wounds. They slept on the bed…" Xylia's voice trailed off. Her fingers scratched her forehead as she tried to recall any other memories. "I cannot recall anything else after that."

"You were both unconscious when we found you," Isaac said.

"Though I am glad to see everyone alive and well, I must say that I am indeed curious as to how Ballard and Petra were able to do what they did." I sheathed my sword.

181

"They saved us, Devin," Demetre said with an edge to his voice. "You should be grateful."

"What did they do?" There was curiosity in Isaac's voice.

Petra and Ballard were quiet, their heads bowed.

"My gratefulness will not be the answer to my questions, Demetre." I bore my eyes into Petra's. "Is there honesty in our midst? Isaac killed a blood-drinker in seconds without moving a single muscle." I pointed my finger to Petra. "You paralyzed that beast with one touch." I scowled at Ballard, shaking my head from one side to the other. "And you cracked the earth open with your fist."

"I don't know how I was able to do that." Petra's shoulders shrugged up.

"You...don't...know?" I let out a quick breath. "And you, Ballard. You are also unaware of how you were able to do what you did, correct?"

A silent nod was his response to my question.

I turned my back to them, walking back to the house. These mysteries devoured me inside. How could they not know how they'd acquired those abilities? Why would they keep these secrets from me?

The pain in my leg set my teeth on edge. These creatures had the power to wound me—a Nephilin. Maybe they were hiding the truth because I had no place amongst them. I was immortal by birth—an aberration.

Athalas had mentored me for so many years. The man I'd deemed to be one of the wisest among men had sold his soul to Lucifer. Had he seen something that I missed? He was the one that opened the door of Justicia to shelter Adawnas and me. Was I allowing this journey to blind me from the real truth? A part of me also wondered where Adawnas was. For so many years, we had lived together, sharing the same pain, the same struggles. Little did she know of the affection that I had for her. If only love was as simple for Nephilins as it was for humans. My heart was shattered when I saw her in Aloisio, standing beside Nephele. She had confided in me in the past. Why had she concealed the truth from me?

I walked across the stall where the horses were being kept. I was surprised when I did not hear their sounds. Flakes of snow started to descend from the sky.

I hurried my pace, worried as to why the animals were so quiet. A rotting stench filled my nostrils. With a heavy heart, I looked at both horses lying on the ground; blood was splattered on the mildewed walls of the stall. Their eyes were a hazy white. There were no signs on their bodies that a wild animal had attacked them.

I looked over my shoulder and saw the others making their way toward the house. I waited for them to come closer.

"We have to leave now," I said as Isaac approached the stall. "Something evil is lurking in these woods." I pointed to the dead animals.

Isaac wrinkled his nose when he saw the horses, resting the back of his hand over his nose and lips.

"Demetre, Petra and I searched these woods. There was no sign of an enemy nearby," he said.

Ballard and Petra studied the horses' carcasses; the girls took one quick look and turned their faces away in disgust.

"What could have done this?" Adara shook her head.

"Judging by the creatures we encountered today, I am sure it was something that we have never seen or heard of before," Demetre said in a somber tone.

"Let's go get the books so we can be on our way," Isaac whispered, his eyes never leaving the dead animals.

"I will keep watch as you all head inside," I said.

They made their way up the short steps, walking through the doorway. Snowflakes fell on my cheeks as the wind blew against the dry branches of the trees.

"Devin." I heard a sudden voice in the air.

I turned around, thinking it was one of my companions, but I did not see anyone.

"I know the evil that lurks in your heart." I shivered as the voice continued. "It must be a great burden to fight against your nature every day."

I unsheathed my sword, walking away from the stall. I searched for the owner of this voice.

"Who are you?" My chest constricted as if being pressed by two hands.

The wind howled while I waited for the voice to respond.

"I am the one that hunts you." The voice deepened, cracking as it spoke.

"Lucifer?" I frowned, watching the pine trees ahead of me dance in the wind.

"We are ready, Devin." I was startled when I heard Isaac's voice. He approached me from behind, the others following.

"Are you alright?" Isaac's eyes analyzed my face. "Did you see anything?"

"No." I did not lie. I had not seen anything, but I was not about to tell him about the voice I'd heard.

"Why do you have your sword in your hand, then?" Xylia inquired, adjusting her satchel around her shoulder.

My right eyebrow rose up.

"I do not have to answer to you." I sheathed my sword.

Her shoulders shrugged upward. She rolled her eyes, walking away from me.

I glanced back at the stall, looking at the lifeless horses. Did that voice belong to the Dark One? Could it be that Lucifer had spoken to me?

XIII

THE SNOW ON the ground deepened as we continued to travel down the Road of Ahnor. The flurries settled on the trees, accumulating atop the frozen ice that already rested on their dry branches. The vegetation grew denser and taller, making limiting my visibility.

Why would the Dark One come to me? Though Lucifer did not have a physical body, his presence lingered, manifesting in different ways. If I heard his voice, did it mean that he was aware of our location? Was he to send an army after us?

Though my heart was troubled by the sound of his conniving voice, fear stood at bay. Perhaps I was making the wrong choice. Since darkness was already inside of me, why should I continue to fight against it?

Above the tree branches, and towering even above the cloudbank, were the mountains that so many men feared.

"There they are," Ballard said in a low voice. "The Weeping Mountains."

"You know where we are?" I asked, looking over my shoulder. Ballard frowned at the ominous landscape.

"Indeed I do. The ruins of Madbouseux lie in the mountains. I will never forget the day I stumbled upon…" His voice trailed off as his hand grasped the rugged satchel around his shoulders. "The day I stumbled upon this book."

"You found the Book of Letters here?" Isaac inquired.

"Yes." Ballard's shoulders rose as he took a deep breath. "I should have listened to my father." He pursed his lips.

An unknown power rested upon these mountains. I recalled King Demyon's accounts of what his soldiers had seen near these ruins.

In an instant, a fog curtain formed around us. It was not long until my visibility was further limited, and I struggled to see what lay ahead of me.

"Stay together," Isaac ordered. Everyone drew their swords. Thistles covered in thick, long thorns rested on the forest floor. The snow no longer descended from the gray sky; there was no breeze blowing against the limbs of the trees.

We were all apprehensive as we continued to make our way through the mist. I looked around me, failing to recall our exact location.

"Do you know where we are, Devin?" came Demetre's voice. I turned my face to him.

"I am not so sure." My right hand tightened. The pain in my leg was almost forgettable, but it was still bothersome.

"Have you ever been here before?" Xylia asked in an impatient tone.

"No."

"Then why do you guide us?" Her voice loudened. "We are lost, aren't we?"

187

My patience grew thin as she spoke.

"Would you like to guide yourself through the mist, girl?" I halted, looking at all of them. "And please, can you at least have the decency of giving me an honest answer?"

Petra pressed his eyebrows together.

"You still do not believe that we are not aware of how we acquired those abilities?" he barked.

I shot him a cold sneer.

"Do not play me for a fool."

"Devin, we are not lying," said Ballard, stepping his way closer to me.

From the woods emerged the sudden sound of rattling hoofs. The loud neighing of horses echoed. The fact that I did not know who or what dwelled in these parts of the world stirred fear within me. With swords ready, we waited for whatever wandered these woods to appear.

"Do we run?" Adara's voice was a whisper.

"They seem to be all around us." Demetre bore his eyes into Isaac's.

"They are approaching us." Xylia stooped her body forward, raising her sword. Her blade stood inches above her head.

My eyes closed as I attempted to control the approaching horses. I focused my mind on the sounds they made as they galloped. They were strong and untamed. The faint beating of their hearts invaded my ears. After a while, I perceived that seven animals galloped in our direction. A throbbing pain invaded my head as I tried to enter their minds. I opened my eyes, pressing my fingers on my forehead.

"What is the matter, Devin?" Isaac asked, laying his hand on my shoulder.

"Nothing." My eyes squinted, trying to relieve my head of the throbbing pain. "I am alright."

The hoof beats and the neighing ceased. We stood together, immobile. I could hear the breathing of the horses and their riders, hidden behind the fog. They whispered to each other, though none revealed the exact location where they stood.

"Show yourselves!" Xylia demanded. "We are not here to be played as fools."

"Neither are we," a deep, disembodied voice declared. "Who are you? What are you doing in these woods?"

"We will only answer your question once we lay eyes on your face." Isaac held his head steady.

A low grunt came from the owner of the voice as I heard him alight his horse. Those around him followed his act. The snow crushed beneath his feet as he walked.

Through the mist came a tall man. He carried a bow in his right hand. The rugged, thick cloak that covered his body was made of sheep's wool. Though the prominent color of the cloak was white, it was stained with dirt.

"Now that you see my face, can you tell me who you are?" His russet eyes were focused on all of us. A scruffy beard covered his heart-shaped face. His brown hair was tied back. He had thick lines around his lips.

"We are travelers." Demetre raised the tip of his sword toward him. "Our business is our own." His right eyebrow shot up, hiding beneath his dark hair.

The man let out a quick breath while he shook his head.

"What kind of business would bring a group like yours to the Weeping Mountains?" His eyes bore into mine.

I lurched forward, leveling my finger in his face. "I believe we can ask the same of you."

His lips curved into a thin smile. "You are not human, are you?"

"He is with us." Isaac stepped in front of the man.

The moment the man laid eyes on Isaac, his face changed. He frowned as his eyes trailed across Isaac's facial features.

"What is your name, young one?" The man tilted his face slightly.

"Isaac."

Upon his response, I heard the men around us murmuring amongst each other.

"You are Isaac?" the man in white asked in a quivering voice. "Isaac Khan?"

"I do not believe we have met." Isaac lowered his weapon.

"No, we have not." The man gave him a half-hearted smile. "But your face is very familiar to me."

Isaac drew his head back, confused at the man's statement.

"What is your name?" Demetre asked the stranger.

"I am Alistar, defender of the Village of Tears." When he finished speaking, the other six riders that accompanied him approached us. They were all dressed in similar clothing as Alistar. All were armed with bows and arrows.

"Tell me, why is the Nephilin with you?" Alistar cocked his head in my direction, keeping his eyes set on Isaac.

I tightened my hands, trying to restrain myself from breaking his jaw. Who did this man think he was?

"I can speak—"

"He is my friend." Isaac cut me off. "He has been by my side since I left home."

Alistar strode forward, bearing his eyes into mine. "Do you all trust him?" he asked.

A part of me wanted to stick my blade into his gut. Another longed to hear the answer my companions would give him.

"Yes, we do," Petra replied in an instant, taking a short step toward the man.

"Who gave you authority to answer for all of them?"

Petra's lips moved as he tried to find words to contend with Alistar. In shame, he returned to his place. Alistar handed his bow to the man on his left.

"Do you all trust him?" He raised both of his eyebrows, creating wrinkles on his forehead.

"If we did not, do you think we'd still have him by our side?" Xylia marched up to Alistar. "Why does it matter if we trust him or not?"

"Do you not fear for your life, girl?" He crossed his hands in front of him.

She lifted her chin, leveling her eyes with his. "If my life is the price to be paid for a just cause, then fear is nothing but a mere enemy that can be easily defeated."

The men around us nocked their arrows, drawing out their bows.

Alistar raised his right hand.

"Lower your weapons." A wide smile appeared on his face. "Girl, your courage is indeed inspiring." He walked

closer to her. "Though pride can sometimes make us forget the danger that surrounds us."

He shifted his gaze to me. "The reason Isaac's face is not strange to me is because his mother and father are in the Village of Tears. They headed there after they left Bellator," he said. "He is the spitting image of his father."

"My parents?" Isaac dropped his sword to the ground. "They are alive?" He raised his eyebrows. "Will you take me to them?" Isaac grabbed ahold of Alistar's right arm.

"I am taking all of you to see them. I have answers to many of your questions." Alistar trailed his fingers across his hair. "I apologize for the way I greeted you all. Our enemy is moving and few are willing to join the war."

"I have never heard of the Village of Tears." The cold wind blew my hair as I sheathed my sword.

"We chose the Weeping Mountains to establish our village because many fear them. You will not find this place on any map the kingdoms possess. The ever-lingering mist shields us," he said.

"How soon until you take us to your village?" Isaac's eyes glistened. "Is it far?"

"We can go now, if you wish," Alistar replied.

"Isaac." The edge of my right hand was pressed on my forehead. "Though I know you want to see your parents, let us not forget the reason we took the Road of Ahnor in the first place." I turned my eyes to Alistar. "We are looking for King Ohmen, King Folletti, and Queen Valleree. We were informed—"

"Please." Alistar interrupted with the raise of his hand. "You must come with me." There was an unsettling urgency in his voice. The men around him exchanged distressed looks.

"Isaac," I said, and his glistening eyes shot up to mine. "It is your decision to follow this man. Let us hope it does not delay our quest."

His shoulders rose as he took a quick breath. "They are alive, Devin," he said in a brittle voice. He shifted his face away from mine, looking at Alistar. "His people must have answers to our questions. It would be wise to follow him."

"I trust Isaac's judgment, Devin," Adara whispered from behind me in her soothing voice. "I also think we should follow Alistar."

"Trust me." Isaac sniffed, wiping his nose with his wrist.

"Trust you?" My chest rose as I took in a deep breath. "I am trying to."

XIV

I LET ISAAC and the others walk ahead of me as we followed Alistar. Though his men were mounted on their horses, he had chosen to walk with us, leading his horse by the reins. Despite the struggle to see as we traveled through the fog, Alistar led us effortlessly. The eyes of his men did not sway from us as they drank from their wineskins.

"I know the thoughts and questions that haunt you, Devin." My heart accelerated as the voice hissed. "Why do you continue to fight against who you are?"

I looked at my companions, realizing that they were unaware of the voice in my ears.

"They are all fools," it whispered.

Lucifer's voice was drowned out by a familiar melody. To my surprise, Alistar hummed a melody that I knew far too well. The words of the song drifted from his lips.

"Through pain and trial, war or rain.
Through storms and calms,
Our hearts steady remain.
Through a journey unseen,
As we walk through fire and water

Victory is found in the light that shines from within."

During the days when I lived with the Council, Athalas would sing the Song of Hope prior to every gathering. He said the Stars had written this song before the fall of Lucifer.

"Where did you learn this song?" I shouted. The tip of a few branches brushed against my cheeks as I strode to him.

"Do you know it?" He darted a surprised look at me.

"I do," I replied. "I remember Athalas singing that song while I lived with the Council."

"Our ancestors valued the old teachings. They thought it was important to preserve the songs that had been passed down to them." His eyebrows rose. "Unlike so many," he placed his hand over his heart, "my people have never abandoned the old teachings of the Creator."

"Do you see this man, Devin?" I attempted to conceal my emotions as the voice started speaking to me again. "In his mind he thinks he is superior to you all. Have you not grown weary of being treated like vermin? Will you continue to waste the power that is inside of you?" From the corner of my eye, I looked at Alistar, walking with his head held high.

My eyes glanced over my shoulder, catching sight of Xylia. Her eyes fidgeted as she pressed her eyebrows. She trailed the tip of her fingers over her ears. Did she also hear the voice?

"Here we are," Alistar said, spreading his arms wide. "Welcome to the Village of Tears."

I looked ahead, failing to see any signs of a village. After we had taken a few more steps, the fog thinned, revealing a wooden wall with a rusted iron gate. Each piece of wood had been painted white, causing the monument to blend in with the surrounding landscape. Atop the wall was a man clothed in garments similar to Alistar's.

Alistar looked up and waved his right hand at the man. A few seconds later, the gate creaked as its rusted doors swung open.

There were very few people walking on the streets of the village. Small quaint houses were built around and atop the snow-covered hills. An old willow tree encircled by a stone courtyard was located at the entrance. The sound of clanging metal echoed to my right. I saw a blacksmith's forge. A slender, tall man held up a sword, analyzing every single detail of his creation. Men shoveled the snow from the cobblestone streets. The occupants of the village watched us as if we were thieves that had been arrested.

I found it odd to see that every building was painted white. Those that were out on the streets wore matching white garments with shades of gray and red.

"Is white your favorite color?" I asked Alistar.

He chuckled. "It conceals us. The white color merges with the lingering mist, creating a natural shield."

Alistar came to a halt, standing next to a frozen lagoon surrounded by five two-story houses.

"I will take it from here, men." Alistar tipped his head down.

"Let us know if you need anything else, Alistar," one of his soldiers said, riding away in the opposite direction. The others followed him.

"This way." He pointed to house that sat on the far right. Across from us was a pub. Though we were on the

196

other side of the road, one could not help but hear the booming laughter and loud bellowing of the men that drank inside.

We walked up the three stone steps to the red door. Alistar knocked three times. He kept looking around while he waited for the door to be opened.

"Are you waiting for anyone else?" asked Isaac. "You seem apprehensive."

"I have to make sure we were not followed. Few outsiders are ever brought to this village." He looked over his shoulder, fixing his gaze on Isaac.

A young girl opened the door.

"Papa." She leaped on top of Alistar, greeting him with a tender hug.

"I missed you, baby girl," he said, bending his body down so his eyes could meet hers. "Where is your brother?"

She gave him a loving smile. "He is upstairs. He was out hunting in the woods."

"Did he catch anything?" Alistar asked, fixing the young girl's hair behind her ear.

"He caught three rabbits. It isn't much, but it will do." Her voice was sweet and mellow.

Alistar smiled, giving the girl a tender shake with his hands.

"Come in." Alistar beckoned us to enter.

"Who are these people, Papa?" The girl grabbed her father's hand, watching us as we walked inside her house.

"They are our new friends." Alistar gave his daughter a broad smile.

I felt the warmth of the burning fireplace. Jars filled with grains and seeds sat on the shelves affixed to the walls. There was a staircase that led to the upper floor; a wooden table with three stools sat on the left side of the room.

"I apologize that I do not have enough seats for you all. I am not one to receive many visitors." He removed his cloak, laying it on top of the settee beside the fireplace. "Please try to make yourselves comfortable. I will prepare us something to eat."

The girls sat on the stools while we sat on the ground, resting our backs against the wall. Petra sat next to me.

"Sela, help me serve our guests some hot tea and bread." Alistar signaled his daughter to approach him.

The girl shot me a dubious stare. "Of course," she said.

"Who is he?" I heard Sela whisper to her father.

"He is with them, Sela," Alistar replied as he laid some plates on the table.

From the corner of my eye, I examined the young girl. Her white dress had long sleeves that covered half of her small hands. Atop her head was a thin silver tiara.

Isaac struggled to remain seated. With great anxiety, he moved his legs as he nibbled on his lips.

"Do you trust them?" Petra whispered, his arms stretched over his knees.

"What other choice do we have now? Isaac seems to trust them," I answered. "At least we will have a roof over our heads and food to feed us today."

Ballard sat by the window. With a pensive expression, he gazed through the glass. Demetre sat beside Isaac.

"Trust no one." I gasped as the unexpected voice sounded in my ear once again, drowning out all other

sounds. Why was this happening? Why was Lucifer speaking to me?

"Where are you?" I thought, hoping that the voice would respond.

"I am everywhere," said the voice, and my heart palpitated. "You desire evil, yet you want to fulfill a bidding that does not belong to you."

I was startled by rapid footsteps descending the staircase.

"Father, I didn't—" The boy's eyes widened as he gasped in surprise. "Who are these people?" He had a young appearance, no older than eighteen. His gray eyes met my own as he walked to his father. I noticed his boots were damp and covered in mud. His white, laced shirt was covered in dirt.

"These people are our guests, Arundel," Alistar replied, handing him a plate with a piece of bread. "Please, help me serve them food."

Arundel tightened his brow into a scowl. In silence, he strolled his way to Isaac while looking at me.

"Is there a problem?" I asked the boy.

He shook his head before speaking. "No. There is no problem," he replied. He handed the plate to Isaac. Wrinkles creased the skin between his eyebrows when he laid eyes on Isaac.

"Thank you." A thin smile crossed Isaac's lips. He tilted his face to the side as he grabbed the plate, noticing Arundel's strange reaction.

Arundel started making his way back to his father. He came to an abrupt halt in the middle of the room. "Are you...a Nephilin?" He shifted his eyes to me.

199

"He is with us," Petra said in a sharp voice.

Arundel strolled his hand through his raven hair. "I am sorry. I did not mean to be rude. You are our guests." He was about to turn his back to us when he looked at Isaac once again. "Have we met before?"

Isaac shook his head. "You have probably met my father, Dustin Khan. People say that we look alike."

"Diane and Dustin are your parents?" Arundel's eyebrows rose. "They are here! They are ups—"

"Arundel, keep handing out these plates, please," said Alistar in a strong voice.

Isaac frowned, standing to his feet. "They are here? In your house? Why did you not tell me?"

"Isaac, you have to listen." Alistar dropped the plate he held in his hand on the table.

"I want to see them," Isaac said, his voice rising.

"Something happened." Alistar crossed his hands in front of him, holding his head high.

"What happened?" Isaac spread out his hands, looking at Alistar with fervent eyes.

"It is not an easy thing to explain…" Alistar's voice trailed off as he made his way to Isaac.

Isaac's chest heaved with heavy breaths. He clenched his hands into fists. In an instant, he turned his back to us and shot his way up the stairs. His footsteps sounded like rocks falling down a cliff.

"Wait, Isaac!" Demetre leaped to his feet, running to him.

"Demetre!" I shouted. He turned to me. "Let him be."

He raised his eyes, looking up at the staircase. "Why would you lie to him?" He turned his gaze to Alistar.

"Your friend is not ready to face the harsh truth that awaits him," Alistar said.

"What harsh truth?" Demetre's shoulders rose with a slight turn of his face. "After all we have been through, no truth or lie would ever have the power to break us again."

With his right hand, Alistar scratched his forehead.

"Do not speak of things that you do not know, Demetre. You know a fraction of the truth."

An uncomfortable silence lingered.

"I am sorry, Alistar," Adara said with her head low. "We should all be grateful for what you are doing here today."

Alistar reached for a plate holding a piece of bread. "Don't worry about me." He walked to Adara. "Your friend is the one that will need your support and courage." He stretched his hand, handing her the plate.

ISAAC

XV

I MARCHED MY way up the stairs, determined to find my parents. Why would Alistar lie to me? What was he hiding? Like a pursuing enemy, rage kept coming after me. I had to forget about him—at least for now.

There was a door to my left. Its silver knob glistened under the candles that burned on the chandelier hanging from the ceiling.

With fumbling hands, I twisted the doorknob.

"Mom! Dad!" I shouted at the top of my lungs.

I peeked inside the room. An empty bed covered by a colorful quilt was sitting next to the window, and a ragged white rug sat at the foot of the bed.

I closed my hand, slamming my palm against the door in frustration.

Another door was in front of me. I repeated my previous act.

"Are you in…" My voice disappeared. Numbness shot up my entire body. My knees trembled.

Here they were. The most important people in my life were lying on a bed, covered in white blankets. They were alive.

I could not move for a while. So many times I had fought against the belief that their lives had been taken. With tears streaming down my face, I tromped my way to them.

"Dad." I took in deep, fast breaths, sitting next to him. His skin was pale, his face covered in bruises and wounds. "Dad," I repeated, this time, shaking him. He did not wake.

I gazed at his face. In my childhood, there had been such pride in me when people talked about how my dad and I had the same face.

"All this time I thought you were dead," I said, disregarding the fact that he was unconscious. "And here you are, right in front of me." I laid my head on his chest; his heartbeat was nothing more than a soft murmur.

On the other side of the room was my mother.

I stood to my feet, making my way to her.

"Mom, I am here." I sat on the edge of the bed.

Her golden hair cascaded above her shoulders. Though she lay unconscious, I found a way to wrap her in my arms.

"It was not easy for me to wake up and not find you in the kitchen that morning. You were gone…" I shuddered at the memories that invaded my mind.

Her skin was pale and cold.

"Can you hear me, Mom?" I waited for her to react to my voice. She did not move. My eyes watched her for a few seconds. I laid her back on the bed, releasing her from my arms.

With elbows rested on my knees, I bowed my head. What had happened to them? What had led them here?

There was a soft knock on the door. I looked back and saw Demetre. It would have been impossible to miss the surprised look on his face as he surveyed the room.

"They are alive, my friend." My trembling lips curved into a thin smile.

Demetre's eyes filled with tears as he rushed his way in.

"I cannot believe it." He stood beside me, looking at my parents.

My smile turned grim. Though I was glad to see them alive, I was also worried.

"We will take this as a sign." Demetre had a soft grin stamped on his face.

"A sign?" I furrowed my eyebrows, tilting my head to the side.

"That we will succeed in this journey. I thought I was never going to see them again." He sat beside me. "Yet here they are, alive."

I placed my arm around his shoulder. "You know, Demetre, I could never have gotten this far without you, my friend. It was because of your companionship that I was able to remain strong in the Wastelands of Tristar."

He let out a low laugh. "Do not forget that it was you that always protected me."

It had been a long time since I had felt hope spring up in my heart. Though the world had changed, the three people I cared for the most in my life had not. They were here with me, inside this room.

"Why do you think Alistar did not want to reveal to me that my parents were here?" I wondered if I had made the right choice by following him to this village.

"Maybe you should go ask him, Isaac. If it had not been for him, you would never have seen your parents again," Demetre replied.

My eyes shied away from his. I nodded, thinking about how I had reacted. Despite the fact that I was uneasy about Alistar, he had brought me to my parents.

"You are right." My hands pressed on my knees.

Demetre and I rose to our feet, walking out of the room. I glanced back, looking at my parents once again.

I descended the stairs, avoiding any eye contact with my companions or my hosts. Demetre was at my heels.

"How are you feeling, Isaac?" Xylia inquired, walking her way to me.

A shy smile appeared on my face. "I am alright."

Her arms wrapped around me in a tender embrace. Her heart was beating at a rapid pace.

"I am glad they are alive," she whispered in my ear.

I returned her embrace.

"Thank you." There was such comfort in her embrace. It was odd having all these positive emotions strike me at once.

"Please sit," said Alistar, pointing to one of the stools.

Devin had his eyes fixed on Alistar as he nibbled on a piece of bread. "How are they doing, Isaac?" he asked.

"They appear to be well," I replied as I took a seat. "I found it strange that they did not move from their beds. They looked unconscious."

"That does not surprise me," said Alistar. He picked up a plate with a piece of bread on it and placed it on the table in front of me. "You have to eat." His eyes bore deep into mine.

I broke the piece of bread in half, waiting for him to elaborate on his previous comment. His son and daughter stood next to the fireplace, watching.

"One of my men informed us that an army of dark creatures arose from the Ruins of Madbouseux. He claimed he saw men with wings like dragons leading this army." He sighed. "There was such fear in his face as he shared the story with me."

"What did these dark creatures look like?" Devin laid the bread on the table.

"They had yellow eyes, similar to a feline's," said Arundel from the corner of the room. His sudden response startled us all.

"Arundel, please," said Alistar, darting him an impatient look.

"Their mouths were long and thin," he continued, disregarding his father's order. "They looked human, though scales covered their bodies."

"Be quiet, Arundel." I was surprised when I saw Alistar's fist pound the wooden table.

"I was the one who saw the creature." Arundel scowled at his father. "I saw them—"

"Hold your tongue. This is my house and you live under my roof. Please refrain from speaking."

An uncomfortable silence lingered. Sela ran to her brother's side. In anger, he wrapped his arm around his sister, walking to the door.

"You'd better not—"

Arundel slammed the door before his father could finish his sentence.

"Please excuse him," Alistar said after a brief silence. He pressed the tips of his fingers between his brows. "My son thinks too highly of himself."

"Arundel saw the army?" Ballard asked, walking closer to Alistar.

"Yes." There was anger in Alistar's voice. "He did leave out a very important detail about this newfound army."

We already had Nephilins, Fallen Stars, and all sorts of dark creatures against us. A part of me did not want to know what this important detail was.

His face shifted in the direction of the fireplace. His eyes watched the fire dance. "They were seen flying away from the ruins." His voice was low and ominous.

"What are they?" Xylia asked, crossing her arms.

"We do not know what they are. There are no accounts of these creatures." Arundel ambled around the room. "Lucifer's army grows strong."

I took a small bite from the piece of bread I held in my hand. All this information was of great importance, but I wanted to know why my parents were lying on a bed in a stupor.

"Two days ago, my men were patrolling the Road of Ahnor when we found three bodies hanging from a tree. They had been burned and mutilated. We only knew who they were because of the royal jewels they wore." Alistar reached into his pocket. With his left hand, he took out three brooches.

He held up one that was shaped like an Aquila with its wings spread wide. "This one is made out of bronze," he said, twirling the brooch between his fingers. "This design can be easily recognized."

"That is the emblem of the Kingdom of Tarsh," said Devin, gazing at the jewel.

Alistar set the object on the table. The next brooch he held was made out of glass. It was shaped like a five-pointed star.

"The emblem of the Kingdom of Watermiles," Alistar mentioned. "They say they are the brightest star next to the Sea of Glass."

With a look of discontent, Petra sighed. "Hold up the other brooch."

Alistar tightened his lips, laying the object he held next to the brooch from Tarsh.

"Do you know who this brooch belongs to, young one?" Alistar had in his hand a golden brooch shaped like a combat helmet. The helmet's thin comb was long and curved.

Petra cleared his throat, scowling at the object. "That is the emblem of the Kingdom of Swordsmouth."

One of our greatest fears was now a reality: Those that we had sought to find on the Road of Ahnor were dead.

"So they are dead," Adara mumbled with a vacant stare.

Alistar set his eyes on me. "Underneath the tree where we found the bodies, we also came across your parents. We assume they were trying to protect the kings and the queen from their murderers. Your parents have been unconscious since we found them."

I closed my eyes, trailing my hand across my face.

"I wanted to warn you before you saw them," Alistar added.

"Who murdered them?" Adara whimpered. "The kings and the queen?"

"We are not sure." Alistar crossed his hands behind his back. "We have been looking for these winged creatures, but we cannot find them."

"I think we might have come across those that led them out of the ruins," said Ballard, sinking his hands into his side pockets.

Alistar's mouth opened, and his face grew pale.

An unexpected, frightening screech echoed from the street.

"What is that?" Demetre asked. We all drew our swords.

The screech continued. From the window, I saw people flocking to the front of the house, their eyes wide in bewilderment.

"What is going on?" Alistar marched to the door.

A bellowing growl resounded. Alistar's shoulders rose up as he let out a long breath, shaking his head in disappointment.

"Are we to just stand here?" Xylia reached for the door handle.

"Do not open it!" he shouted, grabbing her wrist. Her eyebrows rose in surprise.

The moment I saw him lay his hand on her, I pushed his body against the wall, pressing my arm against his neck.

"Don't you dare touch her," I said, bearing my gaze into his. "Do not mistake her for one of your children."

There was great rage burning inside of me. The sudden desire to take his life invaded me.

My companions stared at me, confused.

"Isaac, stop," said Demetre, grabbing ahold of my arm.

Why were such dark desires finding their way into my heart? My hand trembled as I released Alistar.

212

"Be careful, young Isaac," he said, rubbing his neck. "Your courage might yet be your downfall."

The crowd's gasps and murmurs invaded my ears as whatever stood outside let out hair-raising screeches.

Devin pushed Alistar out of the way, swinging the door wide open. The guttural sounds of the creature loudened.

A strange being stood on the street. Thick chains were locked around its neck. Dark stubs stood where its wings had once been. Its menacing, bright yellow eyes were set on the crowd that surrounded it. Arundel held the chain that imprisoned the beast. Sela stood next to him with her hands clutched at her sides. She looked at the grotesque creature, frightened.

"I thought you said you did not know where these creatures were, Alistar." Demetre looked at Alistar and then walked toward the beast.

Alistar had his face fixed in the direction of the crowd.

Drool trickled down the creature's thin neck as it screeched. Its human-like body was covered in small scales.

"Arundel, what are you doing?" Alistar shouted, marching his way to him.

"Dad," Sela whimpered, running toward him.

"Our people deserve to know the truth!" Arundel screamed at the top of his lungs, tightening his grasp on the chains.

"Your stupidity will get us all killed, Arundel." Alistar halted, standing a few feet away from the creature.

"Avoiding the truth will get us killed." Arundel pointed his finger at his father. "Our people need to know what goes on beyond our borders. We have been confined here for far too long."

The crowd murmured amongst themselves as they watched the creature. Fear shrouded all of their faces.

"Have you forgotten the tales our forefathers shared with us?" Alistar turned to the crowd, spreading out his arms. He then turned his eyes back to his son. "Have you forgotten the reason the Kingdom of Madbouseux fell?"

"Of course I haven't," said Arundel. The creature continued to growl. "But we are not them. If you do not show our people the reasons they have to go to war, then I will."

"War…" Alistar scowled at his son. "The fact that we have remained hidden has kept us alive. We are one of the few peoples that have not forgotten the ancient ways."

"But ignoring the other kingdoms makes you useless," I said, walking closer to Alistar. "The fact that you know the stories of the past cannot change the future of Elysium."

"It is none of our business what the other kingdoms do, young one." Alistar's face broke into a cold stare. "My duty is to keep this village confined and protected."

"It was ignorance that led King Bartholomew to fall." Arundel's voice boomed across the crowd. "Do not be like him, Father."

Silence lingered.

"He succumbed to the dark powers of the Book of Letters, leading his people to death. You do not have to do the same." Arundel's eyes glistened as he looked at his father. "We have men that can aid others in this war."

"You talk of war," a man said from amidst the crowd. "What war is this?"

"Are we in danger? Are there more of these creatures?" asked a young girl.

214

All of their voices merged into a single questioning choir. They demanded to know what was happening beyond their borders.

The fact that Alistar knew the truth and had concealed it from his people enraged me. No matter how dark the truth is, it must be told.

The people's murmurs ceased as the neighing and galloping of horses surrounded us. The men that had ridden with Alistar approached us.

"Are you alright, my lord?" one of them asked, holding a sword in his right hand.

Alistar trailed his eyes across the crowd. Arundel's discontentment with his father's actions was stamped on his face. The monstrous creature crawled on the ground, its teeth shimmering as it growled.

Alistar walked to his son, standing inches away from his face.

Arundel's chin quivered as he looked at his father.

"Give me your sword," Alistar said, stretching forth his hand.

Arundel ignored his request.

"Give me your sword," he insisted.

"No," Alistar whispered, stepping away from his father.

With great rage, Alistar grasped Arundel's sword, pushing his son to the left as he marched toward the creature. With a single move, he bore the sword's blade into its skull. The beast's growls turned into gurgles as its body twitched.

Alistar opened his hand, letting Arundel's sword fall to the ground. Its blade was smeared with blood.

"I have kept you all safe in the shadows of the Weeping Mountains," he spoke in a booming voice. "For hundreds of years, we have lived in peace, without the interference of outsiders. I promise that this peace shall last while the village is under my watch." He pointed at us. "I deeply regret bringing these outsiders into our village. We can see that they have brought nothing but chaos to us all."

"What does he mean?" Adara shot her eyes toward me. "We have not done anything."

"Bastard," Devin said behind his gritted teeth. I grabbed his arm as he attempted to approach Alistar.

"I am afraid you have overstayed your welcome in my house." Arundel raised his hand, pointing to a building next to the pub. "I believe the Rest of Ale will be a great place for you all to rest tonight. You shall leave in the morning."

He started back to his house.

"Father!" Arundel pushed the crowd out of his way, walking to Alistar. "Why are you doing this?"

"Ah, I almost forgot." Alistar narrowed his eyes as he scratched his chin. "Men, I believe Arundel has earned himself a night in prison. Make sure he is locked in the darkest cell we have."

"You can't do that!" Xylia huffed as her brows curved. She stomped her way to Alistar. "You would arrest your own son?"

She came to a halt when two guards approached Arundel. They chained both of his wrists and feet with heavy metal chains. The remaining men carried the creature's dead body away.

"I will do whatever needs to be done to keep these people safe. My son's behavior was reckless, so he shall be punished like any other citizen would."

My hands trembled as my heartbeat quickened. I was filled with the desire to take this man's life. His pride and arrogance were repugnant.

My surroundings disappeared when my eyelids pressed together. In the darkness around me, I saw Alistar crouched on the ground, naked. He shivered as he sobbed.

"I will fail like he did," he whispered. "There is no strength in me to fight."

Though I saw him in such a fragile state, my desire to take his life still burned.

"They judge me but they do not know what is inside of me."

I drew out my sword.

"I miss her…" His voice trailed off. "If only they knew…"

With my sword raised in the air, I was prepared to decapitate him. Once again, I wondered why these desires burned inside of me. No matter how proud or arrogant Alistar was, his only desire was to protect his people. I lowered my sword. Its tip pointed to the ground.

Maybe I won't kill you yet, I thought. I calmed myself, returning to my senses.

The guards dragged Arundel from the crowd. He strained against their grasp, but it was no use.

"I regret nothing, father!" he shouted as they took him away. "Tell them the truth!"

XVI

"ALISTAR!" I SHOUTED in anger as I saw him walk inside his house. "Do you expect me to leave without my parents?" I headed toward him, walking up the stairs in front of the doorway.

"Please, leave Papa alone," Sela grabbed my hand, looking at me with glistening eyes. I jerked my hand from hers.

"Look at me, coward!" I demanded, ignoring her innocent request.

He turned around. "There is great darkness surrounding all of you. I do not want you to linger here any longer," he said with fidgeting eyes.

"Have you not yet realized that darkness has taken over our world?" Rage burned inside of me. "Sooner or later, this war will be at your doorstep."

He buried his face in his hand, shaking his head in disdain. My companions walked into the house.

"I know of the books that you carry," Alistar said. Surprised gasps followed. "I know of the powers they possess. I had men in the Kingdom of Bellator. They informed me of the rebellion that took place while you were there. I will not repeat King Demyon's foolish actions."

"Will you do nothing, then?" Wrinkles creased around Devin's eyes as he pressed his eyebrows. "Will you remain hidden in the shadows of the mountains as darkness grows?"

"If it ensures our safety, then yes." He turned his back to us. "The king of Madbouseux failed because he succumbed to the power of the Book of Letters." His eyes looked over his shoulder. "Who is to say that I will not do the same?"

"People are dying!" Xylia shouted as she shook her head, pointing in the direction of the crowd.

"And many more will die, young girl." He marched up to her. I tightened my fists, prepared to strike him. "Tell me, have you felt the power of your book growing on you yet?" Xylia's eyes widened as her jaw dropped slightly. "Can you hear his voice calling for you?" She panted as the words drifted from his mouth.

He circled the room with his fearful eyes. "Soon you will all be taken by him," he said in a scornful tone. "No book-bearer can resist the temptations of Lucifer."

Petra cleared his throat as he stepped forward.

"Tell me, Alistar." He crossed his arms over his chest. "How can you be so sure that we will give in to the darkness? How can you be so sure that we will fail?"

He pursed his lips into a snide smile.

"Lucifer is already finding a place in every single one of your hearts." With quick steps, he made his way to the kitchen. His hands trembled as he grabbed a cup and filled

it with wine. I felt the frigid breeze blowing through the open door behind us.

"Do I lie?" he asked, taking a sip from his drink.

I could see apprehension taking over my companions. I looked at Devin, and his eyes shied away from mine. Demetre approached me, standing by my side.

"I assume your silence is a response in the affirmative," he said, spreading out his arms. "Why would I risk temptation when my people and me are safely hidden inside this village?" He was about to drink from his cup when loud screams were heard.

I looked over my shoulder and caught sight of the fearful crowd making their way out of the streets. The screams loudened as I walked through the doorway.

"What is it?" Ballard asked, following me with sword in hand.

Through the white streets and houses came three dark, hooded figures. Their cloaks covered their feet, dragging on the snow. They marched in our direction, their faces hidden behind a shadow. The one on the far left had within its grasp a soldier's head smeared with blood and dirt.

"Be ready to attack at any time," I ordered, shuddering at the sight.

Petra's hands trembled as they reached for his sword. Adara's eyes glistened while she watched the mysterious figures approach us.

"Now is not the moment to be afraid," I encouraged them.

I felt Xylia touch my shoulder. For a moment, it was as if we could read each other's thoughts—we had both realized that blood was going to be spilled in this village

today. Alistar pushed us from his way as he marched toward the mysterious beings.

"Papa, don't go," Sela begged with tears streaming down her face.

"Stay with me." Adara wrapped her arms around the child. Sela kept her innocent eyes fixed on her father.

"Who are you?" Alistar yelled. "I will have your heads cut off—" His words turned into tortuous screams. I saw flashes of red light surrounding his body. Veins protruded from his neck as he fell to his knees. His teeth chattered as he curved his back. I had not forgotten the last time I had seen this attack.

Rapid footsteps reverberated around us. The sound of beating drums invaded my ears.

"Could it be?" Demetre whispered.

I feared that my thoughts were correct.

"Well, well, well," a familiar voice said. "This is a surprise." The hooded being in the middle removed the cloak from its face.

"Nephele," I said from behind gritted teeth. From the corner of my eyes, I caught sight of Xylia. She cringed her head, looking at the one who had tortured her in Aloisio.

Ballard stepped forward, standing next to Demetre.

Her blue eyes trailed across our faces. "I see your friends have remained loyal…for now," she said in a spiteful voice as her lips curved into a smirk.

"Let's see how long this loyalty will last," a male voice declared. I lost my breath as I recognized his voice. The man removed the cloak from his face.

"Erebos." Great fury rushed into me.

"So we meet again." He raised his eyebrows. "I must say, I liked you better when Mordred dwelled inside your body."

"I hope your whip is stronger this time," I mocked in an attempt to hide the fear that was inside of me. His attack had almost taken my life.

He bit his bottom lip, strolling his way to Alistar. With eyes fixed on me, he spread out his right hand. A red incandescent light in the likeness a whip appeared.

"Please," Alistar managed to say in an agonized voice. "Make the pain stop…" He crawled on the ground, blood pouring from his nose and ears.

Erebos lowered his eyes, looking at Alistar. "I will make the pain go away." His voice was cold.

"Papa!" Sela cried as she pushed Adara to the side, running to her father.

"Sela, come back," Adara ordered, chasing the girl.

The man on the far left dropped the soldier's head to the ground and raised his hand toward the child.

Adara came to an abrupt halt as Sela's feet left the snow-covered ground.

"What is happening? Please, leave me alone." Sela wiped the tears from her face as she hovered in mid-air.

"Don't worry, girl," said a peaceful yet malevolent voice. "You and Daddy will remain together."

"Leave…her…alone…" Alistar's trembling hands touched Nephele's foot. "Please…" Creases appeared on Nephele's forehead as her lips parted. She shook her foot free from his grasp.

The male hooded figure released Sela, dropping her to the ground. She was about to rise to her feet when she was

taken by Nephele's power. Her sudden screams were like a blade piercing my ears. She crawled like a headless insect.

"You would attack an innocent child?" Adara unsheathed her sword. "Release her!"

The mysterious hooded figure chuckled.

"Am I to take orders from a human?" He removed his hood, revealing a pale face; his eyes were as gray as the clouds that hovered above us.

Demetre rushed to her side, keeping his sword pointed toward our enemies.

"It is a shame that we cannot kill any of you." His eyelids rose toward his brow as he gazed at Alistar. "But I can kill him."

With a slight move of his hand, a crimson light wrapped itself around Alistar. Like a snake, it constricted his body. In a matter of seconds, I heard the sounds of breaking bones merge with his grunts and screams.

I wanted to let him die. I watched as he struggled to break free from Erebos's attack, and a part of me did not want this man to live. I stood back.

Xylia stooped her body forward, casting her sword in Erebos's direction.

Erebos ceased his attack, grasping the sword seconds before it could have wounded his body. "I cannot kill you, but my Capios can certainly harm you."

Xylia grunted as she crouched, falling on her knees. Bruises appeared on her skin as she groaned in pain. She squinted her eyes, squirming on the ground. Her groans turned to screams as the Capios tortured her.

The skin on my back ripped, allowing my wings to spread to their full length.

The man on the left raised his right hand, looking at Nephele and Erebos. "Enough, you two," he said.

Nephele released Sela from her devious attack. Her fragile body lay on the snow, immobile. Erebos's whip disappeared, leaving Alistar on the ground. Blood gushed out of his wounds.

"What about Xylia?" I felt sweat descending my brow. "Release her from their grasps." Blood dripped out of her nose. I wished I had the ability to control the new powers that had awakened within me. I much desired to enter Erebos's mind and sink my blade beneath his skin.

Erebos crossed his arms, looking at me with a thin smile. My feet were about to abandon the ground when I heard his orders.

"Let her go." I heard the Capios retreating with quick steps. They probably ran to stand behind their master.

Demetre and I knelt alongside Xylia while Petra and Ballard aided Alistar. Devin and Adara stood next to Sela.

"Why are you all here?" Devin lifted his eyes to them. "I am sure it was not the pleasure of our company that brought you this way."

"Vengeance," said the man with ashen eyes as he took a step forward.

"Who might you be?" I asked. "I do not believe we have met before."

"Xavier, a Fallen Ruler and a servant of Lucifer." He bent his head. "A pleasure."

We were all silent.

"I must say it is indeed gratifying to find you all here in this village, even if you were not the main reason we came." Nephele's voice set my teeth on edge. "We were hunting

224

blood-drinkers when we found your parents trying to protect Ohmen, Folletti, and Valleree from the attack of three Lessers." She took a short step in my direction. "Your parents destroyed two of those creatures, but one Lesser escaped." I struggled to breathe, fearing what she was about to say. "While your loving parents tended to their wounds, Erebos gave them a very special gift."

I gritted my teeth as her words filled my ears like a disease.

"What gift did you give them?" The anger and desire for vengeance that stirred within me grew harder to contain.

"Tell me, Isaac." Erebos raised his finger. "How are Mom and Dad?" He clicked his tongue twice as his lips turned into a cynical smile. "Alive?"

I raised my sword, pointing it to his face. "Bastard, you will be the first one to die."

"That's what Folletti said as we set his body aflame." Xavier tilted his head, looking at Nephele and Erebos. They exchanged mocking smiles.

I soared into the air, aiming to sink my blade into his skull. Xavier's rage and vengeful desire could be seen in his eyes. His feet left the ground as his dark wings came into view. He lifted his sword in my direction, clashing it against mine with a loud clang as I blocked his strike.

His arms trembled as he arched his back in an attempt to push my body downward.

I felt something grasp my ankle. I shot a quick look down, unable to see what had ahold of me.

"Capios are indeed wonderful creatures." Xavier grimaced as I was pushed to the ground with great strength and speed.

The Capios screeched and bellowed as I collided against the snow with a loud thud. Pain spread from my spine to my head. My surroundings seemed to be moving in a circular motion as I attempted to look around.

"Isaac!" I heard Demetre's muffled voice calling my name.

A few seconds later, my vision returned to normal. I attempted to stand to my feet, but the Capios had me pinned to the ground. Devin and Demetre ran to my aid.

I heard the clattering of hoofs drawing near; the neighing of horses followed. Five horsemen approached us.

"The protectors of the Village of Tears have come." Nephele joined her hands together, intertwining her fingers.

These were the men that I had seen on the Road of Ahnor, riding alongside Alistar. They shot a quick look at the man they served, bleeding on the ground. His daughter lay unconscious at his side. They drew their swords.

"How dare you enter our lands and wound others without any remorse or reason?" asked one of the men. He had shoulder-length chestnut hair. Dark, long lashes surrounded the green of his eyes. His narrow face was covered with a scruffy beard.

Erebos cleared his throat. "How dare you presume that we do not have a reason to wound these people?" All five men flinched in fear as Erebos's eyes met theirs.

"Isaac, if we tell the Capios to release you, will you be a good boy and listen to us?" Xavier raised his right eyebrow.

"Why would I want to listen to a word you three have to say?" I moaned, trying to break away from the creatures' strong grasp. But my attempts failed.

"Have it your way, then," Nephele said.

It would be a foolish thing to deny that they were powerful beings. The one with the gray eyes, Xavier, appeared to be one of Lucifer's deadliest and most skilled servants.

"There is one thing that I would like to know," Xavier said. "Where is the Lesser that was here in this village?"

Low grunts and painful moans came from Alistar. His knees trembled as he tried to stand on his feet.

"How do you...know...that one of the Lessers was here?" His legs were too weak to hold the weight of his body. He fell on his chest, striking his head against the ground.

"We are not deaf." Erebos lifted his chin, narrowing his eyes. "We heard the creature's screeches. That is how we found this village."

Xavier's foot encountered Alistar's head, pressing it against the ground. "Tell me where the creature is," he demanded. Alistar moaned as he moved his body around, trying to break free from his torment.

"The creature was killed before your arrival!" Demetre shouted, pointing to the guards. "These men carried its body away."

"Another one lost," Nephele whispered, looking at Xavier. "These blood-drinkers are destroying our army."

"Please, let me go..." Alistar said in a weak voice.

Using the back of his foot, Xavier pressed down on Alistar's skull, crushing it open. I flinched at the sound of his breaking bones. Sela screamed as she watched her father's blood spill on the snow.

"Coward!" I shouted in anger as I tried to break free from the Capios' hold. "All of you!"

"You all deserve death," Devin said behind gritted teeth. He stared at Nephele with a contemptuous stare.

Nephele let out an ominous laugh. "And you don't?" Her dark cloak dragged on the ground as she marched her way to him.

"Dad!" Sela continued to scream, laying her small hands on her father's back. "Answer me."

Nephele raised her hand in attempt to strike Devin on his face, but Devin grasped her wrist and twisted her arm behind her back. He followed his defensive move with a kick, which brought her to the ground.

Nephele's face contorted in fury as she wiped the snow from her garments.

"Imbecile. How dare—"

"Enough, Nephele," Xavier ordered. She shot him a cold sneer.

"Capios," Erebos said. "Release him. I want you to hunt these blood-drinkers until they are found. Bring them alive and unspoiled."

They released me. I grabbed my sword and shot up to my feet.

"We want you to come with us," Erebos said, crossing his arms.

We all had our eyes fixed on him, surprised at his sudden statement.

"You expect us to follow you without a fight?" Xylia asked with a smirk, her eyes focused on Erebos.

He scoffed, looking at Nephele, who still had a death stare on her face.

"There is an army of Nephilins standing outside these walls as we speak. If you hesitate to come with us, we will

kill every man, woman, and child that dwells in this village." Nephele held her head high.

I tightened my hands into fists. "Can you not do your own bidding, Nephele? Must you always bring puppets to do your dirty work for you?"

Her lips went rigid. "A wise warrior never rides out alone, Isaac." Nephele's eyes shifted to Sela.

The girl's tormented screams began once again. She writhed on the ground as blood gushed from her nostrils and ears. The girl fell into a stupor.

"Will you come with us?" Nephele lifted her eyes, looking at us. My companions watched me, waiting for a response.

"We will…" my voice trailed off. The hairs on my neck rose as I caught sight of nine shadows flying across the sky.

"They found us," Petra mumbled. His face grew pale as he watched the shadows.

"We are doomed, my friend," Demetre whispered with eyes fixed on the creatures that descended from the sky.

They landed behind Nephele, Xavier, and Erebos. Their dragon-like wings spread to their full length.

Nephele ceased her deadly attack on Sela. Wrinkles appeared at the edges of her eyes as she turned to them.

"Well, this is a very nice surprise," said Bartholomew with a crooked smile. "I never expected you three to leave the Heart of Elysium." He let out a cynical laugh.

"You thought we were not strong enough to escape?" asked Xavier, pointing his finger toward him.

Bartholomew pursed his lips. "I just did not think you were wise enough to find a way out." A cynical smile followed.

"Maybe you'd like us to put you all to sleep again?" asked Dahmian. His green eyes glistened as smoke enveloped his body.

"If you try that trick on us one more time, we will end your miserable lives right here," Erebos stated with a sneer.

"Do you see that, Erebos?" Nephele leaned her face closer to Erebos's ear. "They are one short."

Bartholomew's face grew cold and emotionless.

"What happened to her? She died?" Nephele shrugged her shoulders as she crossed her hands.

Bartholomew took a deep breath.

"I have not come here to waste my time with you, Nephele." He cocked his head in my direction. "I am here for them."

"Then we are going to have a situation on our hands. We are also very interested in having them come with us," Xavier added.

Bartholomew raised his head. "If you dare try to stop us, I will have my army of Lessers attack this village and kill them all."

"And if you kill them, who will open the books and bring Lucifer back?" Nephele snapped. "Have you thought about that?"

"We care not if Lucifer remains asleep," said one without any hair on his head. He was thin. There were dark circles under his midnight eyes. "We only want the Book of Letters."

"You see." Xavier raised his right hand. "That is going to be a problem."

The blood-drinker gave him a scornful stare.

"Ashtar." Bartholomew turned his piercing red eyes to the bald blood-drinker. "Call our friends, please," he ordered.

Ashtar pursed his lips, letting out a loud whistle. Deep roars filled the atmosphere. From the sky appeared hundreds of Lessers, flying at great speed. Some of the citizens of the village peeked through their windows, their faces filled with fear.

"Did you not see that we, too, brought our own army?" Erebos tightened his fists. "They are outside of these walls."

"They stand no chance against the Lessers," Ashtar said with great confidence.

"I used the Dark Exchange on all of them. A part of my mind is inside each Lesser," Erebos declared. "They will obey me."

Bartholomew gave him a half-hearted smile.

"To your disappointment, Erebos, I have shielded their minds." His tongue caressed the tip of his fangs as he curved the edge of his lips. "They will obey only us."

For the first time, I saw fear on Nephele's face. Xavier stared at the blood-drinkers.

Adara shuddered at the sight of the Lessers hovering above us. They waited for a single command from their masters to begin their attack. Drool trickled down their human-like necks.

"We must flee from here the moment the attack begins," Devin whispered, keeping his eyes focused on our enemies. "We must wait until they are distracted."

I looked at him. "Who is to say they won't come after us once they see us running?" Devin's lips tightened into a thin line. "We have no choice," I said. "We must fight."

Nephele's body disintegrated into a shadow, darting toward the sky.

"Attack them!" Bartholomew shouted.

The Lessers descended from the sky at full speed. At the same time, booming war chants echoed around us. Winged Nephilins crowded the sky, making their way toward the Lessers while others climbed the walls of the village.

I watched in horror as the Nephilins broke down the doors of the houses, dragging the families out into the streets. They pinned them to the ground, sinking their swords and daggers into their chests.

"We must run, Isaac." Demetre clasped my arm. "Nephele and the others will come for us."

Though I wanted to help all of them, I knew we did not stand a chance against them alone. I looked over my shoulder and realized that both Xavier and Erebos had disappeared. Nephele fluttered her wings as she fought in the air, using her dark powers to strike the Lessers. The screams of the people echoed amidst the explosions and clanging of swords.

"Head for the trees!" Devin shouted.

As I followed my companions, a sharp pain stung my right arm. I turned to see what had inflicted such torment upon me. My eyes narrowed when I saw that a Lesser had sunk its nails beneath my skin.

My hands grasped the Lesser's skeletal arm, tossing its body in the direction of the house. As the creature soared, it clung to my arms, dragging me along. I heard the bones

of my back crack as my body thudded in the middle of the living room. I crawled on the floor, trying to reach for my sword. The Lesser's hand tightened around my shoulder, pulling me away from my blade. Drops of its saliva dripped on my face as it held me down with its arms. The hairs on my arms rose while the scales on its body rubbed against my skin. I placed my forearm beneath its neck as it stooped its head down, trying to sink its teeth into my skull.

The Lesser let out a hair-raising screech as I shot my knee against its rib cage. It withdrew its hands, giving me the opportunity to reach for my sword.

My fingers tightened around my sword's cold grip. With my gaze set on the Lesser, I sank my blade in its side.

The Lesser drew its upper lip back and growled, falling on its side. I shot up to my feet, looked down at the creature, and struck its skull. Its screeches turned to gurgles as a puddle of blood surrounded its body.

I turned away from the creature, heading toward the door. I urgently sought my companions.

The pungent odor of burnt bodies filled the air, bringing tears to my eyes. The houses of the village were diminished to cinder and ash. Smoke billowed from the burnt bodies that were scattered around me.

My eyes widened when I saw Sela's headless body lying on the ground. One of the blood-drinkers drank from the blood that oozed out of her wounds. With his tongue over his chin, the blood-drinker licked the ground around the girl. He was dressed in rugged clothing and boots up to his knees. His dark wool cloak was smothered in blood.

"You enjoy killing things?" I screamed, raising my sword above my head. "Then why don't you try to kill me?"

His blue eyes were fixed on me. His dark tangled hair cascaded down his neck. He gave me a menacing smile, showing me his fangs. He wagged his wings, darting his way into the sky.

I was prepared to go after him when I saw my mother and father strolling out of the house.

For a brief second, I watched them.

"Dad!" With great joy, I sprinted my way to them. "Mom!"

I came to a sudden halt. A glazed white mist covered their eyes. With their jaws open, they aimlessly ambled around, their arms dangling in front of their bodies.

"Mom…" I whispered. Her head tilted my way. She let out a single groan, walking away.

She does not know who I am, I thought, keeping my eyes on her.

"Dad…" I ran to my father. "It's me," I said, expecting that he would say something. His eyes remained fixed on the war that raged around us.

I looked at my mom and back at my dad.

"It is me," I repeated. "Your son, Isaac."

No words came from them.

My cheeks trembled as tears filled my eyes.

I reached for my father's face, touching it with my fingertips. His skin was ice-cold.

"You are not in there, are you?" I tasted my tears as they touched my lips. "You are gone."

No pain from my past could compare to this. Hope had already become a distant feeling, and now it was nothing more than a vague memory.

"All the kingdoms of the world will be covered in shadow," my father said in a dark voice. "The reign of Lucifer will expand."

"Foolish are those that have not yet bowed before him," my mother added. Their faces were void of any emotion or desire.

"Such words are not being spoken by you." I used my wrist to wipe my tears. My father lifted his eyes to the sky. I heard him hum a melody, which turned into a song.

"Darker days, moonless nights
A reign of fire will consume every desire
Cries and moans will resound as songs
Fear not the dark, flee from the light"

My chest rose as I breathed in the frigid air. I knew my parents would never have sided with Lucifer. They had done much to protect us all. The words they spoke did not belong to them. Now I understood what Nephele had meant when she'd said they had given them a gift.

"All the kingdoms of the world will be covered in shadow," my father repeated. "The reign of Lucifer will expand."

I rested my hand on my father's shoulder, looking deep into his eyes.

"At least I got to look at your faces one last time." I pressed my eyelids together. The sound of my blade piercing my father's chest was excruciating. I felt his blood trail down my hands, dripping down my arms and onto my feet. When my eyes opened, I caught sight of his pale face.

His body wobbled as his eyes rolled in the back of his head. I placed my arm behind his back, laying him on the snow.

As quick as a breath, I turned to face my mother. A waterfall of tears ran down my face. I bore my eyes into hers.

"Lucifer will reign," she uttered in a raspy voice. "His kingdom will expand—"

Her words turned to groans. My sword penetrated her chest, striking her heart. I turned away as I removed the blade; her body thudded on the ground.

I screamed. I did not care who listened. Though a battle raged around me, the war within my heart was much more difficult to fight now. I fell on my knees, sinking the tip of my sword in the snow.

For a moment, Lucifer and all the other dark forces did not matter. I stared at my parents' bodies.

"Isaac." I glanced over my shoulder and saw Demetre and Xylia sprinting in my direction. They were a few feet away from me when a dark shadow hurled their bodies against an old tree. The shadow assumed the shape of a male figure.

"I have to say, that was a very brave thing you just did." The shadow turned into Erebos.

Though I wanted to help my friends, I could not find any strength within me. Demetre struggled to help Xylia stand. His watchful eyes were set on me.

"Isaac!" he cried.

I turned my head, staring at my blood-covered sword while Erebos approached me.

"Though none of you can be killed yet," he said in a spiteful tone, "you can certainly be harmed."

Vivid memories of my childhood flooded my mind. For a moment, I could see their faces smiling at me. I recalled the sound of my mother's laughter when we went fishing, and my father's awkward advice about life.

Give me death, I thought.

"I have a secret to share with you," Erebos continued, standing inches away from me. "It was I who cursed your parents." My eyes shot in his direction. "I was the one who used the Dark Exchange on them and ripped from them all memory and emotion."

My previous thought was erased from my mind. I clasped the snow beneath my hands. My chin quivered as anger overcame my sorrow.

He laughed. "Your mother begged me to stop while your father squealed like a dying pig."

As the words drifted from his mouth and into my ears, it was as though all other sounds and voices around me had disappeared. Without any reluctance, I landed a punch on his jaw.

He gasped, his eyes widening. He wiped the blood from his upper lip with his right wrist.

"You should not have done that," he said, licking the small cut.

"Should not have done what?" I spread out my arms. "This?" I repeated my previous act.

With great fury, he fixed his eyes on me. Drumming sounds and eerie screeches echoed around me.

"The Capios will teach—"

"I think it is better if you never finish that sentence, Nephilin," said Demetre as his blade cut its way through Erebos's back, piercing the left side of his chest.

237

Xylia approached from my right, standing inches from Erebos's face.

"May death greet you with open arms," she said, sinking her blade into his skull. The drums and screeches ceased as I watched Erebos's body turn to ashes, which were taken by the blowing breeze. His sword disappeared like smoke.

With reluctant stares, they set their eyes on me.

"We have to go," Demetre said through ragged breaths, wrapping his left arm around my shoulder. Xylia placed her hand on my face.

"It will all be alright," she said.

I shied my eyes away from them, not finding the strength to utter a single word.

My wings retracted beneath my skin as we ran. I surveyed my surroundings, looking for our companions, but they were nowhere to be found.

Nephilins, blood-drinkers, and Lessers battled amongst each other, killing as many of their adversaries as possible. They did not seem too worried about our presence. It was as if they battled out of pride, longing to show which kind possessed more power.

I caught sight of a blood-drinker decapitating one of the soldiers who had aided us on the Road of Ahnor. With his hands, he ripped the skin from the man's chest while he screamed. His pain-filled sounds ceased when the blood-drinker ripped his neck open with a single bite.

Some Nephilins struck the Lessers in the air while others attacked them from the ground. I searched for Nephele.

"Where are the others?" I managed to speak with a tremulous voice. "Are they safe?"

238

"Yes," Xylia responded. "Devin led us into the woods."

"You were taking too long," Demetre added as we approached the burning rubble of the wooden wall. "We decided to come looking for you."

Smoke billowed from the fire that consumed the houses. I gasped once when I saw Arundel's body lying on the ground. Wounds and bruises spotting his arms. His clothes were covered in dirt and blood.

Xylia ran to him, kneeling by his side.

"Arundel," she said, shaking his shoulders. "Can you hear me?"

She screamed at the sound of a loud explosion that caused one of the houses to crumble to the ground. My visibility grew dim as the cloud of smoke spread.

"We have to keep on moving, Xylia. We cannot linger!" Demetre shouted.

She gave Arundel three quick slaps on his cheek.

"Can you hear me?" she asked. Her lips curved into a smile when she heard Arundel moan.

Demetre and I rushed his way, helping him stand on his feet. He grimaced, grasping his right shoulder with his left hand. His breathing came out in sharp, shallow breaths.

"It might be broken," he said.

"Ballard might be able to help him," Xylia said. "He might have something that will reduce the pain."

Arundel bowed his head. "Have any of you seen my father and sister?" he whispered.

"They are well." My response was immediate. I did not want to give Demetre or Xylia a chance to answer. They both shot me cold stares; they knew his father and sister were dead. Though I was aware that I had lied to him, it

would bring him no benefit if I divulged the truth at this moment.

I dodged every branch and jumped over every rock as we ran through the trees. I cringed as a sudden sharp pain spread through my head.

"You may run now, Isaac, but know that we will find all of you," Nephele's voice whispered as her face appeared in my mind. My eyes narrowed to thin lines as the throbbing pain continued. "Our ally inside Tristar will soon be revealed to all. No matter where you run, we will come for you."

My lungs gasped for air as the images vanished. My heartbeat accelerated under my chest.

"Are you alright?" Xylia pressed her brows together, setting her gaze on me.

"There is a traitor." My breathing grew shallow. "He is in Tristar."

Demetre stumbled back a few steps. "How do you know this?"

"I heard Nephele's voice." I pressed my hands together "She said that their ally inside Tristar will soon be revealed."

Silence loomed over us. Xylia used her hand to support her body on a tree trunk, her face shrouded in fear. Demetre pressed his fingers against his forehead while Arundel stared at me.

"We must tell the others," said Xylia.

XVII

THE SOUNDS AND cries of battle fell behind us as we ventured deeper into the woods. The wind whistled as it blew through the trees, their dry, ruffled branches crackling as they moved.

Demetre had tied pieces of old fabric to a few trees to aid him and Xylia in finding the others.

"How are you?" Demetre asked, adjusting his sword belt.

"Later," I responded in a cold voice.

He nodded in silence, turning his eyes from me.

Xylia sighed. "Isaac, should you need to talk to—"

"I said, later!" I screamed. "I do not want to talk about this now."

She turned away and furrowed her brows.

I knew they both meant well. The truth was that I was not ready to speak of what had happened. There would be a time when I would mourn their deaths, but this was not it. We were at war.

Arundel cleared his throat. "Are my father and sister with the others as well?" His right arm rested over his chest.

We all ignored his question as our feet sank deep into the snow. From the corner of my eye, I saw confusion forming on his face.

"Can any of you answer me?" he insisted, his voice escalating.

Demetre turned to Arundel. "Isaac will know the answer to your question."

Arundel darted me an angry stare, quickening his pace.

"Did you lie to me, Isaac?" His voice loudened. "Are both of them alive?"

"Arundel…" I sighed as my voice trailed off. I tried to find a way to divulge the truth to him. The real reason I did not want to talk about his family's death was that it would make the memory of the events I had just witnessed even more vivid.

"Are they with the others?" he asked again, his eyes already glistening with tears.

Silence was my response to his question. His chin quivered; his face showed great distress. Tears ran down his cheeks.

So much death, I thought as he sobbed. I was overwhelmed by the whirlwind of emotions raging around me. Arundel rested his back against a tree. He pressed the edge of his hands against his head while cowering.

I continued walking, seeking solitude. These were moments when I wondered whether or not siding with the Darkness would have been an easier choice.

The ground trembled at the roar of a mighty thunder. I looked up and caught sight of threatening storm clouds racing across the sky. Cold drops of rain fell on my face, and jagged bolts of lighting struck the sky.

I wept as the raindrops turned into a torrential flood. I laid my head on a tree and gave in to my thoughts and feelings.

A hand tightened its grasp on my shoulder. From the corner of my eye, I saw Demetre. His blue eyes were swollen, his cheeks red.

"Um…"

"You don't have to say anything, Isaac," he said. "You just to have to keep on being brave, my friend."

My tears mixed with the rain that dripped down my face.

"What I just did will never compare to anything I have done or am yet to do." I slammed the back of my hand against the tree. "I wounded their bodies with my own sword, Demetre."

He was silent. His tears streamed down to his lips.

"The sorrow and agony I felt in the Wastelands of Tristar are like a morning breeze compared to this." My words ceased. I tried to contain my almost inhuman sobs, but they were stronger than my own will.

For a while, I allowed my emotions to flow out of me without restraint. Demetre stood by my side, quiet.

"We have to keep on going, Isaac," he said when Xylia approached with Arundel. "The others are not far from us."

I desired to stay here, isolated from everything and everyone. Part of me wanted to forget that the Diary had ever come into my possession. The hardest part of this journey was that I knew I had to keep on fighting. I closed my eyes and attempted to fill my mind with the memory that always gave me strength.

I saw his scarlet eyes, his fur as white as snow. I recalled his empowering voice. "Know this: I am watching your every move and will be with all of you until the end."

No matter how burdensome our quest grew for me, I had to believe in our victory. Though darkness increased in strength every day, my heart had to cling to the hope that we would live to see Lucifer and his forces defeated.

Demetre walked ahead of us all, leading the way. I slowed my steps, allowing Arundel to go in front of me. His eyes hardened when they met mine. I understood his anger. I had lied to him about the death of his family. He caught up to Demetre, walking by his side.

I waited until Xylia walked next to me.

"How are you?" I asked.

"I'm alright." She gave me a thin smile. "I should be the one asking you that question."

"I will survive, though I am sure these memories will never be erased from my mind. They will haunt me forever."

"At least you were privileged to have your parents for eighteen years," she said. "I can recall the day I started to understand that my family was different." Her fingers trailed through her hair, fixing it behind her ears. "A curious little girl living with a man without a wife. One day, I decided to ask my Uncle Ihvar where my mother was. I was nine."

The wind howled as the raindrops turned into a deluge. The snow on the ground melted, mixing with the carpet of dirt and mud that covered the forest floor.

"Up until that day, he had told me that he was my father." Her face grew despondent.

"How did you feel after you discovered the truth?" It was hard to look at her due to the strong rain.

She sniffled, rubbing her nose with the back of her hand.

"Angry, used, abandoned. After a while, I did come to understand why he had hidden the truth from me." She raised her eyebrows as she pursed her lips. "He wanted to protect me."

My fingertips trailed her hand. She gave me a shy smile as our fingers intertwined.

"You are a strong woman, Xylia," I said, feeling the warmth of her skin against mine.

"The day I turned eighteen, my uncle handed me my book. He shared the tales of its mysterious past, saying it was called The Book of the Justifier. Raziel appeared to me that same day in a dream. My uncle did not seem surprised when I mentioned what Raziel had said to me." She narrowed her eyes. "It was as though he already expected him to visit me. It was hard leaving my uncle behind, but I knew I could no longer be protected by him, no matter how much he loved me." She fixed her eyes on the trees ahead of us. "I miss him. He is the only family I have left."

"Where is home?" I let go of her hand.

"I was raised in the kingdom of Watermiles, near the village of dragonhall. My uncle and I would often go fishing in the ocean in our boat." She shook her head. "I cannot shake off the feeling that the armies of Lucifer will attack Watermiles soon. With the king dead, the kingdom is vulnerable."

I shivered as the raindrops continued to hit my body. Rumbles of thunder echoed, causing the ground to tremble.

"I wonder what happened to Raziel. I have not heard from him since he led the Underwarriors to the Gates of the Fourth Dimension." I tried to avoid thinking on the possibility that he had been killed.

The sudden sound of Ballard's screams echoed around us.

"Did you heart that?" My eyes circled the forest, searching for my companion.

"Where are they, Demetre?" Xylia bellowed, marching up to him.

Demetre darted toward the screams, ignoring Xylia's question. Arundel trudged his way through the melting snow, wiping the tears away from his face.

My wings sprang out of my back. I shot my way into the sky in an attempt to search for my companions. The torrential rain and towering trees made it difficult for me to spot them.

My heart grew apprehensive when I looked ahead and saw two winged shadows fighting in the air. A rush of adrenaline coursed through my veins as I flew in their direction. The raindrops felt like small pebbles hitting my skin. As I got closer, I noticed that one of these shadows was Devin. With his sword in hand, he cast his body against the other shadow being, aiming to strike him with his blade.

I reached for my sword, prepared to stick it into whatever creature attacked him. Hope was crushed within me when Devin's opponent pierced his chest.

Devin's screams sent shivers down my spine. For as long as I could remember, he had never once let out a scream as pain-filled as this one. His body fell to the ground. Despite the limited visibility, I plunged to his aid as I approached their location.

Some joy found its way into my heart when I set my eyes on Adara and Petra standing next to Ballard, who lay on the ground, unconscious. Devin shot me a grimace of pain when he saw me. His left hand was pressed over the right side of his chest in an attempt to slow the blood flow.

My feet sank under the snow while the raindrops continued to fall. In front of me were ten Nephilins—six male and four female. Silver breastplates protected their chests. Spikes protruded from their gardbraces. Their striking blue eyes watched my every move. One of the women had her face hidden behind a helmet with two silver horns.

My eyes searched my surroundings for the one Nephilin I loathed above all others—Nephele. I was relieved when I realized she was nowhere to be seen.

Xavier descended from the sky. The feathers that covered his wings were gray, their tips as black as coal, his rugged garments smeared with blood.

His feet touched the ground.

"This one," Xavier raised his head toward Devin, "has always been a disgrace to his kind. He has not yet grasped the idea that his very blood carries evil."

Devin laid his head on the ground, keeping his hand pressed over the wound.

"What happened to Ballard?" I asked my companions, my eyes fixed on Xavier and his army.

"We are not sure," Petra replied. "Once they found us, Ballard started screaming. After a few seconds, he went into a stupor."

"It would be wiser for all of you to follow us," said the woman with the helmet. She stepped her way to us as she unveiled her face. Her familiar voice increased the anger that already burned in me.

"I was wondering when you would show up, Adawnas," I said with great disappointment. Her golden hair was tied in a long braid.

"We have given you many chances to surrender at your own will, Isaac. If you continue to run, you and your companions will suffer." She lifted her chin, keeping her eyes on me. "None can escape the power of Lucifer. Tristar has also fallen into shadow."

"Ah," said Xavier, raising his finger. "Let us only say what needs to be said. Our enemy does not need to know of our future plans."

"Forgive me, my lord." Adawnas bowed her head in reverence, stepping away.

"Adawnas," I said, pointing my sword to her. "Remember these words. One day, you will think that victory is within your grasp. You will rejoice at the sight of your apparent triumph. When that day comes, I will be the one to stick my blade into your heart."

"I will gladly wait for that day to come," she said with a hard smile.

I tilted my head back, looking for Demetre, Xylia, and Arundel. Had they been attacked? Devin grunted and moaned as blood continued to ooze out of the wound in his chest.

I was startled by Adara's sudden screams. She crouched on the ground, using her hands to cover her ears. The veins on her neck seemed as if they were about to burst from beneath her skin.

"What are you doing to her?" shouted Petra in great distress.

The Nephilins were as still as statues, their striking blue eyes fixed on us. With a calm expression, Xavier smiled.

"I am going to repeat the words that Adawnas said." His fingers rubbed his pointy chin. "Come with us and you will not suffer. If you resist, the pain and torture you now feel will only increase."

Adara's screams were excruciating to hear. I contemplated giving myself up to them. At least the pain and suffering would cease for a while. At this point, I was ready to do anything to find some peace.

Demetre, Xylia, and Arundel ran out of the woods, heading in our direction. Their breathing was labored, their faces tired.

"Ah, the missing companions have arrived!" Xavier's fingers intertwined. "I am delighted to see that you are all gathered."

"What is happening to Adara?" Xylia inquired, staring at her friend with worried eyes. Adara's screams had become sobs; tears streamed down her cheeks.

"I am not sure," I responded, keeping my eyes set on Xavier.

With a wrathful stare, Xylia turned to face our enemies. Demetre, who now stood next to me, glared down at Devin. Special abilities weren't needed to know that he questioned the possibility of Devin outlasting this day.

I was overjoyed when I noticed Ballard moving his fingertips as he awoke from his stupor. He opened his

mouth, catching a long and deep breath. His chestnut hair was damp with sweat and covered in mud.

"Impossible," Xavier mumbled while the other Nephilins stared at Ballard. He shot a menacing look at his army, all of whom appeared confusion.

"You failed, Xavier," Ballard declared in a broken voice. "Your power is not strong enough to take over my mind."

Xavier wagged his finger at Ballard. "Do not consider yourself victorious just yet, boy."

With great struggle, Ballard stood to his feet. His shoulders hunched toward the ground.

Adara's cries had ceased. I set my eyes on her, only to find that she had fallen unconscious.

"What are you doing to her?" Demetre bellowed, pointing the tip of his sword toward Xavier.

With a menacing laugh, Xavier walked our way.

"I am taking over your minds," he replied with a sneer.

Once again, Ballard fell to his knees, letting out tormenting screams. Xylia fell on her back, shrieking as her hands grasped the forest floor. She squirmed in agony. Petra crouched, grunting and moaning in pain.

The feeling of hundreds of needles piercing my skin took over my brain, a pounding sensation spreading throughout my body. A high-pitched screech invaded my ears. My eyes pressed together as I lost feeling in my legs.

I attempted to repel this power that tried to take my mind. I shivered when I felt a creature crawling on my neck. My heart raced when my eyes saw the black scorpions that lurked around me. Their pincers and stingers were of a scarlet color.

Is this real? I thought. *What are they doing to us?*

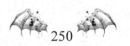

The scorpions let out rattling sounds as they crawled ⌐ my head. The hairs on my neck and arms rose while I lay immobile. I watched the bodies of the scorpions dissipate into a gray shadow, which later took the shape of Xavier.

The landscape around me turned into a dry wasteland. Old tree trunks were dispersed atop the small hills. Roars of thunder and bolts of lighting ripped the sky.

"Do you enjoy suffering, Isaac?" Xavier asked in a low voice.

The unbearable pain inside of my head intensified. I screamed in torment, inhaling the dust and ash that hovered in the air.

"Do you long for peace?" he insisted.

I coughed as every inch of my body was taken by this torment. With my eyes half open, I realized that Xavier had knelt beside me. His body was covered in a red cloak.

"What is it that you desire?" He had a cunning smile on his face.

I nibbled on my bottom lip, struggling to answer.

"Only a fool would desire torment and war," I managed to say.

In the blink of an eye, the dark clouds that hovered above me gave way to blue skies. The ash-covered ground and the old tree trunks sprang up with new life. Grass covered the hills and the chirping of birds filled my ears. As quick as a breath, the pain inside my head subsided.

I furrowed my brows.

"Is this an illusion?" I asked, contemplating the beauty of the landscape that surrounded me.

Xavier had a blissful look in his eyes.

"Only if you want it to be. I know how much you desire to be free from the burden you now carry, young Isaac." He cupped my face in the palms of his hands. "Truth is what we believe to be right."

There was a sweet fragrance lingering in the air. I rubbed the grass beneath my hands, feeling its soft texture. I gazed at the cloudless blue sky, taking in the rays of the sun.

"You may stay here forever." Xavier stood to his feet and stretched forth his hand, attempting to help me stand.

I accepted his help. A warm breeze brushed against my skin.

"What is this place called?"

"Whatever you want it to be called," he replied. "You can make this your world, Isaac."

As I enjoyed the beauty around me, I noticed that the urgency of my journey had started to fade from me. My heart was being taken over by peace and joy—feelings that had grown to be so unusual to me.

"I can make this my world," I mumbled, amazed at the beauty that was around me. I turned my face to Xavier. "Where are my friends?"

"They, too, are enjoying their perfect worlds. I told you that if you followed us, we would end your pain." He wrapped his right arm around my shoulder. "You see, Isaac, all you have to do to stay here in your world is open the Diary."

My eyebrows came together.

"I will erase from your mind all the painful memories of your journey. You won't remember Elysium, the

252

Creator…your parents' death." He touched my chin with his finger. "I can make it all go away."

I was lost in my thoughts, trying to remember the days when there were no rumors of war, no Lucifer or Shadows—no evil desires.

I cleared my throat. "What do I have to do to open the Diary?"

With his left hand, he reached into one of his pockets, removing a silver dagger. I analyzed the intricate patterns and details on its scabbard. The emblem of a dark winged lion was etched at the center.

"I just need you to read the words written on this dagger's blade as you slash a small cut on your wrist. Allow the blood to drip on top of the Diary until the lock opens."

I trailed the dagger with my fingertips.

"Your suffering can end today, Isaac." I felt Xavier's warm breath as he whispered in my ear.

I removed the dagger's scabbard, gasping as I laid eyes on the shimmering blade.

"He is risen," I read the writing etched onto the dagger.

"My son." My heart skipped a beat. I looked over my shoulder and saw my mother and father strolling toward me. Clothed in white robes, their faces were stamped with broad smiles, their eyes glistening with joy. "Do you not want us by your side forever?" asked my mother.

"Isaac, this is your world. You can have everything you have always longed for here." Xavier laid his hands over the dagger.

"And you will make me forget?" My hand rested on top of his. "I won't remember anything?"

"Only the things you want to remember." He gave me a devious smile.

I desired to be free from the burden I carried. My mind would be rid of every ill thought and heartbreaking memory.

In silence, I lowered my eyes, staring at the dagger.

"He is risen," I mumbled.

I reached inside my satchel, taking out the object responsible for all my pain and sorrow. A feeling of repulsion took over me as I looked at the Diary. I released it from my grasp, dropping it to the ground.

With the dagger in my hand, I held up my wrist. My eyes narrowed when I caught sight of the long, thin scar that had always served as a vivid reminder of my hatred for Nephele and Lucifer. Like an unexpected storm, the vivid image of Nephele and Marco slicing my wrists came to me.

"You will forget everything, Isaac," Xavier said once again. "Consider this a fresh start."

I gazed at the scar, feeling anger bubble within me. Though I much desired to have these memories erased, I would only have true peace once Lucifer and his servants were defeated. I saw the face of every child, man, and woman that had died on this journey, and the soldiers of Bellator that had perished in battle. Above all, I reminded myself of the day the Creator had encountered me.

These were moments when my own desires had to be put aside. Would I be willing to allow every single person to perish so I could have peace?

I lowered the dagger, its tip pointing to the ground.

"You are a clever man, Xavier," I said, taking a quick breath. "But I am afraid your cleverness cannot

overshadow my purpose." His joyful expression was replaced by disappointment. "My world is Elysium and my people need me now more than ever."

He let out a malefic laugh.

"You are a fool, Isaac. You have set yourself on a course for disappointment." He clicked his tongue. "But the fact that I invaded your mind shows me that you are as weak as any other human being."

He stretched his right hand in the direction of my parents. The skin from their bodies melted like wax; blood gushed from wounds that appeared on their bodies. They screamed my name in loud voices.

How dare this monster play with my feelings? How dare he tempt me with these sick desires?

"Above all my aspirations, I long for the day that Elysium will be free from your master's power."

I propelled the dagger in his direction. I watched the blade sink deep within the left side of his chest. His knees bent and his body fell.

Like smoke, my surroundings disappeared.

XVIII

MY EYES SPRUNG open. I looked around and saw that all my companions had their faces buried in the snow. They were all unconscious. Arundel lay to my left. Ahead of me, I noticed that the Nephilins had cold stares in their eyes as they gazed at Xavier, who knelt on the ground, his head bowed. I heard his low grunts and moans as he pressed his left hand against the right side of his chest.

Adawnas lifted her head, glaring at me. She ran in my direction, raising her blade in an attempt to strike me. Our swords clashed as I defended myself from her sudden attack.

Her eyes twitched in anger. "It should have worked," she said from behind gritted teeth. "Your mind should have been taken over by the Dark Exchange."

I landed a kick to her stomach, pushing her away. She thudded onto the melting snow, her blue eyes fixed on me.

The other nine Nephilins raised their swords, pointing them in my direction. Xavier's arms trembled as he struggled to stand on his feet. His tattered dark cloak was drenched, covered in mud and dirt.

My eyes widened when I saw the wound on Xavier's chest oozing with blood. He gnawed on his lips as his eyes stared at me in disbelief.

"How dare you wound a Fallen Ruler?" he bellowed, spreading out his arms. "Mark my words, Isaac. Once you are no longer needed, I will be the one to take your life away."

Adawnas stepped her way back to him, keeping her gaze on me. Her golden hair dripped with mud.

Loud clashes of thunder echoed through the sky.

"Awake them," I demanded, looking at my companions.

Xavier, along with all the Nephilins, had a spiteful smile on his face.

"They have not yet awoken from their sleep because they no longer desire to return to Elysium," said the Nephilin on the far left. His facial traits reminded me of Nephele.

"Oh, Duane, we need to be more gentle in the way we share information." Xavier shook his head.

My brows tensed together.

"Only you refused my offer, Isaac," Xavier said with a grin. "Your companions have chosen wisely."

With a heavy heart, I gazed at them all. They were lost in their own dreams, striving to find peace amidst so much turmoil.

Great disappointment took over my heart. In silence, I pondered my decision to return. Should I have remained asleep? My heart would have no longer ached for my current troubles and torment.

Xavier's sudden groans and screams startled me. His chin quivered while his eyes rolled back in his head. His

trembling legs gave out, and he arched his back while his body thudded against the ground. As still as statues, the Nephilins stared at him, confused.

Courage arose within me as I watched Demetre, Devin, and Xylia open their eyes. They gasped for air, raising their bodies from the ground. With a surprised look stamped on their faces, they rose to their feet.

"How come the rest of them are still asleep?" Demetre inquired in a strong voice. "Tell me they have not given in to Xavier's temptation."

Silence was my response to him.

"Unlike you and your other friends, they were wise in the choices they made," Duane said.

Devin managed to rise. He let out painful groans as he limped my way. Sweat trickled down his golden hair, and blood poured from the wound on his chest.

"The one that disgraces our kind has disappointed us all once again," said Adawnas, pressing her lips while raising her upper eyelids. "You should have remained asleep. You would have spared yourself from the shame of a lost war."

His breathing ragged, Devin's legs gave out. Dark circles surrounded his blue eyes; his chapped lips had lost their pigment.

I knelt beside him. "My friend, you must rest." I tried to avoid staring at his open wound. My heart feared that a fate worse than pain was about to come upon him.

He coughed, lifting his eyes to mine.

"Do not prevent death from finding me today," he whispered. "My tormented heart needs rest."

I grasped the nape of his neck, lifting his head toward me.

"Do not say foolish things. We have a war to win, Devin," I said as fear welled up inside of me.

There was a tremor beneath my feet. Xylia and Demetre sprinted in my direction, standing by my side.

"We have company," Xavier said in a dark voice.

The tremor intensified, causing some of the weaker trees in the forest to fall. The wind howled, and the raindrops continued to pour over us like a flood.

Guttural sounds filled the air. Demetre set his eyes on me, recognizing the malefic growls. I looked over my shoulder and saw Duane holding Ballard's body in his hands.

"No!" I darted my way to him, trying to dodge the falling tree branches. I closed my eyes and raised my arms as one of the pine trees fell on top of my body. Its thick branches scraped my face in my attempt to avoid the full impact of its descent.

When I opened my eyes, I realized that Ballard, Petra, and Adara's bodies had disappeared. For a couple of seconds, I stared in disbelief, trying to understand what had just taken place.

Hands dug their way out of the ground as the tremors continued. Decayed bodies crawled from beneath the earth, their bright yellow eyes capturing every detail of their surroundings.

"Shadows." I shuddered at the word.

The tremors ceased. Sweat poured down Xylia's face as she watched the Shadows clump around us like wild animals hunting for their prey. Demetre's brows furrowed, his eyes following their every move.

Seven Nephilins stood around Xavier. Despite his wounds, his face exuded the confidence of his triumphant victory.

"What did you do to the others?" Xylia screamed in fury. The Shadows approached us, saliva dripping down their necks. She darted them a furious stare. "Do you think I am frightened of Shadows? Death has looked me in the eye many times."

"You will not say such foolish things once the Shadows sink their teeth into your skin, girl," Xavier retorted. "I am aware that we need you alive, but it would be my pleasure to torture you."

The snarls of the creatures assaulted my ears like an unrehearsed symphony. These were the moments when I wished I could control the new ability that developed within me. I wanted to enter Xavier's mind and send him back to the Abyss.

"Where are the others?" Anger flowed with every word I spoke.

"Since they accepted my offer, I must keep them safe." Blood rushed to my cheeks as his voice filled my ears. "Soon they will open their books, allowing Lucifer's body to begin to take its shape." He walked in my direction. "Of course, without the Diary and the Book of the Justifier, Lucifer's body could never be whole."

"What do you mean?" Xylia asked.

"Every book represents a part of him." He pointed to me. "Your book is his heart." His gaze met Xylia's. "And yours, my dear." He clicked his tongue, raising his eyebrows. "The Book of the Justifier represents his chest. Without both, Lucifer's body could never come to life."

Xavier let out a sudden pain-filled grunt, and his body doubled over. Xylia, Demetre, and I raised our swords, ready to strike our enemy in his moment of weakness. We ceased our attack when the remaining seven Nephilins flocked in his direction, standing in front of him. The Shadows released angry roars as they watched us with their bright, feverish eyes.

I looked at all of the Nephilins, hoping to find Adawnas in their midst, but she was no longer within sight.

Xylia glanced back.

"Isaac, Arundel is awake," she stammered, surprised.

He reclined his body against a tree trunk, struggling to stand. With a weary face, he rubbed his gray eyes with his fingers while taking in shallow breaths.

"Why was the boy not taken?" one of the Nephilins shouted. "Why did they leave him behind?"

In silence, they exchanged a confused look.

"Fools," Xavier moaned.

A sudden roar filled the atmosphere, followed by the flap of strong wings. From the sky descended a white dragon. A thin smile grew on my face when I saw Nathan flying beside the beast. The Nephilins looked at the creature in horror, and the Shadows screeched in fear.

"We have to leave, Xavier," one of the female Nephilins clamored. "The white dragon will smite us all with its flames if we stay."

As Nathan and the dragon got closer, the Shadows fled through the forest, screeching. Xavier pressed his lips together, bearing his eyes into mine.

"Let us leave. Isaac and his remaining companions will come to us soon."

Xavier and the other Nephilins turned into shapeless shadows, vanishing into the air.

My body grew cold as I caught sight of a dark shadow surrounding Devin's unconscious body. I reached for the shapeless fume, attempting to capture whatever had ahold of my companion, but the shadow disappeared, taking my friend with it.

The wind weakened, and the rain and thunder ceased.

For a few seconds, I shut myself off from everything around me, trying to acknowledge the fact that my companions had been captured. Our enemies had taken Devin, the one that I always believed to be undefeatable.

I cast my sword onto the ground, its blade sinking beneath the mud. My fingers rubbed my forehead as I rested my left hand on my hip, pondering the events that had just taken place.

The loud roar of the white dragon startled me. It whirled its long wings as its paws sunk beneath the melting snow. I lost my breath when I recognized the rider mounted on the beast.

Xylia's eyes widened in disbelief.

"Sathees!" she shouted, running to greet the one who had aided her in the caves of Bellator. He alighted from the white dragon, walking to her embrace. His tattered garments were covered in grime.

Nathan approached and landed. I watched him with weary eyes. He rushed his way to me. Sorrow was stamped in his hazel-green eyes, and bruises marred his face and hands. His fair hair cascaded in front of his right eye. His ragged wings were smeared with blood.

My emotions went on a rampage, racing inside of me. No other desire would be able to suppress my longing for vengeance.

"I am glad to see that you are alright," Nathan affirmed, resting his hand on my shoulder. His silver armor was covered with dents and scratches.

I pulled my shoulder from his grasp.

"Can you not see that we are not alright?" I shook my head, spreading my arms. "Our companions have been taken by our enemies. They gave in to the temptations Xavier offered them." My fingers swept through my hair. "We are far from being alright, Nathan."

"Do not speak as if all hope is lost, Isaac," he said. "There will always be strength within us to overcome the darkness of the world."

My chin quivered. "I no longer have such strength." My voice broke into sobs.

I bowed my head, feeling the tears drip down my cheeks, making their way to my lips. I covered my face with my hand, kneeling on the snow.

I shouted as I grabbed the satchel from around my shoulder, hurling it against a tree. I despised the day the Diary had come to me. Maybe I should have taken up Xavier's offer to erase my mind. Even if we were to triumph over Lucifer, these memories would always haunt me.

I heard heavy footsteps approaching me. From the corner of my eye, I saw Arundel ambling my way, holding my satchel.

Nathan raised his hand, signaling him to stay back. "Boy, I think you should—"

"I would like to talk to him," Arundel demanded, interrupting Nathan before he could finish his sentence.

Nathan darted him a cold stare.

"It is alright, Nathan," I sniffed, raising my shoulders as I tried to contain my sobs.

He turned around and headed toward Sathees and the others. Arundel let out painful grunts as he knelt beside me. His eyes were full of sorrow.

He cleared his throat.

"It's not easy, is it?" he asked in a soft voice as he handed me my satchel. Shivers shot down my spine when I felt the Diary in my hands.

"No," I answered in a low voice. "I had already grown used to the idea that they were dead." My hands wiped the tears from my cheeks. "And then I discovered that they were still alive. Moments later, I had to be the one to take their lives."

Arundel narrowed his eyes. "They are at peace now, Isaac." A shy smile curved his lips. "May the joyful memories you have of them be an anchor of courage when darkness surrounds you. Long before this day, my father was already dead to me. His arrogance and pride killed my love for him day after day." He pressed his hands together. "He did love my sister very much, but after my mother passed away five years ago, his feelings toward me changed." He bent his head to the side, cracking the bones in his neck. "He would always have this spiteful look in his eyes whenever he was with me. I never understood why."

My nose sniffled. "I am sorry," I said.

"Be glad that you mourn their deaths out of love, not regret," he said with his voice caught in his throat, shying his eyes away from mine.

"What do you regret?"

"I regret all the time I wasted trying to be the son he had always dreamed of." He lifted his eyes to the sky. The storm clouds raced against each other as they hovered above us.

"Take your time." His hand tightened around my shoulder. "You have the right to mourn their deaths, but people like you cannot linger in the disasters of the past. You are no ordinary man, Isaac."

He stood to his feet, rubbed his hands on his pants, and walked toward the others.

Though they all talked amongst themselves, I noticed that Nathan and Sathees occasionally glanced at me. Xylia and Demetre kept looking my way, probably waiting for the right time to speak to me.

"Isaac." I heard the familiar voice I had been longing to hear for so long. I turned around, looking for him amidst the trees, but he was nowhere in sight. I shot a quick glance at my companions, wondering if they had also heard the peaceful voice that had called my name, but they still talked amongst themselves. The white dragon rested his head on the ground, napping.

With my satchel around my shoulder, I rose to my feet. My eyes circled my surroundings, expecting to find him.

"You are looking for me in the wrong place, Isaac," he said. His powerful voice was like the sound of crashing waves. "Close your eyes."

My eyelids came together. Though I was unsure of what I was going to see, I obeyed his command.

Amidst the darkness, I saw him—the Creator. His white mane bounced as he approached me. His six wings were covered in long feathers as white as the snow that rested atop mountains.

"You are here." My lips pressed into a tight smile. "After all this time, you have finally come." His scarlet eyes were like sharp blades that could slash my flesh and reveal the depths of my heart.

"I never left." He halted, standing inches from my face.

"It surely felt like you did," I said, shying away from his gaze.

A low snarl came from him. "Do not mistake my silence for abandonment. I have been watching you since the day you took your very first breath."

"Maybe that was the problem. You were just watching." I turned my back to him. "Why did you not help me?" My arms spread. "My companions were taken. I was tempted to accept Xavier's offer."

"Silence can often teach us timeless lessons. If I had not withheld my words, you would have not recognized your weaknesses and strengths." Our eyes met. "Despite all of your abilities, you are still a man, Isaac."

"And yet I have seen things that no man should ever see." I turned my gaze from his. "Done things that have scarred me for the rest of my life."

He listened to my words in silence. I noticed the tears that dripped down the sides of his face.

"I watched all the events you mentioned unfold. After all these years, the consequences of mankind's fall continue

to manifest. The day Lucifer was given the right to enter Elysium, disaster and death followed. Though one man may sow the seed, those around him will reap its fruit, whether it be good or evil." He let out a soft breath. "I am bound by the limits of the universe I created. I decided to give mankind the power to choose for themselves. I cannot interfere with the outcome of their choices, but I can send help and aid them in the battle against the darkness."

"That was a dangerous thing to give us." I sniffled my nose.

"It was my way of showing mankind that I trusted them."

"Do you still trust us?" I feared his response.

"Why do you think I have you and the others going on this journey?" He hardened his scarlet eyes. "My trust stands unshaken. Your journey represents the choice laid out before mankind. You all carry Lucifer's weapons. With such a task also comes the choice to persevere in your decisions to keep these books safe, or to succumb to their temptation."

His voice filled my ears like a beautiful melody. It brought peace to my heart, allowing me to forget, even if only for moment, the sorrow that was inside of me.

He gazed into the darkness, silent.

My hands trailed around my satchel, feeling the Diary that sat inside.

"Is there anything else you would like to ask me?" I felt his strength in every word he spoke.

I clenched and unclenched my hands, thinking of the many questions that needed answers. Two of them required immediate responses.

"Are you aware that there is a traitor inside Tristar?"

His face grew empty of any emotion. He stood in front of me, quiet.

"Are you?" I insisted, pacing in his direction.

"Is there not betrayal inside every single heart?" With tender eyes, he looked at me. "The desire for vengeance? Self-righteousness? There is a rebellious traitor inside each one of us."

I withheld my words, pondering what he said.

"What difference is there between a thief that robs a family's food supply and a man that steals his neighbor's joy by speaking evil words upon him?"

I was incapable of finding a suitable response.

"Worry not about traitors in other realms of the universe, Isaac," he said, letting out a low snarl in his throat.

"There is one more thing that I must ask you." He bore his tender eyes into mine. "Where did my parents go after they died?"

"Home." His voice was calm and soothing. Though his answer was short, it filled my heart with peace. With a smile stamped on my face, I watched as an incandescent light enfolded his white body. His wings disappeared like vapor. The striking scarlet eyes melted like ice under the heat of day.

My eyes shot open and creases appeared on my forehead. Time had stood still while I'd spoken with the Creator. I saw my companions resting against old tree trunks. Demetre sat in silence while Xylia and Sathees talked. I rubbed my hands against my legs to rid them of all the melting snow. I picked myself up from the ground and grasped my sword.

Every step I took felt as if a weight was being lifted from my shoulders. The sorrow that came with the death of my parents and the capture of my companions was still present, but a reassuring feeling of victory filled me with strength.

Sathees caught sight of me. His pale face was shrouded in bruises and cuts. Red veins surrounded the gray irises of his eyes.

"It is good to see you, Isaac," he said in a tired voice. Xylia gave me a half-hearted smile as I stood next to her. Demetre's face was stamped with sorrow.

"It is great to see you, Sathees." I narrowed my eyes, surprised. I darted Arundel a curious stare.

"You both have the same unusual eye color," I remarked, analyzing Arundel's facial traits. The muscles between my eyebrows constricted. "And the same nose." I looked back at Sathees.

Those around me looked at both of them, widening their eyes at the similarities of their traits.

"Eyes like yours are not so common, Sathees," said Nathan, darting Sathees a confused look.

Arundel took three steps toward Sathees. "Have we met before?"

Though confusion shrouded Sathees' face, the resemblance was undeniable.

"No." His voice was cold. He darted me a calm stare, avoiding any conversation with Arundel. "I will go find us something to eat. It will be dark soon." He marched toward the trees.

Arundel watched Sathees until he disappeared amidst the trees. He grimaced, pressing his right hand over his left shoulder.

"What happened to the others, Isaac?" Nathan's face was shrouded with worry.

I drew in a breath, letting it back out with a sigh as I tried to find strength within me to answer his question.

"Xavier penetrated our minds, presenting an offer that was almost too tempting to decline." My brows furrowed as I cleared my throat. "He gave us the choice to have our memories erased if we opened our books." As my words flowed from my lips, a despondent look filled his face.

"So you are telling me…" His voice faded while he crossed his hands. He lowered his head in disappointment.

I noticed that Demetre wept, snuffling as he listened to our conversation. Grave silence loomed over us. We all knew that their acceptance of Xavier's offer gave Lucifer's army even more power.

"Adawnas called this power the Dark Exchange," I added. "She was confused as to why some of us did not remain asleep."

"Where is Devin?" Nathan surveyed our surroundings with curious eyes.

Xylia darted me a concerned stare. Her jaw hung open.

"He was also taken," I whispered, glancing at the spot where his body had laid moments before. "But he was not taken because he did not wake. He was just too weak to fight."

Nathan turned around, looking at the distant smoke that rose from the Village of Tears.

"So the Nephilins and Xavier have within their possession three books and their bearers." He pursed his lips.

"Xavier said that he still needed our books. He mentioned something about the Diary and the Book of the Justifier." His eyes turned to me. "He said that the Diary represented Lucifer's heart, and that the Book of the Justifier symbolized his chest. Without both, Lucifer could not take up his full form."

With an absent look on his face, Nathan crossed his arms.

"Each book represents a part of Lucifer's body," he mumbled to himself, tapping his fingers on his chin.

"Do not forget that the blood-drinkers are also after the third book, the Book of Letters," Xylia added. Chills shot down my spine as a cold breeze blew about, tugging the dry branches of the surrounding trees.

"They will not rest until they have that book within their grasp," Demetre said. "They are determined to capture Ballard and open that book. They said that Bartholomew had opened it before. It was also mentioned that the Book of Letters has the power to awaken a dangerous army."

Arundel listened to our conversation in silence. I was concerned when I saw his colorless lips and pale face.

"Are you alright?" Xylia asked.

"I will survive." He squinted his eyes, letting out low grunts. "I just need to rest."

"Let us know if you need anything," Xylia said with a concerned look.

"Do you think the blood-drinkers will also go after the Nephilins?" Nathan asked.

"I would not doubt it. They murdered an entire kingdom in an attempt to find the book. What would stop them from hunting the Nephilins?"

The white dragon's sudden groans startled me. It opened its striking blue eyes, raising its massive neck from the ground. It flapped its strong wings, letting out loud screeches.

"What is it doing?" Xylia asked in a loud voice, covering her ears.

"I think it is calling for Sathees," Nathan shouted.

Arundel let out a piercing cry as he stood to his feet.

"Make it stop," he begged. "Quiet the beast." His fingers twitched as his hand released his shoulder, falling against his leg.

The white dragon stood on its four legs, letting out a roar that could have been heard from miles away. Arundel crouched on the ground, falling to his knees and sinking his face in the melting snow. With both of his hands, he covered his ears as he continued to scream.

Markings appeared on his skin. Like ink being used to draw a picture on paper, thin lines emerged on his hands and neck. After a while, I realized what these lines had created.

"He has the same markings as Sathees." My eyes absorbed the strange scene.

A glowing blue light shone from the strange patterns. They formed the shape of a white dragon.

The roaring beast took flight, heading in the direction of the trees. A strong wind rushed around us as it flapped its large wings.

Arundel's screams ceased. He uncovered his ears, darting us all a confused stare. He watched the creature soar through the sky. With his hand, he touched his shoulder.

"The pain is gone." He twirled his arm. "The pain…" He let out a loud laugh. "The pain is gone."

He turned his hands, setting eyes on the peculiar patterns on his skin. "What are these?" he asked, frowning at the sight.

"Sathees will be very surprised when he sees you," Demetre remarked with a smile.

There was confusion in all of our faces. Had Sathees told the truth when he said he had never met Arundel?

"What did you feel when the dragon roared?" I asked.

"The moment I laid eyes on it, I felt a warm sensation throughout my body. The pain that struck me at the sound of its growl was similar to a sharp blade cutting through my skin." His fingers trailed over the lines on his hands.

"Perhaps Sathees will be able to tell us why this happened to you," said Nathan.

"Where did the white dragon go?" Demetre asked, searching for the creature.

"Who knows? It is a dragon. It does not answer to anyone." Nathan's eyes ventured through the gray sky.

"What happened after we left Bellator, Nathan?" Xylia asked with a fervent stare.

Nathan scratched his chin as he bowed his head.

Xylia awaited his response.

"The people brought down the gates of the wall that protected the castle. They marched through the doors like an army longing to destroy its enemy, seeking King

273

Demyon and the Book of Letters. The blood-drinkers returned with torches in their hands, setting the curtains and furniture on fire." His hands trailed through his ashen hair, and a grave expression was on his face. "King Demyon and I headed to Sathees' room, only to discover that he was no longer there." Tears welled up in his eyes. "He ordered me to fly away and come searching for you. I was hesitant about leaving him behind, but he insisted."

There was great anguish in the words that he spoke.

"I ascended into the sky, catching sight of the uncontrollable riot." He gnawed on his lips as he creased his brows. "I was attacked by one of the blood-drinkers. At great speed, he chased me through the air. With his strange power, his body transformed into a hand enveloped in smoke. He snatched my ankle, pulling my body toward the ground. While he descended in my direction, my ears were filled with the sound of a white dragon's roar. I looked up and saw Sathees mounted on the beast. Once the blood-drinker saw the dragon, he fled, disappearing into the sky with all the speed he could muster."

Silence hovered over us while we listened to his account of the attack.

"It would be foolish of us to think that these blood-drinkers do not have power." He stared at us. "They were able to cast fear into the hearts of the citizens of Bellator in a matter of hours. We must be careful."

From the woods behind Nathan emerged two boys with burn marks covering their bodies. The shortest had brown eyes that matched the curls cascading down his face. The other had flaming hair. His eyes were as green as the hills of

Mahnor in the spring. Their garments were stained with blood and dirt.

Xylia ran in their direction. They glanced at her with tired eyes. She knelt in front of them.

"Where do you come from?" she inquired.

For a few seconds, they stared at her, speechless. The shortest boy hid his face between his hands.

"What happened to you?" She rested one of her hands on each of their shoulders. They flinched, recoiling away from her touch.

"I am not going to harm you." Her voice was tender and peaceful.

"They are torturing them," said the tallest boy. His body trembled as he struggled to stand. "They locked some of us in the prison. I think they are going to burn them all."

"Some of those people are still alive, Isaac," Demetre whispered, standing beside me as he watched the boys.

"How did you get here?" Arundel paced in their direction.

"After we heard the commotion of the crowd, our parents told us to hide under our beds." His lips trembled. "They barged into our house, taking our mom and dad."

"Will everyone die, Daegan?" asked the shortest boy in a fearful voice.

"I don't know, Cain," he answered his brother. "But I know these people will protect us."

Xylia tightened her hands into fists, rising to her feet. Arundel darted me a determined stare.

"We have to help them." Xylia turned her gaze in the direction of the rising smoke cloud.

A part of me wanted to ignore my surroundings for a while. Not because I did not care for the people trapped in the Village of Tears, but because my heart still ached at the thought of my parents' death. I wanted to mourn in solitude.

"We have to leave at once, Isaac," Nathan remarked in a strong voice. "There is no time to waste."

"We will head there now." I set my eyes on Xylia. "Stay here with the boys. We will be back soon."

She wrapped her arms around both of them. I knew she wanted to follow us into battle.

"Demetre." My eyes met his. "Stay with her?"

"Of course." His voice was low.

"What about Sathees?" Arundel asked. "Will he not join us?"

"There is no time to wait for him," Nathan replied, turning his head in my direction. "We cannot fly, as that would increase our risk of being spotted. We will have to run as fast as we can."

"They cannot suspect that we are coming." There were faint glares of light shining from the patterns on Arundel's skin while he spoke.

Though I was not fond of going to the village on foot, I knew we could not risk being seen by the blood-drinkers.

"Be careful," Xylia whispered under her breath. "All of you."

"We will." I met her tender stare. The thought of leaving them there on their own brought fear to my heart.

XIX

MY COMPANIONS TURNED their backs to me and darted their way toward the trees. I let out a soft breath, following them with a heavy heart.

I dodged every branch, leaped over every log while my eyes searched my surroundings for any sign of our enemies. The ground trembled as clashes of thunder reverberated through the sky. The wind howled as it picked up speed.

A sudden sharp pain invaded my mind. My vision darkened while the pain intensified. The sound of whispering voices echoed around me. I came to an abrupt stop.

"Nathan!" I shouted in despair, trailing my fingertips across my eyes. "Arundel!"

My breathing grew shallow as I realized I could no longer hear the blowing of the wind or the sound of thunder.

"You walk to your doom, Isaac." I heard his voice speaking inside my mind. "Deep inside, you know that you will not triumph in this war."

I felt as if my heart was about to leap out of my chest. At the sound of his words, fear crawled beneath my skin.

"You know I will be the one to defeat you, Lucifer." My voice was strong.

He let out a malevolent laugh. "I eagerly await the moment when I can roam around Elysium in flesh and blood. Once I regain my full power, you will be the first vermin to be visited by me."

A throbbing pain spread through my head. My body trembled at the sound of his voice.

"Three of your companions will open their books soon. My army grows strong." Silence loomed for a while. "Where is your army, Isaac?" he hissed.

"Isaac, can you hear me?" I heard Nathan's faint voice.

"I will visit you when you least expect my presence. I will find you, Isaac, and you will meet your doom."

"Isaac, say something," Arundel begged in a loud voice.

My eyes shot open. Rain descended from the sky. Flashes of lightning brightened the dark clouds.

"What happened to you?" Nathan's voice sounded like a hoarse whisper. "You screamed so loud. I thought you were being attacked."

My head turned to them. "He came to me." I narrowed my eyes. "Lucifer knows that they have the three books."

A grave expression came over their faces.

"What do you mean when you say that he came to you?" Arundel asked, confused.

"He invaded my mind. I could not see him. I only heard his voice."

Nathan lowered his head, resting his left hand on his sword's grip. "Darker days are ahead of us, my friend. We better be ready for them."

"We need to keep moving," Arundel said.

As fast our feet could carry us, we continued running to the Village of Tears. The rain melted the remnants of the snow that still sat on the wet forest floor.

For a moment, I was afraid of what the future was about to bring our way. I did not fear death or pain. I feared the coming of Lucifer. Never had human eyes seen the Dark One in his full form.

Screams invaded my ears as we approached our destination. I covered my nose, trying to block out the smell of burning flesh. I unsheathed my sword, cutting away the thistles and twigs.

"Look up," Arundel whispered in a trembling voice.

I raised my head, squinting my eyes as the drops of rain continued to strike my face. My jaw dropped as my eyes absorbed the macabre sight. Bodies of men, women, and children hung from the tree branches. Most of them were missing their arms and legs. The rain mixed with the blood from their wounds, creating scarlet drops that dripped to the ground. Amidst the dense vegetation, I saw the flames and the smoke cloud that rose from the burning buildings.

There was the faint sound of devious laughter coming from the blazing village. It sounded as if they were celebrating something.

"We need to get closer." Nathan got on his knees. He laid his body on the mud-covered ground, crawling his way to the rubble of the wall. Arundel and I followed.

The rain had melted most of the snow, creating a landscape that recalled my darkest nightmares.

The bellowing roar of a white dragon startled us.

"Is that Sathees?" Nathan asked in an alarmed voice as he lifted his head, searching for our companion. But the rising smoke dimmed his vision.

"What do we have here?" I heard Bartholomew's faint voice shouting. "A white dragon? We will not be hungry for long."

Laughs and mockery were heard from amidst the flames.

"Do you think they have Sathees?" I asked in great distress. Grim stares had filled my companions' faces.

"What do we do?" Nathan scowled in anger, meeting my gaze.

"We distract them." My voice was cold. "Arundel, make your way to the prison and free those people." He darted me a confused stare. "Whatever happens, lead them to safety."

"What are you planning to do?" He furrowed his brow.

My eyes looked into Nathan's. "Nathan and I will surprise them. We will fly our way through the smoke and fire to strike them."

"We are outnumbered, Isaac. They might try to kill or capture us." Arundel said. "What you are saying is madness."

"While they are preoccupied by their attempt to capture us, you will run to the prison and free your people." I lifted my head, attempting to catch a better glimpse of the burning village. "We will be fine."

Arundel's eyes shied away from mine. "Alright," he mumbled.

"Are you with me, Nathan?" I bore my eyes into his.

His lips tightened into a brittle smile. "Until the end."

My wings slithered under my skin, wrenching out of my back. My feet lifted from the ground beneath them. Nathan followed me.

An unbearable odor of burning wood and flesh invaded my nostrils as we rose through the smoke cloud, using it to veil our presence.

My breath failed when I saw the white dragon's skin covered in gashes and wounds. I surveyed the ground, looking for Sathees, but he was nowhere in sight. With my sword in hand, I aimed to sink my blade into Bartholomew's heart.

Nathan drew out his sword, which was adorned with colorful jewels. On its cross-guard was etched the symbol of the lion. From the palm of his left hand shone a dim light.

"I will use flashes of light to blind them. That will be our chance to attack," Nathan informed me, his eyes set on the scene that unfolded before us. "Let us try to wound as many of them as possible."

The bodies of many Lessers lay lifeless on the rubble of the broken houses. Some were enveloped in flames. Two blood-drinkers stood in front of the rugged prison building. One had hair colored like the night. Curls cascaded in front of his face. He was clothed in a dark leather vest. The other had his face hidden beneath a moss-green hood. He rested against the wooden doors of the prison, using a dagger to clean beneath his fingernails. Trembling hands reached through the barred windows as the people screamed in despair.

"Ready?" I whispered, feeling my heart accelerate in my chest.

"Yes." At the sight of Nathan raising his left hand, I plunged my way toward Bartholomew. A bright glare of light beamed through the storm.

The blood-drinkers covered their eyes as the strong light touched their skin. Bartholomew cupped his hands over his face and ducked his head.

My arms raised the sword in my hand as I approached my enemy. With all the strength I could muster, I lashed my sword against him, wounding his right leg. The moment my blade lifted, I felt his hand grasp the nape of my neck, thrusting my body to the ground.

As I was dragged against the mud, I used my hands to propel my body upward while flapping my wings. I tilted my face and caught sight of Nathan throwing himself against Bartholomew.

While he was still in the air, the blood-drinker with the dark curls collided with him, hurling his body against the wounded white dragon. His sword fell from his grasp. The beast wailed as Nathan's body thudded against its rib cage. The blood-drinker with dark curls rushed his way to Nathan, and two others of his kind followed. They pinned his body against the ground.

Bartholomew chuckled. A death stare stamped on his face, his left knee supported his body weight.

"I thought you and your companions had abandoned us all," he said in a spiteful voice. "By now, you should know that a wound inflicted by your blade against my body will heal in seconds."

"I was still the one that wounded you." I wiped the mud from my face. "I was also the one who killed one of your kind."

The hooded blood-drinker that guarded the prison clumped my way with his head held high. He removed the cloak, unveiling his face. A long, thin scar cut across his forehead. Dark circles surrounded his midnight eyes. His beard hid his cheeks.

"Why did you return, huh?" he inquired, biting the corner of his bottom lip. "You could have run off into the wilderness with your companions." His eyes narrowed to slits.

"Now, Dionisius, maybe Isaac missed us." Creases appeared on Bartholomew's forehead. "Or maybe…he misses his friends."

My eyebrows rose.

"Did you really believe those boys had the tenacity to escape this village on their own?" My eyes widened in fear. "I had someone follow all of you while you ran through the forest in a failed attempt to save your friends."

I lowered my sword, my face shrouded with disbelief.

Dionisius clapped his hands in mockery. "It was a beautiful sight to behold." He let out a cynical laugh. "The moment you heard your companion's screams," he lifted his right eyebrow, "you flapped your wings and flew toward him with such grace. You almost looked like a real hero."

"You bastard." The tip of my sword was aimed at him.

Bartholomew marched in my direction.

"We know the Nephilins have the Book of Letters within their grasp." A crooked smile curved on his face. "And we know exactly how to lure them back and make them fall into our trap."

"Where are they?" Anger had taken ahold of me.

"They are locked up in the prison with all the others. I am afraid you will not get to see them." dragon-like wings sprung from his back, stretching to full length.

From the corner of my eye, I saw Nathan straining against the blood-drinkers' strong grasps. The blood-drinker with dark curls had his right knee pressed on Nathan's lower back. The other two had ahold of his arms.

Where is Arundel? I thought, darting a quick stare in the direction of the prison. Had Sathees also deserted us? The people continued to shout and scream for help, banging against the strong wooden door.

Was Bartholomew speaking the truth? Had they captured Xylia and Demetre? How did they know about the two boys?

I lifted my eyes to the sky as two blood-drinkers hovered over us. They flew down like eagles ready to snatch up helpless prey. I had not forgotten Dahmian's flaming red hair and Ashtar's thin, pale face. Dahmian wore a laced gray shirt with a scarlet coat that fell above his knees. Fresh blood stained his boots. Ashtar wore a beige doublet with intricate golden patterns. A brown belt was wrapped around his waist.

"I see you had time to find yourselves some new clothes." Bartholomew scowled, his eyes trailing across their bodies.

They looked at me. Their noses wrinkled as their eyebrows pulled down.

"And I see that you had the time to find yourself a new toy to play with," Dahmian said in a spiteful tone.

Ashtar was quiet; his black eyes fixed on me.

"The service you requested from us has been completed," Dahmian informed Bartholomew.

"Good," he whispered. "It won't be long until the Nephilins and that Fallen Ruler come looking for her."

Confusion stirred within me. Could it be that they had also captured Nephele? Was she the one they spoke of?

My thoughts were interrupted by the white dragon's roars. The creature wobbled its thick neck, rising from the ground. It stood on its four legs.

"Why is the dragon able to stand?" Bartholomew shouted at the top of his lungs. He darted an angry stare at the three blood-drinkers that held Nathan against the ground. "Bhor, did you feed it human flesh?"

"Yes, Bartholomew," replied the blood-drinker with the dark hair and vest. His eyes were the color of fresh blood. "We fed it fresh meat. We gutted those two kids that were with the red-headed girl and the other boy."

I did not want to believe that they had captured them, but after hearing Bhor's accounts, I knew that they had Xylia and Demetre.

The white dragon unfurled its strong wings to their massive width.

"Tame this beast." Bartholomew was desperate. The blood-drinkers did not move from their place. They stood at bay, watching the dragon regain its full strength.

While they had their eyes set on the beast, I glanced at the prison. I was relieved to see Arundel standing at its wooden doors. The patterns on his skin glistened while he lifted the thick log that sealed both doors.

I squinted my eyes as a sudden bright flash of light radiated. Once the light receded, I noticed that Nathan had

broken free from the grasp of those that held him. I glanced around, attempting to find him, but he was nowhere in sight.

"Where is the Underwarrior?" Dahmian's eyes searched the sky. "Where is he?"

Bohr and the other two blood-drinkers stared in a daze.

"Did you see where he went, Daine?" Bohr asked the blood-drinker that stood next to him. Like Ashtar, he had no hair on his head. A tattered red beard hid most of his jaw and cheeks. His eyes had a lively green hue.

"I was standing next to you the whole time. Of course I do not know where the Underwarrior went," he replied with an angry stare. He set his eyes on his other companion.

"Do not look at me, Daine." The other blood-drinker paced away from his companions. "I am as confused as all of you." He had his tangled black hair behind his ears. His eyes were the color of the midday sky. He wore a rugged, brown coat with a thick leather belt. His boots were smothered in mud and blood.

I squinted my eyes, recognizing his familiar face. He was the blood-drinker that I had seen drinking the blood that poured out of Sela's body.

"Anwill, enough babbling." Bartholomew pointed his finger at the white dragon. "We must tame this creature."

No one responded to Bartholomew's order. They feared the consuming flames the dragon could release upon them.

The white dragon's roars loudened. The ground trembled as the beast sank its claws into the damp soil. I was alarmed when I caught sight of its quivering jaw. It glowered at the blood-drinkers; smoke billowed from its

nostrils. The beast flapped its wings, raising its body from the ground. Without warning, it revealed its razor-sharp teeth. It recoiled its head backwards and, in great fury, released fire over the blood-drinkers.

Bohr, Daine, and Anwill dodged the flames, casting their bodies in the opposite direction. In an instant, wings appeared on their backs. Bartholomew, Dahmian, Ashtar, and Dionisius left the ground, soaring into the sky. The dragon was agitated, setting ablaze all that stood in its path.

Without hesitating, I glided to where Arundel stood. I knew it was only a matter of time until one of them saw us.

Before I could reach the prison, Dahmian descended in my direction and, with the sole of his right foot, plunged my body to the ground. My chest thudded against the broken pieces of burnt wood that lay scattered.

"Open the doors, Arundel!" I managed to shout across the sounds of battle as I tried to recover my breath. An uncomfortable pain filled my lungs.

With sweat trickling down his brow, Arundel opened the prison doors. The people raced their way out of the building, screaming as they caught sight of the battle that unfolded around them. My heart accelerated in my chest while my eyes searched for Xylia and Demetre.

Ashtar and Dionisius wheeled in the air and dove their way to the people, attacking them with flashes of light that caused massive explosions. Bodies flew across the village; limbs scattered around us as the blood-drinkers struck them.

I dashed toward the fearful crowd.

"Xylia!" I pushed many out of my path as I looked for them. "Demetre!"

I heard a loud whooshing sound coming from above me. I shot up an alarmed stare, catching sight of the white dragon hovering above the burning village. The buildings that still remained standing were now enveloped in bright, blue flames. An ashen smoke covered the air.

"Xylia!" I shouted once again. "Demetre!"

Two blood-drinkers came into sight through the smoke cloud. As fast as the eye could see, they leaped atop the desperate crowd. They grabbed those that were within their reach and sank their fangs into the people's skins. Like mountain lions feasting on their prey, they ripped off the arms and legs of those that were around them, drinking from the flowing blood.

With heavy breaths, Arundel rushed to my side, dodging the scattered debris that fell like rain. Flashes of lightning lit up the clouds, brightening the darkness caused by the storm.

"Where are the others?" I was desperate. "Have you seen Nathan, Xylia, and Demetre?"

"No, I did not see them," he said between short breaths.

"They were taken." I coughed due to the lingering smoke. "Xylia and Demetre were captured. We must find them."

Arundel scowled, raising his head.

"Look over there," he whispered, pointing to something behind me.

I glanced over my shoulder and saw Bartholomew entering one of the abandoned houses. With watchful eyes, he surveyed his surroundings, ensuring that none followed him.

"Whatever he is looking for must be of extreme importance," I said. "They might be inside that house."

We started toward the house. Agony struck my heart with each scream I heard. I wondered if these people would turn into Shadows. Alistar must have shared with them some truth about the Creator. I struggled to ignore the children being murdered around us by the bloodthirsty creatures that attacked them. A mixture of blood, mud, and rain covered the earth beneath our feet.

"Get down," I said, lowering my body as we approached the house.

From the corner of my eye, I saw Nathan amidst the trees. His gaze was set on us but he made no attempt to come our way.

"Nathan," I whispered. "Are you alright?"

He gave me a quick nod. "Look in there." He mouthed the words to me, cocking his head toward the house.

I lifted my eyes to look through the clouded glass of the broken window. A cold chill shot down my spine as my eyes absorbed the unthinkable.

"What is it?" Arundel whispered, shaking me by the shoulder.

I was at a loss for words. Inside the house were Demetre, Xylia, and the most unthinkable prisoner of all— Nephele. They had pierced her right leg with a rusted sword, leaving the blade inside. Blood seeped from her wounds, staining her dark garments. She was in a stupor.

Demetre and Xylia had their hands tied behind their backs. Their faces were covered with scratches and bruises.

"Well, well, well." Bartholomew spread out his arms as he shrugged his wings. "To think that I have in the same room Isaac's most loyal companions and his worst enemy."

He bent down, grasping Xylia by the cheeks, standing inches away from her chapped lips.

"I wonder how you taste, girl." He trailed his tongue across his lips, his long pair of fangs coming into view.

She recoiled her head, furrowed her brow, and spit on his lips.

"How does that taste, monster?" She shrugged her shoulders.

Bartholomew's lips curved into a menacing smile. He leaned in closer to her.

"Leave her alone!" Demetre shouted, trying to break free from the ropes that tied him.

He trailed his lips across Xylia's ears and neck. She trembled at his touch. My hands turned into fists.

"I will kill you, girl," he said, standing back on his feet. "But not today. I still need you."

Arundel raised his head, glancing inside the house. He gasped, lowering his head in shock.

I darted Nathan a desperate stare.

"We have to help them," I mumbled, feeling my heart race inside my chest.

The thundering roars of the white dragon echoed as the battle raged. The screams of the people were ceasing—a sign that many of them had been killed by the blood-drinkers.

How I wish I had the power to muster this ability that had developed in me. I desired to kill Bartholomew. To see my companions suffering at the hands of this tyrant

infuriated me. A part of me did rejoice at the sight of Nephele's suffering at the hands of the blood-drinkers. She was not worthy of life or mercy.

Nathan laid his body on the ground, crawling his way to us. He rose to his feet as he approached the house, resting his back against the wall. Mud dripped from his garments.

"Stay there," he whispered between heavy breaths. "Save them. Do not come looking for me."

Without warning, he dashed his body against the door, crushing it to pieces. Surprised, Bartholomew turned to him. At that moment, Nathan spread his wings, flinging his body against the blood-drinker.

Wings sprung out of Bartholomew's back. He pushed Nathan against the wall, bringing most of it to the ground. Bartholomew let out a spiteful laugh as dust arose from the wall's scattered fragments.

"Nathan!" Xylia's eyes glistened.

Demetre took in heavy breaths as his eyes searched his surroundings. His face lit up once he saw Arundel and me through the clouded window.

"I thought you had left us," Bartholomew said, wiping his mouth with his wrist. Nathan rose to his feet, unsheathing his sword.

"I had to return, Bartholomew. I could not leave a coward like you alive to roam these lands."

"Coward?" The veins on Bartholomew's neck protruded beneath his skin.

"And to think that you were a king of men once." Nathan raised both of his eyebrows. "Look at you now, king of the vermin. You are doomed to live your days feasting on the blood of the innocent."

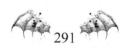

"Hold your tongue, Underwarrior, or I will kill you."

"Empty words from an empty soul." Nathan let out a low laugh. "Do you even have a soul, Bartholomew?"

Bartholomew's wings fluttered as he propelled his body against Nathan. While he hovered in the air, Nathan swung his blade, striking his forearm. They both darted toward the sky, disappearing amidst the rising smoke.

"This is our chance." Arundel and I arose to our feet, running inside the house.

"Am I glad to see you, my friend," Demetre said with a smile as he shook his head. Drops of water dripped down his wet hair.

"I thought you had both been killed," Xylia wailed.

Arundel and I untied our companions. From the corner of my eye, I saw my enemy. Nephele had her head bowed, unconscious of everything that happened around her. It was strange seeing her in such a fragile state.

"Is she alive?" Arundel scowled at her while helping Xylia stand on her feet.

"She is." Xylia darted Nephele a disdaining look. "I hope they kill her."

Xylia rubbed her fingers over the bite marks on her wrist.

"Who did this to you?" I narrowed my eyes, trailing my hands over the scattered wounds. She withdrew her arm, hiding it behind her back.

"She was not the only one." Demetre stretched out his arm, revealing the wounds on his hands and wrists. "Dahmian and Ashtar drank our blood. The moment you both left, we were attacked by three blood-drinkers. Their names were Dionisius, Daine, and Anwill. They pinned us

to the ground and sank their fangs into our bodies. We fell unconscious and woke up here. They wanted to use as bait to lure the Nephilins into their trap. If they had you and Xylia, they knew the Nephilins would come looking for you. They need your books and the blood-drinkers want the Book of Letters."

The blood-drinkers were much cleverer than I had given them credit for.

"Where is Nathan?" Xylia inquired, staring through the opening in the wall. A thick cloud of smoke dimmed our visibility.

"We have to help him," Demetre said.

I tilted my face in his direction. "He told us not to come looking for him."

"Are we to just leave him here?" Xylia walked to the gap in the wall. "He helped us. We cannot abandon him."

"We must trust him," Arundel retorted. "We must leave this place at once." The markings on his skin continued to exude a soft glow.

"Arundel is right. We cannot linger." I marched toward the door. The bellowing roars of the white dragon still thundered in the air.

Xylia's face grew despondent. She knew we could not help him.

"Have you seen Sathees?" Her voice sounded as if it was caught in her throat.

"There is no sign of him," I replied, standing beneath the doorpost. "We have to go now. Once we make it to the trees, we keep on running. Do not look back." I bore my eyes into theirs.

"What about her?" Demetre cocked his head toward Nephele.

"Let her suffer at the hands of her hosts. I am sure she will enjoy her stay with them." Though I desired to take her life, I knew the blood-drinkers would enjoy torturing this Nephilin. She deserved a slow and painful death.

We darted our way out of the house, running as fast as our legs allowed us. The rain poured like a deluge. Explosions and screams were a symphony reverberating around us. I attempted to ignore all the lifeless bodies that lay scattered—men, women, children, and Lessers.

My eyes gazed at the sky, hoping to spot Nathan, but he was nowhere in sight.

A loud roar came from behind me. I darted a quick look over my shoulder and saw the white dragon flying in our direction. It flapped its strong wings as it headed toward the ground.

Arundel came to a halt when he saw the markings on his body glowing with a bright, incandescent light. He frowned at the sight, confused.

"What is going on with you, Arundel?" Xylia widened her eyes.

"I am not sure." He glanced at the approaching dragon.

The white dragon let out guttural sounds as its claws sank beneath the mud. It recoiled its wings and bowed its head.

"What does it want?" Demetre's eyes trailed across the animal.

The white dragon clumped toward Arundel. He stumbled back, afraid that the animal might harm him.

Standing only inches away, the white dragon screeched, lowering its thick neck to the ground.

"I think it wants you to ride it, Arundel." Xylia leaned her head forward, looking at the eyes of the dragon.

"And you just might have to," I said with an edge to my voice, watching as two blood-drinkers flew at great speed, heading in our direction. "Xylia and Demetre, ride with him."

With fearful eyes, they gave me a nod of agreement.

"Head to the mountaintop. We can hide there," I said.

Arundel crawled onto the wings of the white dragon. The light that shone from the markings on his skin grew stronger once he mounted the beast. Xylia and Demetre followed him, sitting closer to the dragon's tale.

The white dragon raised its head, squawking as it flailed its wings. Arundel clung to one of the dragon's dorsal spikes as the animal rose from the ground.

I was surprised when it turned its head toward our incoming enemies. Smoke rose from its snout. It widened its massive jaws, casting fire upon them.

They halted in mid-air. The flames enveloped their bodies as they released loud screams. They thudded to the ground, rolling in desperation; their wings melted like ice. An immediate putrid stench filled the air. One of them stretched out his arm, his fingers twitching as he attempted to crawl in our direction. My companions watched them burn as the dragon flapped its wings, soaring into the sky.

I followed them, darting one last look at my enemies. I knew the flames would only delay them. I did not know how long it would take, but their bodies would heal from their wounds.

The wind picked up. The temperature dropped. The rain ceased. My body ached due to the strenuous effort of moving my wings in such inclement weather.

My eyes glistened with tears as the vivid images of recent events haunted my mind. My parents. My companions. I feared the uncertainty of the future now that the Nephilins had three of Lucifer's books. So much had taken place in such a short amount of time. My heart was overwhelmed with grief and sorrow.

For a while, silence lingered while we hovered in the air. The Weeping Mountains were right below us.

The white dragon released a pain-filled screech. My eyes trailed along the animal's body. Blood trickled down the gashes and wounds spread across its legs and chest. Its eyes were deep and tired. The animal needed to rest.

I gestured with my hand, pointing toward the ground. Arundel nodded his head and raised his hand, showing me that he had understood my signal.

My wings retracted into my back as I dove to the ground. The white dragon followed. I hovered over the forest of pine trees that emerged from the lingering mist. The drips of water on my face turned to icicles as the frigid wind blew against my skin.

There was a valley in the cleft of the mountain with a frozen river that snaked all the way into the forest, disappearing amidst the trees.

I made my way down. The rain had melted all the snow away, creating a vast bog. When I landed, my feet were submerged under the mud-covered soil. The white dragon flurried its wings, landing beside me. The animal's breathing was heavy and shallow.

Arundel and the others alighted from the weary animal. I watched their despondent faces as their feet touched the ground. They were tired.

We were startled by the whooshing sound of the white dragon's wings. It flew away, heading in the direction of the river.

"It must be hungry." Xylia trudged her way to a rock. She sat down, her elbows resting on her knees. She bowed her head, trailing her hands through her red hair.

"Are you alright?" Demetre asked, resting one of his hands on my shoulder.

I wrapped my arm around his shoulder. "I am more than alright, my friend. You are alive. When they told me they had you and Xylia…" I shuddered at the thought that the blood-drinkers could have taken their lives. My breathing faltered when my eyes absorbed the bite marks on his wrist.

He withdrew his hand, trailing the tip of his fingers across the wounds.

"Don't worry." A thin smile brushed his lips. "I was strong."

"I am sure you were," I said, gnawing on the right side of my chapped lips.

Arundel gazed at the horizon, looking at the white dragon as it hovered over the river.

"It is hunting." His hands rested on his hips. "It dove inside the river three times already." He turned his face to me. "I have never felt this way before. I feel power rushing through my veins. It is as if my heart now beats at a different pace." He shook his head, narrowing his eyes. "I

don't know how I was able to tame that dragon—to ride it through the air."

"There are many questions that need answering, Arundel." Demetre's teeth chattered as he rubbed his hands against his arms. "It is futile to seek these answers on our own. We must believe that all of this is happening for a greater purpose."

"We should get a fire going." Xylia's hands hung between her legs and her elbows rested on her knees. "It will be dark soon."

XX

THE FOUR OF us sat around the fire with our hands extended over the flames. Without Devin's hunting abilities, we had to be content with the meat of a few rabbits and two crows. Arundel had skewered the meat on a few branches, placing them over the fire. The white dragon had wandered into the forest to find a resting place.

In the silence that lingered, I pondered the uncertainty of our future. We could go after the Nephilins in search of our companions, but their numbers were far too great—not to mention that they now had a Fallen Ruler on their side. Dark creatures had infiltrated the mountains and forests. The number of Shadows grew at a rapid pace.

Xylia raised her head, bearing her eyes into mine. "I am yet to discover the purpose of all this suffering and pain." She cleared her throat. "All this death…and betrayal. I feel like I am a sheep being hunted by starving wolves." She lowered her eyes, fixing them on her hands. "The tormenting thought that my life could slip through my fingers like water…"

"I know how you feel," I whispered, feeling the warmth of the flames against my hands.

She shook her head from one side to the other. "No, you don't, Isaac. You can fly. You have this sudden spur of power that allows you to enter someone's mind and kill them, if you wish."

"I would not wish such power upon any of you." I rubbed my hands together, trying to stay warm.

"Such words would not be coming out of your mouth if you were in my place. I am not used to running from my foes." A doleful look clouded her face. "Throughout my whole life, I always found strength in my ability to overcome my fears. Today, I see myself as weak as a prey fighting against its predator."

"Tell me, Xylia," Arundel spoke in a low voice, holding up one of the skewers, smoke ascending from the cooked rabbit meat. "Do you long for power to achieve your own desires or to fight for a greater cause?"

Xylia's intertwined her fingers. She bit the sides of her lips. "I long for power to bring justice upon those who are lovers of wickedness, Arundel."

"Courage is the greatest weapon we could ever hope to wield." Demetre leaned his body toward the flames. "We must believe that we can be a light amidst this darkness."

She lowered her shoulders, dropping her head between her hands. "Do you not think that I believe, Demetre?" She wiped her nose with her wrist. "I just witnessed our companions being taken by our enemies. Who knows what they are doing to them now. What can we expect to see once those three books are opened?" Tears trailed down the sides of her face as she closed her eyes.

I pressed my fingers against my head, listening to her low sobs. My heart ached with the memories that invaded

my mind. I saw the dimples that appeared on my mother's cheeks when she laughed; heard my father humming a joyful melody when we used to go fishing at the shores of the River of Agalmath. I missed lying on the soft grass of the Hills of Mahnor. Would I ever see Agalmath again? Would I ever return home? My eyes brimming with tears, I looked at Demetre. He rested his chin on his crossed hands. With a pensive expression, he watched the fire dance.

"Food is ready." A thin smile crossed Arundel's lips as he reached for one of the skewers. He was about to take a bite when his eyes widened. He laid the skewer over the fire, standing to his feet. His lips curved into a long smile.

"Look at that…" His voice trailed off as he raised his finger to the sky.

I turned my head to see what had caught Arundel's attention. The dark clouds that had veiled the moon and stars for so many months were dispersing. The thin, bright, curved line of a new moon appeared, surrounded by bright stars.

"Are my eyes being cheated?" Arundel stepped closer to me. "Is that the moon?"

Xylia broke out in laughter, mesmerized by the sight. Demetre smiled, his eyes trailing across the firmament.

"Do you think we will see the sun rise in the morning?" There was joy in Xylia's voice.

"I hope so." I took in a deep breath, absorbing every detail of the wondrous sky.

"What do you think happened?" Demetre reached for one of the skewers. "What could have caused these clouds to disappear?"

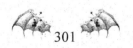

301

"Do you think the books were opened?" Arundel grasped the skewer he had laid over the fire.

"I want to believe that this is a sign." Xylia looked at Arundel with a smile. "No matter how dark the clouds, the sun and the moon still shine above them."

My ears were filled with melodious sounds that emerged from the forest. The chirping of crickets merged with the high-pitched screeches of cicadas. The howling of wolves came from deep within the forest. Though it was night, the forest awoke as the soft light of the moon shone above.

I reached for one of the skewers, devouring the well-cooked meat. For a while, we sat quietly, listening to the wildlife of the Weeping Mountains.

It was strange to see joy in my companions' faces. I allowed myself to enjoy this moment. For a short while, I decided to ignore the danger we were all in.

After we were done eating, Demetre made himself comfortable beside the fire, laying his head against a rock. Arundel strolled to a tree trunk located to my far right. I walked to a sycamore tree that sat near the river. I reclined on its trunk, allowing the sound of the running water to soothe me.

Countless stars shone above me. There were so many of them that it was if a large hand had tossed diamond dust across the sky.

There was a sound of twigs being crushed by slow footsteps coming from my right. Xylia met my gaze with a smile.

"Can't sleep?" I cleared my throat, watching her approach me with tired eyes. The soft breeze blew against her red hair.

"Do you mind if I sleep somewhere here?" Her lips trembled as she spoke.

"No, of course not." In haste, I picked up the wet scattered leaves and broken branches that were next to me, tossing them to the other side of the tree. "You can sleep here if you want."

"Are you sure? I do not want to disturb your rest, Isaac. You are tired."

I scratched the back of my head. "I am sure."

Though there was not much space. I dragged my body to my left, giving her some room to lie down.

She reclined against the tree trunk, leaning her head back. I watched her with attentive eyes while she looked the stars.

"What a sight to behold," she said. "The sky is so vast and endless."

"My father once told me that it takes thousands of years for the light of the stars to reach us." I looked at her. "What do you think?"

"I do not care about the amount of years it takes for their light to reach us. The important thing is to have them shine in the dark sky, don't you think?"

I felt the warmth of her breath brush against my cheeks as her eyes searched mine.

"What?" I whispered, putting my right arm around her.

"How do you do it?" She rested her head on my shoulder. "How do you stay sane through all this?"

A shiver shot down my spine when I felt a cold breeze touch my skin.

"There is no sanity in me. Have you not noticed?"

She let out a soft breath. "Do you regret not accepting Xavier's offer? I mean, you would have forgotten all of this. You would have been rid of all the pain and the hurt."

My head leaned against the tree trunk.

"I cannot deny the fact that I wanted to have this weight lifted from me, but my purpose speaks louder than my desires. I hung by a thread when he offered to erase my mind." My breath rasped in my throat. "I have to accept the fact that even if we win this war—"

"When." She raised her right eyebrow. "When we win this war." There was an edge to her voice.

I chuckled. "When we win this war, I am aware that these memories will haunt me forever. I guess that is the price I will have to pay. Every decision has both good and bad outcomes."

She leaned in closer to my face, her nose inches from mine. "Are there any memories that you want to remember?"

I felt the softness of her skin as I cupped her face with the palm of my hand.

"Yes." My thumb rubbed on her cheek. "This one." Our lips touched in a tender kiss. My heart raced when I wrapped my arms around her. The smell of her red hair reminded me of a garden of roses. Her fingertips trailed across my cheeks and down my neck.

"Was this kiss worthy of remembrance?" she asked, her lips parting from mine. I could smell her breath as our foreheads touched.

"Most definitely," I said, my fingers entwined with hers.

She reclined her head on my chest, wrapping her right arm around me. I leaned back on the tree trunk. There was

no denying that since the first time I had laid eyes on Xylia, I had felt something special for her. It was a strange thing to feel this way during these times when there was so much darkness and destruction around me. I fought against my eyelids as I watched her fall asleep. After some time, my eyes shut as I listened to the sound of the river.

Flames as tall as trees encircled me. My eyes glistened, striving to see beyond the blinding cloud of smoke. The stench of burnt flesh made my stomach turn. Confused, I took a few cautious steps, trying to get a better view of my surroundings. There was nothing familiar about this place.

"Do you think you can hide from me, Isaac?" The sound of Lucifer's foul voice stung my ears. "I am coming soon."

My steps turned to running. My eyes traveled through the landscape, trying to spot Lucifer's location. I felt a hard, sharp, and uneven surface beneath the soles of my feet. With every step I took, there was a crushing sound coming from the ground. I lowered my eyes, attempting to see what it was.

My throat closed at the sight. A carpet of human skulls sat on the uneven terrain. Some had strands of hair and pieces of rotten flesh hanging from them. Using the tips of my fingers, I shut my nose, trying to avoid the odor.

"Look at your future, Isaac." There was a hiss at the sound of every word he uttered. "These skulls belonged to those that you loved. Like an untamed lion when it feasts upon its prey, I will devour every single one of them."

Desperation crawled beneath my skin as the tormented wailing of children bellowed in my mind. I crouched to my knees, covering my ears in an attempt to avoid the screams.

"Their cries are like music to me." A thick, gray mist rose from the ground, dimming my sight. "What kind of music will you make when I crush your bones, Isaac?"

"Isaac!" The breaking voice of a young boy shouted. "You failed. I am burning because of you."

"No, no." My right fist came against the ground.

"I watched my younger brother die because you did not save me, Isaac," the tender voice of a young girl whispered. "Will you let me die? Will you not save me?"

All the voices joined together in a disturbing choir, shouting my name.

"I will kill every man, woman, and child who stands in my way. Join my kingdom or confront your fate." The hovering mist moved in the air like a snake. It circled around my face. With every breath, it entered my body through my nostrils. My fingers grew numb. My eyes rolled back in my head. I lost feeling in my legs.

"You cannot hide." Lucifer's voice was a whisper in my ear.

My eyes burst open. Sweat dripped down the side of my face. With ragged breaths, I stooped forward. Xylia had rolled over to her side, sleeping on top of her hands. Demetre still slept in the same spot, snoring with his arm on his forehead. Arundel rested with his arms crossed and his head bowed.

I reached inside my satchel. A shudder spread through my body when my fingertips felt the object. I sat up straight, taking the Diary out and laying it on my lap. Though I had been its bearer for quite some time now, I was still not used to laying eyes on it. The mysterious etchings on the cover sent shivers down my spine. I touched the rusted lock that kept the Diary inside of its case, pondering the mystery and secrets that were written on its pages.

Had it been a dream or had Lucifer entered my mind?

I saw a dim red light shining from the symbol that was etched on the case. The straight line surrounded by a wide circle shimmered as the light coursed its way to the etchings of the Diary. From the corner of my eyes, I noticed a bright light shinning from within Xylia's satchel.

In a few seconds, I felt a rising heat on the palms of my hands. A chill shot down my spine when I heard the voices from my dream echoing through the forest.

"We are here." I heard the voice of a young girl coming from my right. "Please, help us."

My eyes circled the trees around me in an attempt to spot these children. Cries and screams merged in a dark symphony, causing my mind to think back on all the families that had perished at the attack on the Village of Tears.

In a matter of seconds, the Diary was enveloped by fire. I released it from my grasp, dropping it to the ground.

"Wake up!" I shot all my companions an alarming stare. "Wake up, all of you!" My heart pounded in my chest.

Arundel rubbed his face, lifting his head in my direction. In haste, he stood to his feet. His eyes widened in surprise when he saw the Diary engulfed in flames.

"What is going on?" asked Demetre, raising his body from the ground. "What is that smell?"

Xylia still lay on the ground, immobile. I knelt next to her.

"Can you hear me?" My eyes were fixed on the light shining from her satchel. She did not answer. "Xylia?" I grasped her by the arms, shaking her body in an attempt to wake her. I removed the satchel from around her shoulder, tossing it next to the Diary. Arundel and Demetre approached me.

"Why won't she wake?" Arundel bore his eyes into mine.

"I don't know..." My voice trailed off when I caught sight of Xylia's satchel taken by flames that were as blue as the sea. I found it strange that though the books burned, there was no sign that they were being destroyed.

My throat closed once I smelled a foul odor that lingered. The smell was strong, bringing tears to my eyes.

Xylia's eyes shot open. Once she saw my face, she pushed me against the tree trunk, staring at all of us.

"Where is he?" Her chest heaved with heavy breaths. "Did he follow me?"

"Who are you talking about?" Demetre looked at her, confused.

Xylia threw her body against the tree trunk, wrapping her hands around her arms.

"He is going to find me." She broke into tears. "He is coming for me."

"Who is 'he?'" I asked, fearing that I knew the answer to my question. I leaned in closer to her, resting my hand on her knees.

There was a grim stare in her eyes.

"Lucifer. I saw him." She grasped my arm. "He tortured me. There was the sound of children crying. They said they burned because of me. I saw fire..." She furrowed her

brow, looking at the burning books. "He is coming for us all."

I sensed a change in the sky. I turned my head east and saw that dawn had broken—a mixture of red, yellow, and orange on the horizon.

"The sun is rising." Part of me wanted to see the first sunrise after many months of darkness, but I feared that though the clouds had vanished from the sky, darker days were coming.

A breeze as warm as a summer's day brushed on my cheeks. We all exchanged a surprised look.

"He is coming..." Xylia's voice was a whisper. "He is rising."

The water from the river glistened as the light of the sun broke through the clouds. I looked to the ground to find that the books still burned. The stench of decomposed flesh arose from the books as the sunlight touched them through the canopy of trees.

"Hear me now, book-bearers," Lucifer's voice echoed through the air. "The quest to retrieve my books is almost at an end. Their bearers have opened three of them. Your companions are of no use to me anymore." My teeth chattered at the sound of his voice. "A servant of mine awaits you in Agalmath." My jaw dropped at the sound of the last word he uttered. "Meet him there in two days or your friends will be killed and I will dispatch all my forces to hunt you until you are found." Demetre crouched on his knees, covering his ears. Arundel had his eyes fixed on the burning books. "Ballard, Adara, Petra, and Devin are waiting for you."

The whispers and screams that echoed around us ceased. The pungent smell of putrid flesh was replaced by that of the morning dew. The flames that enveloped the books disappeared like the early morning mist. The chirping of birds filled the air.

Xylia's breaths were heavy. She rose to her feet, reclining against the trunk of the sycamore tree. The light of the sun reflected on her green eyes and pale skin.

"What are we going to do?" With his fingers pressed to his forehead, Demetre sat on the ground.

I squinted my eyes, feeling the heat of the rays of the sun against my skin. My heart hammered under my chest.

"What other choice do we have?" I asked, turning my face to them. "We must do as Lucifer requested. We cannot leave our companions."

"It could be a trap, Isaac." Xylia approached me.

"It is a trap, one that we cannot run away from. We must be prepared for whatever fate awaits us in Agalmath."

"I HAVE FALLEN SO FAR FROM THE LIGHT,
THAT I AM NOW DOOMED TO BE
AN ETERNAL SLAVE TO MY WICKED DESIRES."

DEVIN

ACKNOWLEDGMENTS

God, any talent that I possess was given to me by you.
I am forever grateful.

It would have been impossible to finish another novel without the support of my friends and family.

Mom, Deborah, Carlos, and Dad, thank you for always believing in me. Your support has been an anchor to me during times of confusion and doubt.

I started writing this novel on a flight to Denver, Colorado on January 15th, 2013. As I typed the first chapter, I was sitting next to some of the people I love the most in this world.

Henrique and Maile Siqueira, thank you for always believing and for always listening. I love you.

Marcos and Mariana Debossan, Joel and Hannah Lemes, Katharine Siqueira, Filipe Catarcione and Mariana Novaes; the laughter, the jokes and the countless hours we spent together helped shape many of the characters in this novel. I will never tell you which ones!

Ronaldo and Jaise Alves, thank you for your friendship. It must be a terrible burden to bear being friends with me for over twenty years!

Fernanda and Gleison, thank you for always believing in

my potential. Your friendship is precious to me.

Flavia Duddey, this is another opportunity for us to look back on the days we used to daydream together and see one of those dreams completed. You are awesome.

"Though our dreams may have one thousand reasons to fail, believe in the one reason why they should succeed."

Thank you, Cristiano Piquet. These words will be carried with me for the rest of my life.

Sasha Alsberg, words fall short to describe how thankful I am for your love and passion for this series. You have helped these books reach so many different readers. I am forever in your debt.

I honestly believe that my fans, the Army of the Fallen, are the most devoted, passionate, crazy and creative people in this world. Thank you for all the tweets, Facebook posts, Instagram pictures, drawings and fan accounts. I wish I could hug each and every one of you.

You inspire me every day!

CPSIA information can be obtained
at www.ICGtesting.com
Printed in the USA
BVOW08s1541250717
490002BV00001B/6/P